THE GOLDEN MOONBEAM

ANGELA JAMES

Acorn Independent Press

Copyright © Angela James 2012

Published by Acorn Independent Press Ltd, 2012.

The right of Angela James to be identified as the Author of
the Work has been asserted by her in accordance with the
Copyright, Designs and Patents Act 1988.

This book is sold subject to the condition it shall not, by way
of trade or otherwise circulated in any form or by any means,
electronic or otherwise without the publisher's prior consent.

Cover artwork by Louise Millidge, cover lettering by Sue Quick
and all line drawings by Angela James

ISBN 978-1-908318-83-1

www.acornindependentpress.com

Acknowledgements

My grateful thanks to Leila and Ali for their guidance and continued support, Jill Sharp and Emma O'Neill for their feedback and encouragement during the earlier drafts, and Matt Holland and the Swindon Festival of Literature for making dreams come true.

For Steve, Ellie
&
William

Contents

For
Sarah
May the magic
of reading stay
with you!
Angela James
21/6/13

Chapter 1
*D*isappointment

'You're just an old fossil… you've forgotten what it's like to be young!' Mailliw shouted at Aunt Foggerty.

'Mailliw! Go to your room!' yelled Forthright, his sister.

'Just because you're two years older, doesn't give you the right to keep bossing me around and I'm not going to my room!' Mailliw argued as he jumped up from the oak dining table. The tablecloth caught in his belt and dragged the pewter water jug over the edge. It clattered to the flagstone floor. Forthright took out her wand, muttered an incantation, and watched the water flow backwards into the jug and the jug fly back onto the table. She exhaled with exasperation as Mailliw rushed passed her.

'Don't shout at me and don't speak to your sister like that!' warned Aunt Foggerty. Mailliw heard the rise in tone and knew he had pushed her patience to its limits. He ran from the room, slammed the door and headed outside.

It was late afternoon on the longest day of the year, summer solstice day, and the heat enveloped Mailliw as his ocean-blue eyes stared at the main gates. It was the day that school broke up for the summer holidays and the day his parents should have been waiting for him at home, instead of stuck on site at some stupid archaeological site. He didn't even know where the location of the site was because it was all hush-hush, top-secret

1

stuff. He yanked off his school tie, threw it down, and dug his hands into his trouser pockets. Well, he'd show them. He broke into a sprint towards the gates. Anger pumped through his body as he ran down the cobbled streets towards the market town of Feyngrey.

Mailliw sped through an alleyway, where grey stone terraced houses had cream coloured shutters still closed against the afternoon heat. Red geraniums spilled out of window boxes and family dragons dozed on doorsteps. Mailliw was breathing hard when he arrived at the market square. His white shirt hung loose over his school trousers and his blond hair stuck to his perspiring forehead. An old wizard sat on a bench and stared at him.

'I used t' be able t' run like that once,' he said with a toothless grin and a face creased like a piece of old leather. Mailliw acknowledged the wizard then slowed to a walk to get his breath back. As he walked, the shouting at his aunt and arguing with his sister yet again kept nagging his brain. It said, 'You shouldn't have done it… what would your father say?'

Mailliw knew exactly what his father would say… that Mailliw had let the side down; especially as he had wanted Aunt Foggerty to have some help in looking after the children when he and his wife, Agnetha, had to be away for long periods. Aunt Foggerty had insisted that just because she needed a bit of help from a walking stick, it didn't mean she was an invalid, she was quite capable. And she had been until she caught summer flu last month. Since then, Forthright had taken control and, over the last four weeks, their arguments had become intolerable. Nowadays, Mailliw's temper was constantly simmering, just waiting for Forthright to turn up the heat for him to boil over again and again.

Mailliw fumed as he paced the market square like an imprisoned lion. 'I hate her! I hate her! I wish she was dead!' he muttered, but even as he said it, he was appalled at the intensity of his own feelings. He kicked the kerb. A shooting, jarring pain in his big toe made him yelp. Mailliw dropped onto the kerb and nursed his throbbing foot.

A breeze ruffled his hair, like small fingers trying to brush aside the damp locks from his forehead and then it whispered... *be careful what you wish for... there's magic in the air today.* Before Mailliw could look around, the breeze swirled over a couple of ice-cream wrappers, made some dust eddies and was gone. The words echoed until the swifts screaming and reeling over the town hall drowned them out.

Apart from the swifts, the market square was unusually quiet. The shops were all closed. Even the café was shut. Sparrows hopped under café tables, seeking crumbs of seed cake or buttery flakes from the light pastries people dunked into their hot chocolate or chamomile tea. Everywhere had closed early to prepare for the summer solstice celebrations tonight. The celebrations Mailliw had been excited about for weeks, especially as it was going to be Forthright's debut moonbeam collecting night and, best of all, Mum and Dad would be there too!

Mailliw remembered how proud he'd been after Forthright had asked if he'd like to operate her moondial while she collected the moonbeams. Now Forthright was fourteen, she had to learn this skill before progressing to the next stage of advanced magic – using moonbeams in spells and potions. She had studied all year in preparation and it was the benchmark for determining a student's maturity and whether they were ready for more powerful magic. Mailliw felt jealous. He had to wait another two years before it was his turn, but deep down he knew he needed to study much harder if he wanted to succeed. He sighed. It was difficult to follow in Forthright's footsteps. The tutors expected him to be like her – studious, always reading books and doing her homework. It was also very annoying how she always made magic look so easy!

The pain in Mailliw's foot eased. He stood up, but the words… *be careful what you wish for… there's magic in the air today,* came back to him like a troublesome incantation refusing to go away.

After completing a circuit around the square, Mailliw limped home to their small chateau. It was built out of the same grey stone as the other buildings in the neighbourhood and the colour of this local stone gave the area its name – Feyngrey, a grey town that nestled alongside the River Feyn. The chateau rested on its own small hill and, being enclosed by a stone wall, there was only enough ground for a terrace and a courtyard garden with a clock tower.

Mailliw entered the chateau. *Be careful…* echoed in his mind as he closed the front door. The air smelt of beeswax and lavender polish as he roamed towards the dining hall. He looked in. All evidence of his uneaten herb omelette, the fresh bread and pats of butter, the sliced tomato salad with basil and olive oil had gone. The room was at rest, but Mailliw felt sure it was breathing in and out, trying to inhale cold air and exhale warm air in an attempt to cool itself down.

Mailliw continued to the snug where he slumped into a carved wooden recess overlooking the terrace. His fingers traced the letters P H I L L E A S that were carved into the wood. His father told him he had put them there when he was twelve, the same age as Mailliw. The only sound in the room was the heartbeat ticking of the Four Times Clock, so named because it struck just four times a year: one gong each for the two solstices and the two equinoxes. It resembled a grandfather clock with its long case and round face; a face with three-hundred and sixty-five engraved lines radiating out from the centre, one for every day of the year. With a fixed hand in the twelve o'clock position, it was the face that rotated a small movement for every passing day.

4

He'd only been sitting in the snug five minutes when Forthright burst in.

'Where have you been?' she said in a loud interrogating manner, 'I've been looking for you everywhere!'

'Well, now you've found me… what do you want?'

Forthright sucked in her breath, 'Do you know I could almost pull out my own hair worrying about you!' she said, grabbing her hair and tugging hard. Her hazel eyes watered as several strands of brown hair came away in her hand.

'Sometimes you are sooooooo impossible!' Forthright said, 'And I want to know why you've been so rude? Why did you shout at Aunt Foggerty? She was only trying to help. Aunt Foggerty is one of the nicest people I know and she's been quite ill over the last few weeks. You've really upset her, now she's got a migraine and has had to go to bed. Go and apologise!' She pulled at his shoulder, but he shrugged her fingers away. 'Do you think you're the only one disappointed?' she continued, 'I am too! But that's what happens when both parents are archaeologists and have to report directly to the Council of Wisdom! Excavations get delayed or something exciting and unusual is uncovered and they have to stay. They've said they'll be back in three to four weeks. At least we've got decent parents… unlike Drabder…'

'That's not fair! Leave my friend out of this!' Mailliw growled and stared out of the window. Forthright, however, recognised Mailliw's weak spot and she pursued it like a hunting tigress.

'Let's face it… every day he straightens his tie, smoothes his gown and rubs his shoes on the backs of his trousers because he's terrified of his father and…' Forthright paused for breath, 'and you know as well as I do that if his cousin Monity hadn't been there to look out for him, you'd have only been too willing to stay and put off seeing our parents until you knew he was okay…'

'Finished yet?' snapped Mailliw. His fingers tapped the window sill with increased speed as his irritation escalated.

'No, I haven't...' Forthright said furiously, and then she stopped, screwed up her face and began counting. In between numbers, she inhaled and paced uncomfortably around Mailliw. When she ceased counting, she forced her voice to a more measured tone.

'Look, I'm sorry I said those things about Drabder. It was very unkind, but I guess I wanted to hurt you like you hurt me earlier. When I saw you sitting there acting as if nothing had happened, I got angry again... I really... I mean, I really came to ask if you're still going to help me collect moonbeams tonight?'

Spite squeezed Mailliw's heart, 'Why should I?' he said, jerking his knees into his chest so hard that he caused several clumps of hair to fall over his eyes like a heavy curtain.

Blood rushed to Forthright's face, 'If you don't, I'll fail a whole year of school work just because you're acting like a spoiled brat!'

Mailliw buried his face into his knees. He heard Forthright slam the door as she left.

***

Forthright returned to the dining hall. She looked up at the vaulted ceiling and blinked back the tears stinging her eyes. Mailliw was so unpredictable when he was in this sort of mood and lately it had been increasingly difficult to reason with him. He ignored his homework, he didn't keep his room tidy, he was late for school and Forthright even had to nag him to comb his hair. With Aunt Foggerty's illness, Forthright felt responsible for him. She was aware Mailliw thought her bossy, he'd told her often enough.

Forthright moved to the sideboard. A casket lay open with gifts sent from their parents. It was their apology for not returning in time for the summer holiday. They had sent Forthright an illustrated antique book on wild flowers, but

Mailliw hadn't seen what they had sent him. Forthright picked up the gift. It was an elongated black diamond and she had never seen anything like it before. As she held it up to the light the facets glinted, but it was so black, no light penetrated the crystal. With a sigh, she put it in her pocket. Forthright was angry with Mailliw, but she desperately wanted him to help with the moonbeam collecting tonight. She banged the casket shut and made her way back to the snug. Her slippers pattered across the stone floor, causing whispered echoes from the dark oak panelling. They only became silent when she tapped on the snug door. Forthright could have walked straight in, after all, it was a family room, but she was trying to appeal to Mailliw's better nature by acting with respect.

'Mailliw, I have something for you.' There was a long silence before Mailliw opened the door. She tried a smile, but he slunk back to the recess. 'I'm really sorry about being bossy again… and also that Mum and Dad aren't home. I miss them too you know.'

Mailliw did not respond.

'I have the present they sent you,' she said and drew it out of her pocket, 'look… it's a black diamond with a very unusual shape, it's elongated with a fine point. I've no idea what it's for… perhaps you should look at it.'

She held it out for Mailliw. He ignored her.

'Well… I'll leave it on the window sill. How about adding it to the collection in your bedroom with all the other artefacts they've given you?'

Forthright put the black diamond on the sill and sat down. It was difficult keeping calm when Mailliw was being this awkward. She tried again. 'Mailliw, I really want to collect silver moonbeams this evening because it is a very special occasion. We have a full moon on the summer solstice and it only happens once every nineteen years! Tonight's moonbeams will have extra strong magical powers, so it could be dangerous.

That's why I need someone to operate my moondial, so we know exactly how many moonbeams I've collected. I asked you because you're my brother and I really wanted to share this with you. It wouldn't be the same without you… will you come?'

There was a pause for several seconds before Mailliw gave his answer. 'No!'

'Why?'

'Because!'

'Because what?' Forthright's patience snapped, 'If you don't, it's because you're too selfish and can only think of yourself. Mailliw it's time you grew up!'

Forthright strode to the door. Disappointment poured into her stomach like a bitter potion of snake venom. It was such an important occasion and there was no one in her family to share it with, Aunt Foggerty was ill in bed, her parents were away and Mailliw had stubbornly refused.

'I'll be at the clock tower in the courtyard garden at nine o'clock… just in case you change your mind,' she said, then left the room keeping her fingers crossed. Mailliw could tell by the knotted tone in her voice that she was trying not to cry.

***

The household tensions were no better down in the dragons' kitchen. Situated next to the main kitchen, it was for all the family pets, but because three dragons resided there, they regarded it as their kitchen. House dragons were smaller than their wild cousins, but even so, a full-grown house dragon was still about the size of a small pony, but with twice the strength. Forthright's dragon, Dingle, was half-grown and he was there along with Norgruk, a dragon who belonged to Mailliw and Forthright's mother and father, Agnetha and Philleas. Norgruk was the largest of the household dragons, but he still had some growing to do. In the absence of their parents, Norgruk had become too fond of eating and sleeping. Then there was Cleopatra, an old dragon belonging to Aunt Foggerty. She was full size for a female, but still smaller than Norgruk.

Tonight, Peculiar, Mailliw's pet vampire cat, arrived in the dragons' kitchen carrying a saucer of goat's blood. Norgruk had eaten his plate of roots and was settling down for the night with his claws linked together over his belly and Cleopatra was snoring with a crocheted blanket draped over her scaly back.

'What's the cat doing here?' demanded Norgruk, 'Dingle, get rid of it!'

'Why me?' asked Dingle.

'Because it's your friend.'

'It's not my friend,' Dingle muttered and then in a loud voice to Peculiar he said, 'please leave and take that with you.' His claw pointed at the saucer of blood. The smell of it permeated the whole kitchen. Dingle felt faint.

'No!' growled Peculiar.

'Leave now and take your dinner out of here. It's making us feel ill.'

'You sissies,' hissed Peculiar, 'get used to it. I'm not leaving!'

'Yes you are!' insisted Dingle.

'NO! I'M NOT!'

'YES YOU ARE!'

Dingle ground his back teeth to ignite the gas collected in the chamber above his stomach and, with a WHOOSH, a stupendous emerald green flame roared from his mouth. The heat clotted the goat's blood in the saucer and Peculiar flew from the kitchen with her tail on fire.

'Yep! Those peppermint and parsley patties Aunt Foggerty makes produce fantastic green flames,' he said turning back to his plate of roots. Norgruk grunted his approval, but suddenly Dingle felt a pang of foreboding. He had crossed Peculiar and no doubt, he would pay for it! But how? A jab in the leg with a sharp claw as he passed on the stairs or a blood-drained mouse left in his bed, or even worse... have Peculiar leap out from behind a door with fangs at the ready to puncture his neck. Dingle shuddered. He looked at his plate of roots and lost his appetite. He nudged the half-asleep Norgruk.

'Want them?' enquired Dingle.

'Stupid question!' replied Norgruk, his eyes popping open to see how many roots remained.

'Right!' said Dingle and pushed the plate to Norgruk. All he thought about was where and when Peculiar would strike!

Chapter 2
Moondials & Moonbeams

At ten minutes to nine, Mailliw stood in the shadow of the clock tower. He observed the fading light, noticing how colour was fading to monochrome. The perfume from the courtyard roses hung like heavy damask and he could almost smell the colour from every bloom.

Their small chateau, in its raised position, overlooked much of the town with its backdrop of volcanic cliffs and gorges filled with ancient woodlands. From here, he could see the River Feyn that flowed beside the market town. Looking west, Mailliw saw silhouetted trees on top of the cliffs against a salmon-pink sky blended with apricot and grey, whilst overhead, the sky deepened to indigo and the first stars of the night appeared.

Mailliw breathed deeply to relax. Plagued by earlier events in the market square, Mailliw's guilt had multiplied because he had deliberately rejected Forthright's attempted reconciliation.

'Look… if there is magic in the air today,' he whispered to the sky, 'I didn't mean what I said, honest I didn't,' then he glanced around nervously to ensure nobody had heard him talking to thin air. A soft breath touched his face. It was almost like his mother blowing him a kiss and it sounded like two paper-thin words. What was it? What had he heard? Then he understood and his body recoiled with fright. The words... *too late...* shot into his brain like a bolt of lightning.

'No! No! I didn't mean what I said!' he answered in alarm and put his hands over his ears, but it was no good trying to undo the sound, they were now there, fixed in his brain. Mailliw leaned back against the clock tower with his legs sapped of strength when a movement caught his attention. It was Forthright. She carried a broomstick, a couple of moonbeam collection boxes and a large rucksack with a moondial poking out of the top. She was wearing a black ceremonial gown and it swished smoothly as she walked. He saw how sophisticated she looked and... Mailliw's heart pounded when he thought it... how much she resembled a younger version of their mother. He leaned deeper into the shadow of the tower, his legs still weak.

Forthright looked around anxiously for Mailliw. Her shoulders wilted with disappointment when she realised he wasn't there. After putting her gear on the ground, she paced towards the rose beds, turned and paced back, then returned to the roses. She bent her head to inhale their fragrance. A rustling made her turn.

'Mailliw?' she asked hopefully, 'Oh! Sorry Peculiar, I thought it might be Mailliw...' then she stopped and sniffed, 'what is that smell? It smells like... burnt fur.'

The vampire cat stalked by holding her burnt tail high, but before Forthright enquired further, Mailliw stepped out from the shadows.

'Your cat smells peculiar,' said Forthright.

'Are you being funny?' asked Mailliw. The question sounded sharper than he intended and his guilt mounted.

'I'm sorry, I wasn't being rude about her name, it's just that as she passed by I smelt burnt fur...' said Forthright and paused mid-sentence. She was grateful he had turned up and didn't want to aggravate him in case he decided not to go after all, so she changed the subject and smiled nervously.

12

'Can you hold this for me please?' she asked, picking up the broomstick. 'I expect it'll be busy tonight with hundreds collecting moonbeams as well as those going for the celebrations. Here… put the rucksack over your shoulders so I can check the moondial is safe inside and then buckle it up.'

Mailliw looked at her, not sure what to do first, hold the broomstick or put on the rucksack? Forthright continued talking, 'I'll clip my moonbeam collection boxes onto my belt, then you can get on the broomstick behind me and we can go.' Her fingers were fumbling trying to organise everything.

'Why can't I do the flying and you carry the moondial?' Mailliw asked. He was now afraid that something might happen to her and he was a good flier. If he was in control of the situation, maybe he could protect her from harm.

Forthright gave a small snort and immediately regretted it.

'What's that supposed to mean?' Mailliw retorted.

'Sorry, sorry… but I've just told you… it's going to be busy…'

Mailliw interrupted, 'I'm the best flier in my class…'

'And I'm the best in mine! Has your class done the Stingetty manoeuvre or the pike somersault?' she asked tilting her head to one side as if talking to a five-year-old.

Mailliw clenched his teeth and shook his head.

'I guessed as much, therefore, I'm doing the flying,' she said sweetly and smiled. Mailliw grabbed the rucksack and put it on.

When they were ready Mailliw asked, 'Aren't we going to wait for Aunt Foggerty?'

'She's not coming. Her migraine is so bad she can't even stand up. I've taken her some chamomile and willow bark tea,' said Forthright.

Mailliw sat behind Forthright with his arms around her waist and felt the warmth from her body. She smelt of vanilla and honey from the soap he had given her on the last winter solstice. She had been delighted when she lifted the lacy lid on the small box and the fragrance blossomed like a warm bouquet.

For the first time, Mailliw imagined how Forthright must be feeling, knowing he was the only family member present with her tonight.

***

Take off was smooth and as Forthright steered the broomstick skywards, her gown fluttered over Mailliw's feet. They flew over the terraced cottages and alleyways towards the outskirts of Feyngrey. Mailliw was on guard for any signs of danger waiting to descend on Forthright.

The skies were congested with witches and wizards on broomsticks all flying towards a large flat area of common grassland. It was the usual meeting place for everyone from all the surrounding areas to use for events such as this.

'Hey! I think there's Monity and her mother in front,' said Forthright and pointed to just ahead of them. Mailliw tried to peer over Forthright's shoulder to see Drabder's cousin, Monity. 'If we catch up and land in the same area, you'll have some company,' said Forthright and tilted the broomstick. Mailliw's stomach lurched as the broom dipped and sped forward.

As they caught up with Monity and her mother, a small bat flitted around their heads.

'Bit is saying hello,' shouted Monity.

'Hi Bit the bat,' said Forthright, laughing as the bat circled around her head, 'look Mailliw! Look at the crowds. It's bedlam! I can smell candy floss and popcorn and there's even the Tinker Acrobats.'

Forthright landed close to Monity's mother and helped Mailliw take the rucksack off his shoulders. Monity had been carrying one for her mother.

'My shoulders are stiff. Those moondials are so heavy,' said Monity as she strolled towards Mailliw and stretched her thin arms above her mousy, wind-swept plaits. She had changed from her school uniform into a knee-length blue polka dot skirt and white T-shirt, but her skinny knees looked just as grubby as they had done this morning, after she had weeded the herb beds at school.

'Mmm, the popcorn smells delicious, but I haven't any money,' Monity said, trying to grin and sniff the hot buttery popcorn at the same time.

'Nor me. I had other things on my mind,' Mailliw confessed.

The noise and crowds increased. Witches wearing ceremonial attire bustled in and out of stalls buying pre-prepared potions, magic remedies, fresh and dried herbs, rare ingredients, new models of moondials, broomsticks, hats, wands, crystals, moonstones, toffee apples, popcorn and candyfloss. Vendors called out bargain prices and offers 'Not to be missed!' and voices filled the air so it was hard to hear what the person standing next to you was saying.

'Mailliw,' Forthright called, 'the moon is rising so I'm going to start setting up. It'll take me about five or ten minutes to polarize the collection boxes and sync them up with the moondial, so why don't you go and have a look around?'

Mailliw hesitated.

'Go on,' urged Forthright, 'take Monity. Just make sure you're back in time,' and, with that, she turned her attention back to her moondial.

'Can I go Mum?' asked Monity as her mother, Roo, started to set up her own moondial.

'Yes, but only for ten minutes,' answered Roo, pushing up the voluminous sleeves of her ceremonial gown, 'the sooner I get airborne the better. Don't forget the full moon coincides with the summer solstice this year so the moonbeams are coming up for maximum strength in the next half hour. Oh! Forthright,' she said turning, 'I can check your synchronisations when you're ready if you want me to.'

Forthright flashed a smile at Roo and nodded.

Mailliw reluctantly followed Monity into the crowds. He glanced back to reassure himself Forthright was okay.

'How are your parents?' Monity asked, 'Did they have loads to tell you? Did they bring lots of treasures back?' but she stopped when she saw Mailliw's frown.

'They aren't home yet,' he replied and Monity felt his disappointment. She didn't know what to say, so just squeezed his hand as they pushed through the hordes. Then Mailliw halted.

'Look! Drabder's over there with his father… but why has he got a dog?' he asked.

'Drabder doesn't have a dog,' replied Monity.

'I know! That's what makes it so odd.'

Mailliw tapped Drabder on the shoulder but before he had a chance to look around, Drabder's father, Turnbull Fink shouted, 'I'm going for a tankard of brew, keep outta mischief AND get rid of that dirty mutt!'

Drabder nodded at his father and watched him go. Only when he saw Mailliw and Monity did his pale face break into a smile. With combed hair, clean shirt and trousers, he looked as fresh as when he'd dressed for school that morning.

'What's with the dog?' Monity asked, suddenly aware of her own dishevelled appearance. She spat on her hands and tried to rub the dirt off her knees, but it just smeared into streaks.

'I d-d-don't know. It keeps f-following m-me,' said Drabder, leaning down and stroking the dog's ears. Mailliw realised Drabder was stressed, because his stammer was more noticeable than usual. The dog gazed at Drabder, then opened its mouth and clamped its teeth on his sleeve, pulling and tugging him.

'I think it's t-taking me somewhere!' he said trying to grab Monity's arm before he was pulled into the crowd. Mailliw and Monity jostled along trying not to lose sight of Drabder. The dog led him to a caravan where a woman, with a roosting grey pigeon on her shoulder, sat in front of an open fire stirring a cauldron. She looked up and smiled. Drabder stood staring at the woman.

Mailliw and Monity caught up with Drabder and also stared at the woman. It was difficult to guess her age. She looked young and old simultaneously as she pulled her red and white checked shawl around her shoulders.

'Who are you?' enquired Mailliw.

'I'm Mother McGinty. I travel everywhere, collecting goods from one place and transporting them to another, before selling them to people who are unable to get the goods locally.'

'Like what?' asked Monity.

'Oh, precious items and rarities such as bluebell honey and pickled moths' tongues,' Mother McGinty replied, 'my dog, Gypsy, is expecting puppies and she's been looking for prospective owners for them. She has chosen you,' she said looking at Drabder, 'because she knows you have a kind heart.'

'M-m-my father will never let me have a p-p-puppy,' Drabder stammered. He looked at Gypsy and saw the deep amber eyes inspecting him. She trusted him and he knew it, but he had no idea on how to convince his father.

'He's right,' said Monity, 'his father will never allow it.'

She looked up at the rising moon as she spoke and remembered they needed to go, 'It's been nice meeting you and your dog, but we have to get back.'

As they left, Drabder caught Mother McGinty smiling at him. It made him feel all warm inside and he smiled back. But, once Mailliw and Monity left Drabder with his father, the tight knot inside his stomach returned.

***

Mailliw and Monity hurried back to Forthright and Roo. Hundreds of moondials were positioned like dwarf soldiers standing to attention. Every moondial consisted of an identical dial covering a small circular basin which sat on top of an individually styled column about forty-five centimetres high. The cost of a moondial depended on the complexity of the column design. Cheap models were mostly plain, but the expensive versions had intricately carved patterns created by master craftsmen.

Mailliw saw Forthright observing other witches and wizards switching on their moondials and she proceeded to do the same. Instantly, the dials emitted a soft luminous glow onto everyone, tinting their clothes and skin green. As the moondials hummed, Mailliw's skin prickled with the strange vibrations pulsing through the air.

'Oh good! You're back just in time,' said Forthright looking up at Mailliw. 'Now this is what happens – we keep exchanging these moonbeam collection boxes,' she said, unclipping the two boxes from her belt, 'until I've collected sufficient moonbeams. You will store the moonbeams in the moondial like this – lift the luminous dial and place the collection box into this square area inside the basin,' she said pointing to the centre of the basin, 'replace the dial and press these four buttons in the directions of north, south, east and west to seal in the box,' she checked to see if Mailliw was still paying attention. 'Place your hand over the dial and turn it clockwise, one full rotation. This empties the moonbeams into the basin storage container and stops them from escaping.' Forthright paused, took a deep breath and continued, 'To retrieve the collection box, turn the dial anticlockwise and press the four buttons in reverse. To see the moonbeam status, look at this inner ring on the dial. The silver hand on the inner ring registers the amount of moonbeams collected.' Forthright looked at Mailliw again and was satisfied to see him still concentrating so she carried on explaining, 'When the silver hand reaches this green marker,' she said, showing him, 'you must tell me, because one more refill will take it to the red marker and the moondial will be full. Whatever happens, I must not collect anymore once the hand reaches that point. Is everything clear?' she finally said with a concerned look.

'Yes, I think so,' Mailliw replied.

'Are you sure? It's important I stop collecting at the red marker.'

'Yes! I've got it!' he said, wishing she'd stop treating him like a child.

'Good,' said Forthright as she took a collection box and mounted her broomstick.

***

The air became alive as witches and wizards took flight. It was an extraordinary sight. They swooped and dipped, manoeuvring to avoid colliding with other broomsticks and when they rose into the air, they flew in formation like a vast flock of starlings. Gradually, the numbers spread out and the collection of moonbeams began. The more experienced collectors gathered swiftly and were back within minutes. Roo landed quickly, exchanged her box and started another collection.

Mailliw's eyes scoured the sky trying to locate Forthright. He turned on his heels, but couldn't see her anywhere. Panic flapped inside his chest like a caged bird trying to escape. Where was she? He turned again. No sign of her. He kept his eyes skyward and spun round once more. Suddenly, Mailliw's foot hit the base of the moondial.

'Ow! Ow!' he howled, as pain ripped through the big toe which was already bruised from when he kicked the kerb earlier. Stunned with pain, Mailliw hopped onto the other foot. He tottered as he tried to lift his injured foot. Unbalanced, Mailliw fell against Forthright's moondial. He felt the impact, the wobble, and as he fell, his eyes watched the moondial fall too. With outstretched hands, he reached for it, but then he heard the sickening thud as it hit the grass. His heart echoed the thud, his mouth went dry and he couldn't breathe for fear. Ignoring the throbbing in his toe, and with trembling hands, Mailliw picked up the moondial and set it straight again. The dial still emitted a luminous glow, then Mailliw put his hand on the column and found it was still humming. It was only then that he exhaled. Just as he swung round, Forthright landed with her first collection and gave her box to Mailliw.

'I was getting worried. I couldn't see you,' he said anxiously trying to keep the fear out of his voice, but Forthright was too engrossed in moonbeam collecting to notice.

'This is so exciting Mailliw. Hand me the other box quickly!' she said breathlessly, beckoning with her hand for him to give her the other collecting box. She looked happier than she had done for weeks and her face shone with pleasure and pride. Mailliw handed Forthright the box and she took off again. He commenced emptying the full box of moonbeams into the moondial, exactly as Forthright had instructed him, and the silver hand on the inner dial moved round to register the collection. From then on, Mailliw remained glued to the spot, only moving when Forthright returned and he emptied another collection of moonbeams.

After four more trips, Roo's moondial indicated it was full, so she and Monity started to tidy up.

'I expect Forthright will be finished collecting soon, Mailliw,' said Roo. 'How many times has she been up?'

'I think this is her fifth collection,' he replied.

'I'm impressed with her speed of collecting,' said Roo and smiled, 'when I've finished depolarising everything and packed away, we'll both come over.'

Forthright and Mailliw exchanged another box and she made another three collections before Roo and Monity joined him.

'Forthright must be nearly finished, everyone else has now. Let's have a look at her moondial,' said Roo ambling towards him with her ceremonial gown in full sail.

As Roo examined the moondial, she looked concerned. The silver hand on the inner dial indicated the moondial was only half-full. Even allowing for Forthright's inexperience, after the number of times she had been up, the moondial should be almost full, especially as the moonbeams were more powerful tonight.

'Mailliw... when transferring the moonbeams into the moondial... did you make sure you sealed the dial every time?' Roo asked.

'I promise I've been very careful,' he replied.

'Is anything wrong?' asked Monity, pushing her plaits over her shoulders as she studied the moondial.

'Well... there shouldn't be, I checked everything myself,' answered Roo.

Roo tapped Forthright's moondial. Mailliw watched. In horror, Roo saw the silver hand on the inner dial slide backwards from being half-full to a quarter-full.

'Oh no! Oh no!' Roo wailed and frantically grabbed Monity, 'Where's Bit?' she shrieked, 'Get her to find Forthright and drive her down immediately!'

Mailliw's heart pounded so hard that he thought his chest would burst. Monity whistled for Bit and gave instructions to fetch Forthright down from the sky. The bat whizzed through the air, sending out clicking noises as she attempted to locate Forthright.

Monity turned back to her mother, 'What is it Mum? What's wrong?'

'Wrong! There's something very wrong with this moondial. The registering mechanism is broken!' she said wringing her plump hands in distress. Monity paled. Mailliw stood still, his heart now pounding in time with the words... *too late... too late!* But the lump in his throat forced him to stay silent.

Bit flew in the moonlight and continued sending out radar in every direction. Now the skies were clear of other witches and wizards, it was easier to identify other flying objects like bats, moths and night flies. She ignored these in her search for Forthright.

***

Forthright was enjoying the moonbeam collecting and really wanted to appreciate the experience. A full moon on summer solstice wouldn't happen again until she was thirty-three. She wasn't unduly concerned about being the only person left flying the skies, because the whole purpose of using a moondial was to ensure you only collected the correct amount. She glanced down and observed small campfires, but as she was flying high, the sounds from the melee below were muted. The air rushed by in her ears and she was at peace with the freedom of space. Once more, she held out a collection box in direct line with a stream of moonbeams.

Without warning, her peace was shattered as a bat dive-bombed her. Forthright flinched from the attack and swerved to avoid the assailing creature. She reeled her broomstick around, but the bat returned again and again, thrashing against Forthright's head, skimming her ears, her cheeks, her lips and her eyes.

'Get off me!' cried Forthright, swinging the hand holding the collection box at the bat, 'What's the matter with you? Are you crazy?'

Bit continued with the attack. Her instructions were to drive Forthright down and this was the only way she knew how. She flew in a frenzy, driving Forthright lower and lower, until Forthright had no option but to abandon her collecting and head back to Mailliw. Forthright plunged to the ground, grabbed her broomstick from underneath and used it to take one hefty swipe at Bit. The broom thrust the bat sideways and hurled it to the ground.

'What's the matter with that stupid bat?' screeched Forthright, 'Is it demented?'

Monity ran to where Bit lay and picked up her little bat.

'I think she's dead,' she sobbed.

'Is it Bit?' Forthright demanded.

Monity nodded helplessly.

'Is she insane? What is going on?' Forthright asked angrily.

Roo took Bit from Monity's hands and cradled the small creature.

'Forthright! I had to give Monity instructions for Bit to fetch you down. It was vital to get you down immediately. She was only doing the job she was asked to do,' Roo said, 'I never... never imagined this. I'm so sorry Monity...'

'But why?' asked Forthright, 'What was so urgent? What couldn't wait until...' she paused leaving the question unfinished and then the blood that had suffused her angry face drained away. She scrutinized Mailliw's face.

'No! No! Please tell me you didn't mess up. You didn't... did you?'

Mailliw hung his head.

Roo saw Mailliw swallow several times before he whispered, 'Yes... I messed up.'

Forthright stepped towards him, 'What did you do this time? What didn't you understand?' she said with her throat so constricted with fear that the words were forced out in a high-pitched shriek.

'It was an accident! I was looking for you, I couldn't see you and then I knocked your moondial over... I thought it was okay, it still looked like it was working,' the words gabbled from Mailliw's mouth.

Forthright's brain hammered with thoughts seeking to wipe out the memory of what Mailliw had just said. The hairs on her skin stood on end, and her heart felt as though it was jumping in her mouth. A cold, terrible despair surged like a tidal wave as one thought dominated her mind... Mailliw had wanted to punish her for all the arguments, for telling him what to do, for not being Mum and Dad.

'You did this on purpose didn't you? Didn't you? Have you any idea of what you've done? Do you have the slightest notion of what might happen to me?' the cold edge in Forthright's voice was as sharp as a diamond cutting through rock. For Mailliw, this was more frightening than any amount of bellowing and shouting. He was astounded at the accusation and gaped at Forthright, speechless. Mailliw shook his head in denial and glanced at Monity. In the moonlight, her cheeks glistened with tears.

'What Forthright means Mailliw, is that there is a serious risk she has been exposed to an overdose of silver moonbeams,' explained Roo urgently.

'You mean... silver moonbeam sickness?' Monity gasped and clapped her hands over her mouth.

Roo's mouth twisted. How was she to tell this boy that what he had done tonight could result in his sister's death? When a small movement fluttered in her hands, Roo handed Bit back to Monity.

'Take care of her Monity. She's alive, but needs careful nursing.'

With her hands now free, Roo seized Mailliw by the shoulders so he had to face her. Her thick fingers dug into his flesh, 'Look at me Mailliw,' she demanded, 'this is a dreadful, dreadful situation and we are talking about silver moonbeam sickness!'

'How serious is it? I mean... it's not like she's going to die... is it?' Mailliw asked so huskily it was barely audible.

Roo fought back the urge to shake Mailliw senseless. Mailliw's terrified eyes stared at Forthright. He didn't need spoken words to know the truth. Forthright's sheer look of bleached terror confirmed the answer for him.

24

Chapter 3
The Sickness

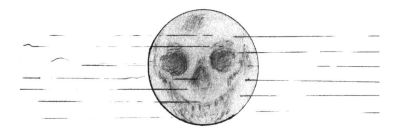

Peculiar, Mailliw's vampire cat, sat on his four-poster bed and watched a moth bashing against the leaded window. It had been a bad night all round. At supper, the dragons had rejected her and Dingle even had the audacity to throw flames at her. She growled at the thought that her tail would take months to recover. Mailliw had gone out without her, then he returned in a filthy black mood, so had Forthright. Aunt Foggerty was ill in bed and now there was Monity blubbering downstairs with her mother pacing up and down wringing her hands. Peculiar decided the full moon had affected everyone but her and the safest place was Mailliw's bedroom.

The moth flitted across to the lamp on the desk where Mailliw did his homework. It danced senselessly around the glow a few times, and then flew to the empty fire grate, before falling to the flagstone hearth where it lay exhausted. Peculiar jumped down from the bed and tiptoed around the usual junk littering Mailliw's bedroom floor – items such as shoeboxes containing various collections of dragons' teeth or smooth polished pebbles, then there were the adventure magazines and odd socks, half-eaten biscuits and empty sweet bags – all of this contributed to the general air of a messy boy's room.

Now that the moth ceased to hold Peculiar's attention, curiosity was getting the better of her. She left the room and was making her way downstairs when she noticed Forthright's open bedroom door. She glimpsed in and was surprised. The normally pristine room was a mess. Books lay scattered everywhere and a ceremonial gown lay in a ragged heap on the floor. It looked more like Mailliw's room, not Forthright's!

'I'm going to die!' Forthright moaned as she lay on her bed wearing only her ceremonial undergarments. She buried her head in her arms and Dingle, her dragon, sat on the floor not knowing what to do.

'I'm going to die! I'M GOING TO DIE!'

Peculiar decided this was not the time to barge in, so carried on downstairs to the drawing room. Mailliw was standing by the empty fireplace so she went and joined him. His hair was sticking up on end from where he had pushed his fingers through it repeatedly.

'You must get Aunt Foggerty immediately,' Roo commanded.

'She's ill in bed!' Mailliw answered back.

'I don't care, she must be told without delay. Now go!'

Mailliw ran up the spiral staircase leading to Aunt Foggerty's bedroom and banged on the oak door.

'Aunt Foggerty, I must speak to you, it's urgent! Please open the door.'

He waited a few seconds and then banged again. The heavy door creaked open. Mailliw was appalled at the sight of his aunt. She stood in front of Mailliw in her nightdress with one hand on her walking stick. Since being ill with flu, her skin had become drawn over her cheekbones, giving her face a frail, translucent quality. But now he saw she had been crying, and with puffy eyes and strands of her silver waist-length hair clinging to her wet face, she looked dreadful. Seeing her like this, he became aware of how much he had upset her earlier, and what he had to tell her about Forthright was only going to make things worse.

'I've done something terrible! Monity's mother is furious and Forthright is-is-is…' Mailliw stammered worse than Drabder.

'Mailliw, I'm not in the mood to deal with any more of your squabbles with your sister today. Go and sort it out between yourselves,' she said impatiently and retreated to her room. Mailliw gripped her arm.

'You don't understand,' he shouted, 'silver moonbeam sickness!' he yelled at her.

Aunt Foggerty whipped round, 'What did you say?'

Her face froze hard like a glacier, 'Where is she?' she demanded, 'Take me to her immediately!'

Aunt Foggerty grasped him for support. Mailliw had never seen her try to run before, but she tried now, dragging on him as one leg buckled beneath her time and time again. She strained with the effort and cried out with pain, all the way to Forthright's room.

***

Mailliw waited downstairs with Roo and Monity as he was told to by Aunt Foggerty. Nobody spoke, but the suspense in the drawing room felt as if all the air was being sucked out and they were going to suffocate. Time dragged its heels like a reluctant child.

When Aunt Foggerty came in, her face was grave and one hand gripped her walking stick so tight, her knuckles were white. She held out the other hand in a desperate plea to Roo. Roo hurried over and wrapped her plump arms around Aunt Foggerty.

'I can't thank you enough for bringing them home Roo,' said Aunt Foggerty wearily, 'and I'm sure you and Monity must be very tired, so it'll be easier if you return home on my flying carpet. Norgruk will escort you and make sure you get home safely. He's waiting outside ready,' she said, 'but if you stop first at Doctor Poonar's house in Riverside Lane and tell him it's an emergency, I'd be very grateful.'

'Of course… it's the very least we can do. You stay here, we'll let ourselves out,' Roo replied and nodded to Monity who followed, carefully carrying Bit in her handkerchief.

As she passed, Aunt Foggerty thought how similar Forthright had been at that age and in a few more years, how Monity would lose her skinny waif-like look and become an attractive teenager.

Aunt Foggerty focussed on Mailliw. Their eyes met and her black eyes flecked with gold searched deep into his ocean-blue ones.

'I want the truth Mailliw,' she said, not taking her eyes off him, 'Forthright says you did this deliberately, did you?'

He stood there, dumb. He was confused and avoided Aunt Foggerty's penetrating gaze.

'Mailliw!'

Aunt Foggerty's stern voice pierced his ears.

'Answer me!' she insisted.

Thoughts flashed through his mind. How could Forthright think he had done it deliberately? The moondial broke when he fell. It wasn't deliberate. Nevertheless, his conscience reminded him of the incident during the late afternoon, when he had wished Forthright was dead. Mailliw's brain clamoured with denial, it was an accident… but he had said he wanted her dead… so was it his fault? Was he guilty? Mailliw really didn't know. The uncertainty was disorientating his thoughts and he was incapable of finding a truthful answer.

'I… I…' but the words refused to come, 'I don't know,' he finished lamely.

Peculiar was still standing by Mailliw and she could almost touch the heat radiating from Aunt Foggerty. It was like a low smouldering fire, under control at the moment, but very dangerous if the right material came along to spark it into an inferno. Mailliw was very close to being that spark.

'Come with me!'

It was a command and he obeyed. Mailliw followed her down the hall to the front door.

'Forthright needs me, so I want you to wait here for the doctor and, while you're waiting, I want you to think about your parents and what you have done. When the doctor arrives, bring him straight to Forthright's bedroom. Afterwards, I want you to go to your father's library and start looking for anything you can find on silver moonbeam sickness.'

Aunt Foggerty turned from him abruptly. He watched her walk to the stairs and go step by painful step, back up to his sister.

* * *

After taking the doctor to Forthright's room, Mailliw left the library door open so he could hear when the doctor left. Peculiar followed Mailliw into the library and waited as he gawped at all the books. His father was proud of his 'collections' as he called them and, when he was home, he spent hours sitting at his desk researching and writing. Agnetha, his mother, preferred to relax on the old leather sofa to do her reading. She'd kick off her slippers and curl her feet under a cushion. Mailliw had seen Forthright doing the same recently.

The books lined the library walls from floor to ceiling and Mailliw didn't know where to begin. There were thousands of them; red, blue, green, brown and black leather bound books; thick, thin, medium thicknesses and collections where each volume was half the size of his father's desk so that it required two people to lift one of them. There were miniatures no bigger than a postage stamp; gold leaf books; books with illustrations and illuminations; books written from centuries ago; contemporary books; there were rolls of manuscripts, maps and charts, and they all contributed to the library's bookish smell of paper, leather, glue, inks and something else… knowledge.

Mailliw heard voices in the hall and crept to the library door. He listened to Doctor Poonar's deep rumble and the tap of Aunt Foggerty's walking stick as they progressed towards the front door.

'Er… you see… although it used to be an all too common sickness for yours and previous generations, I haven't actually seen a case of silver moonbeam sickness before. Er… with the invention of the moondial some fifty years ago and because of its effectiveness… er… the Council of Wisdom has always put the emphasis on the prevention rather than the cure. Er… as such… er… the decline in the sickness is almost one hundred per cent, er… I mean the statistics speak for themselves, therefore no further research was required into finding a cure… er… I'm afraid there is nothing I can do, er… I'm very sorry.'

The doctor's voice became muffled as he departed and Mailliw heard Aunt Foggerty say goodnight.

She entered the library. Mailliw could see how weary she was, but he still blurted out 'Is she going to die?'

Aunt Foggerty winced as if he had struck her. She swallowed several times before she was ready to speak.

'I honestly don't know, Mailliw. Silver moonbeam sickness is fatal if the exposure was too high and the moonbeams tonight were more powerful than normal. The problem is, we don't know how much of an overdose of silver moonbeams Forthright has had, if any at all.'

'When will we know if she has it?' he asked.

'The next few days will be critical. Doctor Poonar has never seen a case before, but I have though, many, many times when

I was growing up,' a haunted look came into Aunt Foggerty's eyes, 'but even I only know of one person who survived a fatal overdose and I have no idea how they did it.'

'If she gets it, why can't we magic her better?'

Aunt Foggerty gave a long drawn sigh, 'Oh Mailliw! Magic cures are only achieved by the construction and deconstruction of potions and spells. It takes years of trials before the knowledge becomes available for the treatment of many illnesses. You know it's the law that trained doctors and herbalists can only treat serious illnesses. For ourselves, we can only use magical potions and herb remedies where the information is readily available from any good medical book.'

'So why isn't there a cure for silver moonbeam sickness?' he asked miserably, remembering Dr Poonar's words.

'Because they still don't understand why the sickness occurs. It has something to do with moonbeams being "other", that is, their source originates from outside our world. So, at the moment, our best defence is on prevention rather than cure, and the reason why moondials are so important.'

'Can I go up and see her?'

'No! Doctor Poonar's given her a strong draught of poppy juice. She's sleeping now. Mailliw... I have to know, so I'm going to ask you again, did you do this to Forthright deliberately?'

Mailliw's face crumpled, 'I don't know!' he sobbed and slowly, through tears and deep gulps of breath, he tried to explain how something heard him say he hated Forthright and he wished she was dead and then he confessed as to how the accident occurred. Aunt Foggerty flinched at his words, but at last she understood why he didn't know and couldn't give her an answer.

'Mailliw oh Mailliw!' she said, her voice trembling, 'It was Fate, Mailliw...'

He looked up and wiped his cheeks with his shirtsleeve, 'I don't understand.'

'Of course you don't! But many a person has been undone by Fate, by a said word, an action or deed. Today, of all days, was a magical day and you tempted Fate. Unfortunately, she heard you and accepted your challenge. Fate, it seems, has decided to grant your wish,' she paused and looked at Mailliw's distressed face, 'Mailliw, you are guilty of having said something terrible, but you are innocent of any deliberate harm to your sister.'

Aunt Foggerty's explanation did nothing to alleviate Mailliw's anguish. The words, 'you tempted Fate' only increased the torment in his own mind. As far as he was concerned, it was his fault and he was guilty.

His aunt patted his arm in a comforting manner, but it was as if hot metal splinters stabbed her own heart as it grieved for both Forthright's sickness and Mailliw's despair. Aunt Foggerty tried to rationalise her own feelings of helplessness, but without success, and there was no one there to comfort her. She felt so alone and wanted to curse Fate, but kept her lips pinched.

When Mailliw was calmer she said, 'You ought to go up to bed, there's nothing to be done for now.'

'I don't think I'll be able to sleep.'

'Me neither,' replied Aunt Foggerty. 'Shall we stay here with some blankets?'

Aunt Foggerty went to a chest near the desk and took out some blankets. Peculiar crept out from behind the sofa and climbed onto Mailliw's lap.

'Why does her tail look burnt?' asked Aunt Foggerty.

'I don't know,' sighed Mailliw.

Aunt Foggerty handed Mailliw a soft woollen blanket, 'Try this. It's woven out of something called llama wool. I got it about five years ago from a woman called Mother McGinty, a traveller, but I haven't seen her for a long time now.'

'That's odd,' said Mailliw, 'we met her tonight before all this terrible business happened. She's got a dog called Gypsy who took a fancy to Drabder.'

'Yes, you're right Mailliw, it is very odd… after all this time she turns up again, but she didn't have a dog when I knew her.'

'How are we going to tell Mum and Dad about this?' he asked, his lower lip quivered as he spoke.

'Mailliw, you have asked a very serious question. I'm afraid I don't have an easy answer, but they must be told and I'm thoroughly terrified at the thought,' she said hoarsely.

Aunt Foggerty turned down the lamps and they both sat in silence, eyes staring into the dark, waiting for sleep to arrive.

***

Early the next morning, Mailliw threw off the llama wool blanket. Aunt Foggerty was nowhere around. He yawned and realised he must have slept at some point.

'What a crazy night! I blame it on the moon,' said Peculiar stretching out her claws.

'So what happened to your tail?'

'Don't ask! You have enough to worry about… your sister might be going to die, remember!'

'I'd better go and see her,' Mailliw said and sprinted up the stairs.

Aunt Foggerty was already in the bedroom and Mailliw gasped at the sight of Forthright. Something was definitely wrong.

'Go away Mailliw! I don't want to see you!' Forthright yelled when she saw him standing in the doorway. He ignored the order, stepped into the bedroom and studied her. She was pale. It was to be expected after last night, but there was something else about her. Around the edges of her body, Mailliw could almost see through her.

He looked to Aunt Foggerty, 'What's happening to her?'

'She's disappearing!' she replied.

'Where?'

'I'M PROBABLY GOING WHERE ALL MOONBEAMS GO!' shrieked Forthright.

'Where's that?' he asked uneasily.

'I DON'T KNOW!' she shrieked again. Forthright thumped the pillow on her bed then threw her face into the feathery softness. In a muffled voice she cried, 'I'm most likely going where the light goes when you blow out a candle... and if I knew where that was... I'd be able to tell you where to find me,' she said snivelling. She continued to sob into the pillow as her body shook with convulsions and her heart pounded with trepidation, because nobody, nobody at all was capable of helping her.

Chapter 4
Decisions

'I'm NOT going to let you DIE!' Mailliw shouted as he punched the oak wardrobe. 'Aunt Foggerty knows somebody who survived silver moonbeam sickness. I'll find them and ask how they were cured. You can't die... I promise to save you! I have to save you!'

'Mailliw! Stop it!' ordered Aunt Foggerty, 'You don't know what you're saying. You have no idea of what's involved in such a promise...'

Mailliw looked hard into Aunt Foggerty's eyes, 'Answer this,' he said, 'is there a chance, even the slightest chance my sister can be saved?'

Aunt Foggerty twisted round and looked out of the window. The early morning sunlight was dancing on the river, the sky was blue and the birds were singing, but she didn't notice.

'Well?' he persisted.

A tear rolled down Aunt Foggerty's cheek and she groped for a handkerchief. Finally, she said quietly, 'I'm not sure...' then she paused and said apprehensively, 'maybe there is a very, very small chance, but first there is something you need to know. You'd better come and sit.'

Forthright stopped weeping and looked up from her pillow. Mailliw stepped over the ceremonial gown on the floor and sat on a velvet-covered stool. Neither of them looked at nor spoke to each other while they waited for Aunt Foggerty to speak.

'Yesterday, Mailliw, you called me an old fossil. It may seem to you I've always been old, but there was a time when I was young and had my whole future in front of me, just like you two. Many years ago, when I was working in the capital, Panir, at the head office of the Institute of Historical Events, I was researching archive material and came across some papers which meant an important historical book had to be rewritten. I collaborated with a wizard who was a senior lecturer on the subject. We spent so much time together and got on so well, we ended up falling in love. But, he was already married and unfortunately, his wife was one of the most powerful witches around. When she found out, her anger was so violent that she cast a spell and fried his brain. He became mentally devoid of any thought, an invalid unable to work and I was not in a position to give him the constant care he required.'

Mailliw fidgeted, he didn't want to know about some sordid romance and certainly not something like this about Aunt Foggerty. He was shocked to think his aunt had experienced a life before them and he had no knowledge of it.

'But what has this got to do with me finding a cure for Forthright?' he asked trying to change the topic of conversation.

'It's her isn't it? The lecturer's wife…' Forthright said slowly, 'she's the one who survived the silver moonbeam sickness isn't she?'

'Regrettably, yes,' Aunt Foggerty replied.

'So,' said Mailliw, 'how do I find her?'

'Patience Mailliw! Let me finish. Because of the terrible harm she caused to another human being, there was a court hearing conducted by the Council of Wisdom in Panir. As punishment, they banished her to the Carnivorous Swamp… for life!'

'What happened to him?' asked Forthright.

'She was going to take him with her, but he died before her sentence at the swamp commenced. Before all this, she was called Merry Willows. On her husband's death, she became Merry Willows the Widow. I know she survived silver moonbeam sickness, because, after the Council of Wisdom court hearing, a member of the court said it was a shame to have survived the sickness only to spend the rest of her days in such a place.'

'Merry Willows the Widow. Her name doesn't sound too dreadful,' said Mailliw.

Aunt Foggerty looked at him and suddenly realised she had made a terrible mistake. She was so desperate to help Forthright that she wasn't thinking clearly and should never have told either of them about Merry Willows the Widow. How could she have been so stupid? She couldn't let Mailliw go off and find her. It was far too dangerous!

'Don't be fooled by her name,' Aunt Foggerty replied angrily, 'the nature of the spell she used, aged her beyond her years. She became a hag living in the centre of the swamp. It is surrounded by putrefying flesh, which is devoured by the carnivorous plants that grow there. The swamp is immune to spells and she can't cross it without being eaten alive. It's an abominable place and I can't allow you to go there. Besides, I have absolutely no knowledge as to whether she's still alive… it was many years ago and you may waste precious time on a fruitless journey.'

'Do we have another choice? I mean… we're not exactly brimming over with solutions are we? You tell me how long Forthright has before she disappears completely.'

Aunt Foggerty's dark eyes narrowed, 'Judging by the speed of her deterioration overnight, it's likely she'll be gone…' she hesitated, struggling to get the words out, 'by the next new moon.'

The horrifying answer registered on both Forthright's and Mailliw's faces.

'So short a time?' whispered Forthright, and she lay down and buried her face in the pillow once more.

'Two weeks! In that case, I don't have any time to lose,' said Mailliw striding towards the door.

'Mailliw! Stop right there!'

He halted in the doorway as Aunt Foggerty commanded.

'I can't let you go to somewhere like the Carnivorous Swamp! Think of the danger! Think of what might happen! Think of your parents! It's torture to lose one child, but to risk losing another is just…' Aunt Foggerty faltered as her throat clammed up with emotion and words failed her.

Mailliw reeled round, his face scarlet with anger, 'And how do you think I can face my parents after what I've done, without even trying to do something to save her? Is that what they would want? How could they look at me without remembering… or be able to love me without hating me at the same time?'

'STOP IT! STOP IT!' cried Forthright.

An uneasy silence followed.

'If I was in Mailliw's position, I'd want to do the same,' Forthright said quietly, 'I'd have to know I'd tried my best to save him, even if it meant putting myself in danger or failing in the attempt. I'd have to do it or I'd never be able to face my mother and father again.'

'What, even if it meant they lost both of you?' cried Aunt Foggerty in distress, 'You don't think they'd be comforted by at least having one child still safe and living?'

'They might be, but I wouldn't and I'd have to live with the knowledge for the rest of my life,' Forthright replied in a disturbingly determined voice.

'I agree with Forthright,' nodded Mailliw, 'that's exactly how I feel. I have to try,' and for the first time in weeks they were both in agreement with each other.

Aunt Foggerty looked at them. She was deeply troubled. What a time for both of them to be of the same mind! And how was she going to explain any of this to Philleas and Agnetha?

Forthright observed her anguish, 'I know you feel responsible for us, but Mum and Dad will have to understand this was our decision. It isn't reasonable for you to take the blame on our behalf,' said Forthright.

Aunt Foggerty thought it was strange how at times they were still so childlike and at others, so grown up like right at this moment.

'No...' Aunt Foggerty replied, pulling her shoulders back, 'there will be no blaming. We're going to be in this together and I'll do my utmost to help, because I would never forgive myself if I didn't. If there's a punishment for what we are going to do, then it will either be worth it because we have saved you, or it won't come anywhere near to the pain of losing you,' she finished saying. But, in Aunt Foggerty's heart, sorrow weighed like lead as she thought of what these children might have to face.

'Mailliw, come,' she said briskly, 'we must hurry and prepare. Forthright, you must stay out of the sun. If sunlight touches your skin, it will speed up the rate of your disappearance. But, for now, try to rest, you're going to need your strength as the days pass. As soon as I've sorted Mailliw out, I'll start researching all the books in your father's library to find out what I can.'

Forthright leaned against her pillows to think. If Mailliw failed to find Merry Willows the Widow and discover how she survived silver moonbeam sickness, or if the Widow was already dead, then they needed another plan of action. So, with such a short time remaining, lying around in bed was the last thing Forthright wanted to do.

She pulled herself up and swung her feet over the side of the bed. When Forthright bent down to put on her slippers, she noticed her feet didn't seem to fit into them properly anymore. She snatched her dressing gown and made her way downstairs to her father's library.

Chapter 5
The First Journey Begins

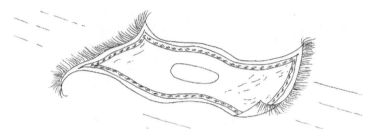

Norgruk was in the dragons' kitchen eating breakfast. He grumbled about being called out for duty last night to accompany Roo and Monity home, and then grumbled about having to carry home the rolled up flying carpet on his return journey. It was a stupid carpet if it didn't work unless somebody sat on it. It didn't help matters when Cleopatra asked why he hadn't sat on it himself and let it bring him home instead!

'Would you sit on it?' he retaliated, but Cleopatra was helping herself to a plateful of water lily roots dressed in horseradish sauce and didn't answer. Dingle was regarding a stack of corncobs on the floor with suspicion, – there might be a spider lurking in there somewhere. He was just about to remove a cob and bite into it, when he saw something twitch. He peered uneasily at the leathery snake-like thing poking out from the bottom. It twitched again. He really didn't like this. The thing moved again, this time from side to side.

'Yah!' yelled Dingle as he leapt from the floor onto the table and landed in Cleopatra's plate of water lily roots. Sniggering erupted from the corn stack and out strutted Peculiar. Dingle's dragon scales went from green to bright red as he watched the vampire cat exit the kitchen with her leathery tail held high and her nose in the air.

'Get off my roots!' barked Cleopatra as she slapped at Dingle's feet. Dingle wiped the horseradish sauce off his feet, chucked a couple of corncobs into his mouth and followed Peculiar to the drawing room. He wanted to know the latest news of Forthright's condition.

'Peculiar and Dingle are here,' said Mailliw to Aunt Foggerty as he looked up from a map they were studying.

'Good. You'll need to take both of them. Dingle will be for protection...' said Aunt Foggerty. At this remark, Peculiar smirked. 'And Peculiar will be the first one to fly over the Carnivorous Swamp on the flying carpet. She'll do an initial survey to get some indication as to whether Merry Willows the Widow is still alive. I don't want you taking the risk until you have a better idea of the situation.'

Hearing what her task was, the smirk evaporated from Peculiar's face. Did they have the slightest clue about what they were asking her to do?

'Can't Dingle fly over instead?' Mailliw asked when he saw the fur bristle on Peculiar's back.

'Good gracious no! A dragon would be hopeless with such an abominable stench! You know how sensitive they are to smells... he'd pass out, fall into the swamp and be devoured. A vampire cat copes much better with that sort of thing.'

Dingle's haunches quivered at the thought of being eaten. He sincerely hoped dragon scales were inedible and would cause the swamp plants to have eternal indigestion.

Mailliw looked at Dingle and Peculiar. His face was flushed with nervous tension as he said, 'I need you both for this journey. I can rely on you to help me save Forthright, can't I?'

Dingle and Peculiar glanced at each other and then averted their eyes. Just for a split second they hesitated, but neither was going to back down in front of the other so they nodded in agreement.

'Excellent!' said Mailliw and took the map Aunt Foggerty was handing to him.

'Keep to the plan Mailliw and don't enter the Carnivorous Swamp. If you do, you'll never get out alive. Do I make myself clear?'

'Crystal clear,' he replied.

***

Outside, Aunt Foggerty's flying carpet had been loaded up with food, water, spare clothing and blankets. Peculiar sat on the carpet as it floated about a metre off the ground. Dingle noticed that her fur was bristled all along her back. He decided he was lucky he could fly.

Aunt Foggerty was holding something out to Mailliw.

'What is it?' he asked.

'I've put this together for you to wear like a mask when you fly over the swamp,' she said, giving him a thick padded length of sheeting. 'It's been soaked in essence of lavender, jasmine and honeysuckle. I've put a renewal spell on it to keep the fragrance from evaporating too quickly. They are the strongest perfumes I have I'm afraid and I don't know how effective they'll be in masking the smell, but try it anyway.'

Mailliw took it and placed it on the carpet underneath the clothing and blankets.

'Now, you've got your wand?' asked Aunt Foggerty.

'Yes, but I thought you said the swamp was immune to magic,' replied Mailliw.

'I did. The swamp is immune to magic, but you're not and neither is Merry Willows the Widow.'

'But I don't know much magic yet,' he said, wishing he had worked harder at school.

'I know that but in the face of danger, your enemy won't, will they? It might be good enough to deter them. Most importantly, eat regularly to maintain your energy levels,' she said pointing at the food packages, 'you never know when you might need to use magic. Remember, low energy creates weak magic,' she said and then paused as she handed Mailliw a locket.

'Take this Mailliw.'

'What's it for?'

'If Merry Willows the Widow refuses to help, use this locket to persuade her. It contains a lock of hair. She'll know who it belongs to and she will desire it. Barter with it wisely.'

Mailliw took the locket and put it around his neck. When he glanced at the library window, he saw Forthright standing in the shadow of the curtain.

'Tell her, I'll be back as soon as I can,' he said and climbed onto the flying carpet.

'I'll ask Monity and Drabder to stay for a few days. They will be of valuable help in the library and I think Drabder would prefer to be here than under his father's feet,' said Aunt Foggerty, '... and Mailliw... be very careful... don't take any unnecessary risks!'

'I'll do my best,' he said, balancing his body in the centre of the carpet. When he was ready, Mailliw spoke the required instructions and the carpet rose into the air. Then Dingle spread his wings. He flapped upwards, aligning his body alongside the flying carpet to position himself ready for any directions Mailliw gave him on the journey. Mailliw had pinned the map to the carpet, ready to compare it with the landmarks below. The sun warmed the backs of their necks as they headed north. They left Feyngrey behind, with its people milling below as they set up for the day's market in the square.

'Say goodbye to civilisation,' warned Peculiar, whose claws gripped like prickly holly leaves on the carpet.

As they travelled, Mailliw looked down at the common land where the moonbeam collecting had taken place the night before. Everything felt unreal. It seemed impossible to believe that something terrible had happened and how, last night, Forthright's short-lived happiness became a nightmare within minutes. He took the carpet lower and observed a few people still packing up, but everyone else had gone. It looked desolate with thin trails of smoke rising from the odd smouldering fire. He saw windblown candyfloss ensnared on a gorse bush, glinting in the morning sun. Spilt bags of popcorn littered the grass, inviting birds to feast on the discarded leftovers.

In the distance, Mailliw peered at a small caravan being drawn along by a horse. It was accompanied by a woman wearing a red and white checked shawl, and a dog walking along by her side. This time, instead of the grey pigeon sitting on Mother McGinty's shoulder, it was now hitching a lift on the back of the horse.

'So much for Gypsy choosing Drabder to have one of her puppies. I don't expect we'll see them again,' he said. Peculiar gave a scathing look as if to say, 'Who wants a puppy anyway?'

Then Mother McGinty looked upwards. She saw him and raised her hand. Gypsy stopped and barked. Mailliw waved back, astonished to find they recognised him, not only from such a distance, but also from their brief encounter last night.

Mailliw took the carpet upwards and Dingle kept at a steady flying pace. They flew over villages, farms, cornfields, olive and orange groves, lavender fields with rows of beehives and hedgerows studded with poppies. In the distance, the mauve haze on the hills loomed ahead of them. Mailliw studied the map. On the other side of the hills was a vast lake called Gillyfrec and once there they'd stop, have some food and allow Dingle a short rest.

As they drew nearer to the hills, the mauve hues faded, turning to gold and green where ripening cornfields and vineyards grew. Higher up the hills, wild goats scrabbled about the boulders and stones searching for vegetation.

'I spy a feast down there!' said Peculiar peering over the side and eyeing the goats.

'Don't worry. I'm sure, at some point, you will be required to source your own food. We've only enough supplies for today and tonight, so I'm hoping we won't be gone for more than a couple of days at the most,' said Mailliw.

'I hope I'll find something more substantial than rats. Their blood is so thin,' moaned Peculiar.

Dingle ignored their conversation and saved his energy for flying.

They gained height, rising above the hills. At the highest point, they looked ahead and there was Lake Gillyfrec. In the middle, the lake was coloured deep blue, but towards the shallows, the water blended into soft shades of aquamarine with clear ripples at the edges, gently ebbing and flowing onto shores of white sand.

'Wow! It looks fantastic! Come on!' said Mailliw to Dingle, 'Let's go down for a quick break. You deserve a rest.'

'We can't go down,' said Dingle as he turned his head from side to side and sniffed the air.

'Why? What's up?' asked Mailliw as he looked around nervously, 'I can't see any problem.'

'The wind is turning colour. It's changing from red to purple.'

Dingle, like all dragons, had the ability to smell subtle wisps of colour in the wind, but only for a short period during the change.

Mailliw frowned, 'That's not good! Which direction is the storm coming from and how much time do we have?'

'It's moving from the east and I estimate it will cut across our path in about twenty-five minutes. If we keep going, we might just get across and outrun the storm, so try to make the thing you're sitting on, go faster. I'll do my best to keep up, but if I fall behind, just keep going. I've got a better chance of surviving the storm than you have.'

45

Mailliw urged the carpet on, and Peculiar's claws dug deeper into the woven cloth as her whiskers became pinned back against her cheeks when the carpet accelerated. After fifteen minutes of top speed flying, Dingle tired. He'd already had a long flight and his burst of speed was faltering. Mailliw looked over his shoulder and watched Dingle falling slightly behind. Then he checked to the east and scanned the brewing purple and yellow tinged clouds. Flashes of lightning streaked across. The light was fading fast, making it difficult to focus on the distant shore.

They were just over halfway across, when the wind howled with eddying swirls buffeting the carpet. A large bump threw Mailliw off balance and he helplessly watched the food, clothing and blankets slide perilously close to the edge. With another bump, the wind whipped them away. Mailliw tried to grip the carpet and wished he had claws like Peculiar. A flash of lightning lit up the sky and Mailliw looked back to see where Dingle was. He glimpsed the dragon hurtling down towards the lake.

'I think Dingle's been struck,' he bellowed at Peculiar, 'he's going down! We've got to get him!'

'No!' growled Peculiar, 'He was aware of the risks and he told us to keep going. Anyway, he might be going lower to get out of the lightning. It's what I'd do.'

Mailliw wasn't so sure. The speed he saw Dingle drop had been frightening. He was going to lose his sister and now Dingle had gone. When Mailliw noticed the perfumed sheeting flapping over the edge of the carpet, he shifted towards it and tried to grab hold. But, just as his fingers touched the fabric, another strong gust caught it and whisked it away. Mailliw swore at the wind, but his words were swept soundlessly into the sky. He clamped his mouth and edged back to Peculiar. Another thrust of wind jolted the carpet and Mailliw was sent sprawling. Peculiar could see his feet close to the edge.

'Hold on to me!' she bawled.

Mailliw stretched out his arms and wound his fingers into Peculiar's fur. He clung on so tight, he was scared of pulling out huge clumps. The clouds rumbled towards them, but the carpet continued heading towards the other side of the lake.

After another ten minutes, Mailliw's fingers were numb. The temperature had dropped and he had no spare clothing to put on. Hailstones the size of golf balls, pelted everywhere. They smashed into Mailliw, Peculiar and the carpet before bouncing over the side. Peculiar screwed up her eyes and searched for somewhere to land the carpet.

'We're nearly there!' she screamed as another hailstone thwacked her ear, 'Start the descent!'

'Land quickly!' Mailliw bellowed at the carpet.

The carpet tore downwards and with alarm, they found it was going too fast to land safely. They went down and down.

'Hang on for a crash landing!' shouted Mailliw, but the warning came too late. The edge of the carpet caught the top of a tree and was deflected sideways. It shuddered and spiralled towards the sand.

'Jump!' roared Mailliw, and Peculiar released her claws from the carpet. She rotated and twisted with Mailliw still clinging on and she landed, as all cats do, on her feet. Mailliw thudded into the sand with his hands holding clumps of fur ripped from Peculiar's back. He forgot about his bruised toe from yesterday as he lay winded and his ribs aching from the impact. Peculiar picked up the carpet and scampered to a couple of protruding rocks where she placed the carpet over the top.

'Come on… there's just enough room for both of us to get under here,' she said, trying to push Mailliw as he staggered to the rocks and crawled beneath the temporary shelter. The hailstones were relentless, lightning forked down towards the lake and there was no sign of Dingle. They both sat together shivering and waited for the storm to pass.

***

With the lightning flash, Dingle had seen the clothes, blankets and food falling overboard from the flying carpet. He folded his wings and raced forwards at an angle he hoped would intercept them, before they sank into the depths of the lake. He dropped and dropped, knowing the flying carpet was increasing its distance between himself and the others. His feet skimmed the water as he opened his wings. Then he stretched out his arms and caught the food and clothing packages. With his arms and claws full, Dingle watched as the blankets hit the water and sank. He flapped his wings, but was too tired to gain any height, so he settled for flying a few metres above the turbulent waves. The problem with flying at such a low level was not being able to see the other side of the lake, and the gathering gloom did not help. He flew on and soon heard a clang in the distance, followed by another, and another. As Dingle drew nearer to the noise, he spotted a buoy swaying in the water with a bell at its centre which was the source of the sound. It wasn't much, but it was enough for Dingle to take refuge until the storm passed. He landed on the buoy and felt his weight tip it to one side. His toes bobbed in and out of the water but at least he could rest.

After a few minutes, the bell drove him crazy with its continual clang, clang, clang, so he unpacked a piece of clothing and wrapped it around the clapper. Then, feeling hunger pangs, Dingle unwrapped the food. When he opened the package and found half a dozen peppermint and parsley patties, his eyes lit up. Aunt Foggerty must have put them in especially for him. Well, they were definitely worth saving from the murky depths of the lake! He took one and nibbled. It took enormous willpower not to gobble it and finish the entire lot, but as he didn't know what lay ahead, it was best to reserve the rations for as long as possible.

So, Dingle remained on the buoy with the silenced bell, hoping and wishing for the storm's speedy departure. The hailstones, when they weren't sploshing into the water all around, were hitting him and even with horny scales, they hurt. But worse, the swaying buoy was making him seasick.

***

The hailstones gradually ceased and the storm clouds continued their journey, taking the lightning and thunder with them. The waves on the lake became calmer and rippled towards the sand again, instead of crashing in like unwelcome visitors. Mailliw crept out from their shelter and searched for anything to make a bonfire.

'The sodden carpet can't fly in this condition,' he told Peculiar, 'we'll have to dry it out as best we can, so we need to build a fire.'

They collected bits of driftwood and broken branches from the storm. From time to time, they scanned the horizon to see if there was any sign of Dingle. Neither of them wanted to admit it seemed hopeless.

Mailliw took out his wand from his pocket and aimed it at the bonfire. Using a basic survival spell, sparks shot out from the wand, and soon flames danced and crackled as they stood holding the carpet close enough to dry without scorching it. Steam rose from Peculiar's fur, and Mailliw's shirt and trousers hissed as they dried.

Suddenly, Peculiar pointed skywards, 'Look! He's found us!' and sure enough, Dingle was flying towards them.

'He's not flying straight!' commented Mailliw, as they both watched Dingle fly to the left, then to the right and back again. He landed clutching the food and clothing.

'Went to get these... landed on buoy... then saw fire... beacon...' he rambled at them, then he keeled over and was violently sick.

'Eugh! Not a pretty sight!' muttered Peculiar.

'Food and clothes!' yelled Mailliw, and he pounced on the packages Dingle had discarded on the sand.

Dingle lay on his back, his sides heaving as he gulped for air. Sleep! That's what he wanted more than anything, to stop the memory of the sea churning him backwards and forwards on the buoy like a demented chicken. His eyes closed and his mind drifted away.

Chapter 6
In The Library

Mailliw, Peculiar and Dingle had only been gone for a few hours, but Forthright and Aunt Foggerty had been hard at work in the library ever since they had left. Norgruk had been sent with messages, inviting Monity and Drabder to stay at the chateau and help with the research on silver moonbeam sickness.

Aunt Foggerty was sitting at Philleas' desk, searching in the *Encyclopaedia Magica* for a formula to create a speed-reading spell. Strands of unbrushed hair fell over her face as she bent over the pages. Forthright stood close by. Now that Mailliw had gone, she was already missing him. Their relationship had been terrible over the last few weeks, but at least he was there for meals, or rushing around trying to get things done at the last minute, or sitting in the snug, or walking to and from school. The rooms felt empty without him and it was as if they also missed his presence. They were silent and sleepy, waiting for his energy to infuse them like sunshine bursting through the clouds.

'Aha! This formula is just the thing,' said Aunt Foggerty, stabbing at the page with her finger, 'by using a speed-reading spell we will be able to cover hundreds of books every day.

I'm going to combine it with an automatic alarm, so when the words "silver moonbeam sickness" are found, the pages will stop and a whistle will blow so we can identify the book immediately. The only problem is... the spell will have to be done individually for every book. I sincerely hope Drabder and Monity can come and stay because we need to be organised and methodical. It will be of enormous help if they can assist by getting the books from the shelves, keeping a record of which shelves have been completed, and then returning the books correctly.'

Forthright cast her eyes over the thousands of books on the shelves.

'Do we have to go through every one? Surely we only need to research the potions books?' she asked Aunt Foggerty.

Aunt Foggerty scanned the books, 'It's best we start with potions and if we can't find anything there, we must continue with the rest. From my experience of working at the Institute of Historical Events, you never know where a useful bit of information might be waiting.'

Forthright removed numerous potion books from the shelves and placed them on any spare space in the library. Aunt Foggerty touched each book with her wand. The covers opened and she chanted a long incantation for each book. The first book turned a few pages and then the pages flipped faster and faster, creating a small breeze like a fan. When all the selected books were underway, the sound of whirring filled the room.

***

As Norgruk delivered the invitation to Roo, she wasn't sure if Monity would want to go after Bit was nearly killed last night, but Foggerty had confirmed Forthright had contracted silver moonbeam sickness.

'Foggerty has invited you to stay at the chateau for a few days. She's hoping you will help them to research silver moonbeam sickness in the library. She says she's also sent a message to ask if Drabder can go as well. What do you think?'

Monity read the message and sat down, 'I don't really want to go after Forthright hurt Bit last night.'

'I understand and respect how you're feeling, but Forthright desperately needs help,' said her mother.

'And so does Bit!' Monity retorted. She thought about the potion that her father had created when they arrived home. He used a recipe of liquidized mosquitoes blended with the herb, healwort, before feeding it to Bit through a tiny dropper. Bit had gone into a deep sleep and was still sleeping.

'Anyway, you told me last night there's no cure for silver moonbeam sickness, so what's the point in researching something that doesn't exist?' argued Monity.

'That's not what it's about! Forthright must be terrified of what's going to happen and her parents aren't there to comfort her. How would you feel if your friends deserted you in your time of need?'

Monity's face flushed.

'If Drabder goes along, then I'll go as well,' said Monity and she went to inspect Bit, asleep in her handkerchief bed.

'I'll send a message to say you're going then,' answered Roo, knowing Drabder was unlikely to decline.

***

Norgruk handed the replies to the Aunt Foggerty and he stared about the library in astonishment as open books flipped page after page.

'Oh! Thank goodness, both Drabder and Monity will be arriving after lunch. It will speed things up tremendously,' she said and Forthright noticed the tired circles under her aunt's eyes.

'I feel awful about what I did to Bit and Monity was so upset, I'm rather surprised she has agreed to come,' said Forthright as she took another tome from the bookshelf. Aunt Foggerty rose from the desk and took her walking stick.

'There are enough books going at the moment. I'm going to need plenty of energy for casting so many spells, so I'll go and make lunch now before Drabder and Monity arrive. Then we'll really be able to get cracking. Will you be alright here?'

'Worried I might disappear somewhere without telling you,' Forthright said, trying to smile, but by the look on Aunt Foggerty's face, she wished she'd never uttered it.

'I'm sorry, it wasn't funny, I don't know why I said it,' Forthright mumbled and groaned as a wave of nausea passed over her. She sat down at the desk and put her head between her hands.

'Forthright! What's the matter? What is it?' asked Aunt Foggerty urgently, 'Do you feel sick?'

'Yes,' moaned Forthright.

Aunt Foggerty put her hand on Forthright's head and was startled to find her fingers move through the outline of it without touching her hair.

'Damn it!' cried Aunt Foggerty.

Forthright looked up in alarm, but Aunt Foggerty was already halfway to the door.

'I'll get you some mallow root and barley medicine. It should help the nausea,' she said, unable to look at Forthright. She didn't want Forthright to see her fear... she had just learned the silver moonbeam sickness was accelerating faster than she had initially estimated.

Forthright lifted her head and slowly opened the book sitting on the desk in front of her. She turned the pages while she waited for Aunt Foggerty to return with the medicine. The book's title was *The History of Magical Potions During the Reign of Katrin II, the Queen of Amshir.* She experienced another wave of nausea and closed the book. She tried to think about her early history lessons in school, when they were taught about their country being ruled by the kings and queens of Amshir. But being ruled by kings and queens ceased over five hundred years ago, when Queen Katrin II's only child, Solaré, was stolen. Queen Katrin II bestowed the gift of speech upon all her court favourites such as dragons, unicorns, vampire cats, changelings, and all the more unusual creatures who had their own legends, enabling them to travel and communicate in their search for the stolen child, but Solaré remained lost. When Queen Katrin II died, there was no heir, and battles were fought to put a new ruler on the throne. After many years of fighting without success, a government called The Council of Wisdom was created. The Council gave Amshir a new name and called it Samborca.

Forthright tried to concentrate, but the nausea overwhelmed her and she flopped forward over the closed book. She desperately hoped Aunt Foggerty returned soon with the medicine and it would quickly soothe the urge to vomit.

**

When Drabder and Monity showed up, Aunt Foggerty took them to the library. Like Norgruk earlier, they looked astonished when they observed open books on every available space with pages flicking over fast, all by themselves.

'W-where's Mailliw?' Drabder asked looking around the room and when Monity saw Forthright, she gave a small gasp.

'Thanks for coming,' said Forthright, 'and Monity, I can't tell you how sorry I am about what I did to Bit.'

Monity reddened and said, 'Dad says she's going to be alright, but I think she'll be nervous about coming near you again.'

It was Forthright's turn to go pink as she admitted, 'I don't blame her. Anyway, if we can't find a cure in the next couple of weeks, she won't need to worry because it seems I'll have disappeared by then,' she said, fighting back the tears, 'as for Mailliw, he's gone to find someone who was cured of the sickness many years ago. It's a gamble, because she may be dead for all we know. He should be back in a day or two.'

Drabder glanced at Monity. Why hadn't she told him how serious the situation was?

'We've decided to start with this section and can I just say, thanks again for coming,' said Forthright waving her hand at the potions books, 'we thought a rotation system would be best. Aunt Foggerty is casting the speed-reading spell on each book, so if I take the books from the shelves, Drabder can return them once the reading is finished, and Monity can update the record sheets on which books have been completed to avoid duplication. This way we should make fast progress. Is that okay?'

Drabder and Monity nodded, then looked about the room when a couple of books shut their covers with a snap and lay waiting to be replaced on the shelf.

They began work in earnest with Aunt Foggerty chanting, Forthright and Drabder moving books around and Monity diligently keeping a record of every book. With books opening and closing, and pages whirring like fans, the library sounded like a fat, sleek cat purring.

***

While they worked, Aunt Foggerty kept a watchful eye on Forthright when she thought she wasn't looking. The medicine appeared to have controlled the nausea for the time being, but the dose had to be repeated frequently.

She also noticed with so many books fanning their pages, more and more dust wafted around the library and with all the incantations, her throat had become dry and irritated.

'I need a cup of tea, would anyone else like one?' she asked. Everyone nodded and carried on with what they were doing. Monity continued recording details with black inky fingers from the quill pen, but when Aunt Foggerty left the library, she sidled up to Forthright.

'Can I ask you a personal question?' she said looking at her. Little needles pricked Forthright's stomach in anxiety, but she felt she couldn't say no, so she nodded even though her shoulders became tense.

Monity drew in her breath, 'Why do you call Aunt Foggerty your aunt? She's looks too old to be your dad's sister, she's more like a grandmother.'

Forthright's shoulders relaxed. She thought Monity was going to ask about her disappearing outline. That was something she didn't want to discuss because it made it too real.

'She's actually our great aunt, but it's too much of a mouthful, so we just call her aunt. She raised my dad when he was a boy. His parents died when he was a baby and now she looks after us when Mum and Dad are away. She's always lived with us and I can't imagine it being any different.'

'Oh! I see… I hope you didn't mind me asking, but I suppose it's a bit like Drabder being looked after so much by my mum. Drabder's mother left when he was tiny and his dad, my Uncle Turnbull, didn't know the first thing about babies, so Mum being his sister an' all, helped him out, even though she says he's a bad tempered old so-and-so!' Monity's hand flew to her mouth, 'Oops! I'm not supposed to repeat things like that… even if it is true,' she whispered to Forthright, 'although, my Mum has never understood why Drabder's mother left him behind.'

Drabder replaced another book on a shelf, looked at Monity squarely and pronounced, 'Perhaps she had no choice. I mean, if she ran away or something, maybe she had nowhere to live and found it impossible to take me with her. I don't believe any mother would deliberately leave her child unless she had to.'

Forthright and Monity were astounded. He spoke with a firm tone of voice and he hadn't stammered once.

'One day, I'm going to look for her…' but before he said anymore, there was a sudden shrill noise piercing the room.

'What's that?' Monity shrieked, 'I nearly jumped out of my skin,' she said, her heart thumping with fright. Forthright's heart thumped for a different reason. It was the alarm. The words 'silver moonbeam sickness' had been located.

'Drabder! Run to the kitchen and get Aunt Foggerty!' she said urgently, but as Drabder reached the door, Aunt Foggerty entered. Forthright's blanched face pivoted towards the book with the motionless pages… the one containing the words she so desperately wanted to find. They crowded round the book, nobody uttering a sound. Forthright's heart pumped adrenaline around her body and soon her arms and legs were shaking. Aunt Foggerty leaned over the book and started reading and as she read, her shoulders sagged.

She shook her head and said, 'No… not this time.'

Forthright gazed in disbelief, the disappointment was like a sharp knife being held at her throat.

Aunt Foggerty glanced up, 'It did find the words, but only in relation to the person who invented the moondial.'

***

By late afternoon, Aunt Foggerty's energy was too weak to be effective. Pages turned slower and slower as her energy levels dropped, and she needed a break with food and drink.

'I'm going to the kitchen to make tea,' she said and noticed Monity's eyes drooping, 'come and help Monity, you need a break as much as I do.'

'We'll all come,' said Forthright and they followed Aunt Foggerty down the stairs to the large kitchen. Copper pots and pans hung on the stone walls and a vast range stood in an inglenook fireplace. Although it was summer, the range was still in use to provide the kitchen with enough hot water for the domestic chores and several hot baths.

There were four oak doors on the left-hand side of the kitchen and each was engraved with the category of goods stored within. The first door read, 'Jams, Jellies and Other Preserved Things', the second, 'Dried Herbs, Flowers and Spices', the third, 'Brews, Potions and Beverages' and the fourth door read 'Potent Spells, Medicinal Remedies and Unpleasant Things'. A drying rack hung from the ceiling and dried bunches of lavender and mint perfumed the warm air.

'I say,' said Monity, her eyes widening in admiration, 'this kitchen is fantastic! Ours is a pokey affair in the cottage.'

Drabder wandered around. His fingers touched the pots and pans to feel the burnished copper. Then he stopped in front of a large dresser where an enormous glass jar was filled with peppermint and parsley patties.

'May I t-try one?' he asked.

'Of course you can, but don't expect to breathe emerald flames… breathing those is a privilege for dragons only!' Aunt Foggerty told him. 'Can you bring the kettle from the range Monity and we'll make a pot of tea.'

Aunt Foggerty poured hot water into the teapot and heard Drabder munching.

'How's the patty Drabder?' she asked.

'Scrumptious!' he replied with a mouthful of crumbs, 'No wonder d-dragons love them! The peppermint is ice-cold, b-b-but it melts in your mouth with the peppery heat from the parsley... incredibly yummy!'

They brewed the tea and placed it on the large oak table in the middle of the kitchen. Forthright laid delicate floral china cups and saucers with silver spoons on the table, followed by a matching milk jug and a sugar bowl filled with sugar crystals.

Before long, they were sitting down eating toasted teacakes with cinnamon butter, followed by sticky flapjacks and a rich dark fruit cake.

'What happens if Mailliw doesn't return in a c-couple of days?' asked Drabder eating his teacake with his usual impeccable manners.

Aunt Foggerty looked at him and said, 'We'll have to organise a search party with Norgruk, but I truly hope it won't come to that. I'm repeating "keep safe" incantations when I'm not concentrating on the books.'

Forthright chewed her flapjack and wondered if she was really hungry or whether it was comfort eating. Monity had finished hers and was slurping her cup of tea.

'Sorry,' she said, realising Forthright was staring at her, 'the tea's rather hot. I don't normally make such rude noises when I drink.'

Drabder gaped at her and said, 'Yes you do! You're always d-d-doing it and it annoys the living daylights out of your m-mother!'

'Okay! So I slurp! Makes the tea taste better. Can't understand why everyone makes such a fuss about the drink anyway,' muttered Monity with embarrassment.

A sound from upstairs stunned everyone into silence. They heard the shrill clamour of not one, but two whistles! Forthright jumped up from her chair in astonishment, she couldn't believe it, but it was true... upstairs in the library, there really were two books sounding the alarm.

Chapter 7
The Carnivorous Swamp

Dingle slept whilst Mailliw and Peculiar continued to dry the carpet. Mailliw impatiently turned it in front of the fire, hoping to dry it more quickly. He wanted to get on with their journey to find Merry Willows the Widow.

'We can't let him sleep any longer. We need to reach the Carnivorous Swamp before dark and it's been a long enough day as it is,' Mailliw said. It seemed like days since they had left home.

Mailliw dried out the map and re-pinned it onto the carpet. It was slightly smudged from being wet, but still readable. Then he and Peculiar loaded up the remaining food and clothes. His own clothes were nearly dry, but Peculiar's fur was becoming frizzy and full of static, so before long she resembled a great furry puffball. It did help to hide the bald patches from the missing fur on her back, but her spindly bald tail looked even more pathetic.

'How much further do we have to go?' asked Peculiar.

'An hour or so of flying should see us there, as long as we don't meet anything else unexpected. So we should arrive before nightfall. We'll have to make camp before sending you over the swamp.'

Peculiar regarded the lake. She had heard rumours about the swamp; how the smell was enough to drive any living creature within the vicinity to madness. Being a vampire cat she was able to stomach strong smells, but Dingle couldn't even cope with the smell of goat's blood. And what about Mailliw? How would it affect him?

Mailliw shook Dingle awake and waited for the sleepy eyes to register who was shaking him.

'We must get going if we want to avoid travelling in the dark,' he said.

'Not a good idea in strange country,' Dingle mumbled and clambered to his feet. Grains of sand between his scales irritated him, so he shook his body and sent the sand flying in all directions.

Once back in the air, they could see how calm the lake was. The sun shone on the waves and they glittered like stars. It was difficult to believe that a few hours ago, they'd been lucky not to have perished. At least now, Dingle was almost flying straight again as they continued their journey.

***

With the shores of the lake left behind, they looked down at the changing landscape. There were no green fields or vineyards revealing the fertility of the land. Instead, the land was flat with sparse, shrivelled vegetation.

Peculiar sat staring ahead when her nose began twitching. She sneaked a sideways peek at Dingle and saw he was also aware of the malodorous taint in the air. Every minute the smell increased, until even Mailliw noticed.

'I think we must be almost there, judging by the pong!' he said.

'It'll get a lot worse yet,' replied Peculiar, 'can you and Dingle find something to wrap around your noses like masks?'

Mailliw pulled out a pair of trousers and a thick jumper from the clothing Dingle had rescued. He held out the trousers for Dingle, who flew as close as he could to the carpet, before taking them. Mailliw rolled the jumper in half, and then he secured it over his nose and mouth by using the arms to tie around the back of his head. Dingle held the trousers in his claws but had trouble in concentrating on two jobs at the same time. Flying and dressing did not go together. Eventually, he placed the trousers on his head, pulled the legs down behind his ears and then brought the legs forward to wind down the length of his snout like a bandage. He finished by hooking the hems over two top teeth, to stop the trousers from unravelling. Peculiar stole a glance at him through the corner of her eye. If the smell hadn't been so bad, she would have thought it extremely amusing.

'There's the swamp!' said Mailliw in a muffled tone as he spoke through the jumper, 'I'm going to take the carpet down and just skim the ground until we reach the edge.' The carpet descended and as the speed decreased, they became aware of a loud humming noise.

'I think it's coming from the swamp,' said Dingle, pointing ahead of them, 'we ought to stop here.'

'Flies!' said Peculiar.

'What?' asked Mailliw.

'Flies! You know, small, annoying buzzy things,' replied Peculiar, 'there are millions of the little blighters. They're attracted by the smell.'

'I can't go any closer,' said Dingle mumbling through the trousers, 'I really can't.'

'I agree,' said Mailliw, 'this is as far as we go. I'm not sure I can stick it for much longer. I suggest we retreat further back to make camp for the night. Then first thing tomorrow morning, Peculiar, you can do your reconnaissance and then rendezvous back at camp.'

'I'm going to throw up any second!' moaned Dingle as he hovered behind the carpet.

Mailliw veered the carpet around and they headed away from the swamp. By the time the smell was at a bearable level, dusk was falling. There was just enough light to gather some dried debris to make a carpet support for an open-ended tent, and enough wood for a small fire. With the fire stacked and lit, Mailliw took his wand and stepped several paces away.

'Will it work?' asked Dingle.

'What… the magic circle? Well, put it this way… I'd prefer to stay here overnight knowing I've drawn one around the camp rather than not drawn one,' Mailliw replied. He murmured a protective incantation to evoke the Guardian Spirits of the night as he completed the circle in the dust.

***

They ate supper as they sat around the fire and Mailliw said, 'I suggest we take it in turns to sleep. I'll take the first watch. Peculiar, if you have the second watch, you'll be able to get some more sleep before setting off tomorrow, and Dingle can do the last one.'

'In that case, I'm going to bed now,' said Dingle. 'Wake me when it's my turn,' and he curled up underneath their homemade tent. When Peculiar thought Dingle was asleep, she moved closer to Mailliw so he could scratch her ears.

'So, what's the plan?' she asked.

'We'll wait for your return tomorrow. If there are signs of the witch and you have some bearings for me, I'll go and find her…' he said and paused, 'if I'm not back by tomorrow evening, you must return home. Promise me you will return home with Dingle.'

Peculiar sat in silence.

'Promise me!' repeated Mailliw, and he waited for her to respond.

Eventually, Peculiar answered, 'I promise,' and Mailliw was satisfied.

'Off you go… go and get some sleep,' he said, and gave her a gentle push towards the tent.

Peculiar begrudgingly lay next to Dingle. Mailliw sat alone listening to the night air. There was the odd crackle from the fire, but everything else was silent. Too silent! There were no hooting owls or rustlings from nocturnal creatures. The smell from the swamp seemed to have driven every living thing away. It was like death stealing across the night sky, an unseen enemy, waiting, waiting, waiting.

***

Dawn arrived, and Dingle stared blearily as his turn at night watch ended. The sun was rising and he was grateful nothing eventful had occurred during the night. Maybe the magic circle had worked! He was still tired from yesterday's flying, and today he hoped to have enough rest before the flight home. He watched Peculiar stretch as she moved her body out from under the tent. At home, she might be a very annoying creature, but he was glad she was here now. There was something reassuring about having her around. He was beginning to like her, but he wasn't going to admit any such thing to her!

Mailliw emerged from the tent rubbing his eyes, 'Morning Dingle, everything okay?'

Dingle nodded and ambled over to join Mailliw as they took the carpet off its supports for Peculiar's journey. When it was ready, Peculiar leapt on and flexed her claws.

'You're keen aren't you?' said Dingle looking at her in surprise.

'The sooner I go, the sooner I get back,' Peculiar replied, but Dingle noticed she didn't make eye contact. When Peculiar fixed her claws through the carpet, the fur on her back bristled again. With trembling whiskers, she gave a nervous smile, then she raised her bare tail and flicked it across Dingle's face.

'Ouch!' he complained, 'What was that for?'

'For setting fire to it the other night,' she said and gave Dingle a devilish smirk. Dingle was in two minds about liking her after all.

Mailliw patted her shoulder and said, 'Ready when you are Peculiar.'

'Ready,' she replied.

Mailliw watched the carpet. It rose into the air and headed towards the swamp. Peculiar stared straight ahead. Not once did she look back to see Mailliw and Dingle waving as the carpet flew further away from them.

When Peculiar had vanished from view, Mailliw said, 'I need to keep busy, so we'd better gather some more dried vegetation for the fire, in case we need one later.'

They continued with the task of collecting and as the sun rose higher, the heat cooked the dried earth. The crisp vegetation was scattered some distance apart and there were no signs of any streams to quench their thirst in the increasing heat.

'Do you want me to go and look for water?' enquired Dingle, squinting up at the sun.

'We've gone from being completely drenched yesterday to bone dry today,' said Mailliw fanning his face with his hand. 'Can you remember seeing any water sources near here when we flew over yesterday?'

'Apart from the swamp you mean? Can't say I noticed anything, so if I go, I don't know how long I'll be gone.'

Mailliw thought. Was it wise to let Dingle go? If they were all separated, how would any of them know if the others were in difficulty and needed help? If Dingle or Peculiar failed to return, he would be stranded. But did he have any choice? Without water, they would die anyway. He was just about to tell him to go when Dingle waved frantically.

'Look! It's Peculiar!'

Mailliw strained round and his eyes searched the direction indicated. As the carpet drew closer, there was Peculiar with her head in a position which indicated she was still staring ahead. When the carpet landed, Peculiar panted with relief as her feet touched solid ground once more. Mailliw grabbed her and hugged her tight.

'Good grief! You smell disgusting,' said Dingle putting his claws over his nose.

'If you'd been where I'd been, you'd smell too!' she replied as her tail twitched from side to side in the sand. She stepped back from Mailliw, 'She's there! But she's a nasty piece of work!'

'What do you mean? You found her then? She's not dead?' Mailliw asked, firing out the questions before Peculiar had time to answer the first one.

'There's an island in the middle of the swamp and when I spotted it, I flew lower down to see if there were any signs of her. The next thing I knew, she cast a lightning bolt from her wand and it blew a hole in the carpet,' Peculiar explained and pointed to a hole about ten centimetres in diameter near one of the corners.

Mailliw looked in the direction of the swamp. His stomach churned. Encountering Merry Willows the Widow could mean facing death… and immediately Mailliw understood the kind of fear Forthright was experiencing; the knowledge that life was not eternal, that it might be snuffed out sooner rather than later, and the only remaining thing would be you in somebody else's memory.

After a few moments of silence he said, 'I must go.'

'Mailliw… it's horrible, very horrible,' Peculiar warned him, 'you must wrap something really, really tight over your nose.'

'I'll use the trousers Dingle used and tie a big knot at the back of my head,' he said picking them up.

'And Mailliw…'

'Yes?'

'Keep your eyes shut whenever you can.'

67

Chapter 8
Meeting The Widow

Mailliw sat on the carpet and instructed it to return to the island in the swamp. It floated up and surged forwards. A fist gripped his insides like a vice when he thought about what he was doing. He was now on his way to see the terrible Merry Willows the Widow, the witch who survived silver moonbeam sickness, the witch who had fried her husband's brain, the witch who was then banished to live the remainder of her life in the Carnivorous Swamp. Nevertheless, he had to do it for Forthright.

The smell in his nostrils rapidly increased as he approached the swamp. It was unbearable even with the trousers tightly wrapped around his face. He pressed his hands to his nose and breathed through his mouth. Mailliw didn't know which was worse, the smell or almost being able to taste the decomposing matter. Before long, Mailliw heard the thunderous buzzing from the flies. The sound ran like a cold razor over his spine and he shuddered. With the combination of the stench and the deafening flies becoming excruciating, Mailliw wanted to rip the trousers off his face and scream.

The carpet continued over the swamp and Mailliw lay face down, unable to control the rising sick in his throat. He swallowed over and over, attempting to hold it back, but the sour, watery sensation in his mouth persisted. Eventually, he retched over the side and watched, as thousands of flies descended onto the vomit when it splattered into thick red sludge. Too late, Mailliw remembered Peculiar's words, 'Keep your eyes shut whenever you can' and he saw numerous half-decomposed corpses being devoured by plants with needle-like teeth. The corpses were flayed open and suddenly the grisly truth pummelled into his mind... the red sludge was congealed blood! He trembled as bodies with dead eyes stared up at him out of half eaten faces. With terror, Mailliw observed the plants halt in their feasting and look towards the carpet, charting its progress. Yet, they were sightless... it was as if they could smell him! Thousands of them knowing and waiting. Mailliw groaned and forced his body back to the centre of the carpet. How much longer was the journey? His head spun and then... he started to laugh. It became a loud hysterical laugh. He couldn't take much more of this. Why didn't he just fall over the side and end this madness? He ceased laughing as he rolled onto his back and squeezed his eyes shut, trying to block out the sickening images beneath him.

He maintained this position and suppressed the urge to vomit again. Anything to avoid the risk of seeing what was over the side. It was a living nightmare and instead of wanting to open his eyes to wake up, he wanted to sink into a deep sleep and forget about the smell, the flies and the flesh-eating plants waiting for him to be their next meal.

***

'BOY!' shouted a voice.

Mailliw opened his eyes and discovered he was lying on the motionless carpet. At last it had landed on the island in the middle of the swamp. He pushed himself to his knees and tried to determine where the shout had come from. About ten metres away, there was a small figure dressed in black.

'STAY WHERE YOU ARE!' the voice shrieked, 'TELL ME WHY YOU ARE HERE!'

Mailliw remained on his knees, but to be able to answer, he had to remove the trouser wrap, and what about the smell? He couldn't talk if he was being sick! While these thoughts tore through his mind, his nose registered the absence of rotting odour, and instead he smelt an overpowering sickly-sweet honey fragrance. Cautiously, he untied the trousers and took a quick sniff. The air, at last, was tolerable.

'I'm here because I need your help!' Mailliw replied in a loud voice.

'HELP? WHY DO YOU THINK I WOULD HELP YOU?'

The black figure shuffled towards Mailliw. He looked to see the speaker's face, but it was covered with a black fine mesh veil. He couldn't even see her eyes. Mailliw's heart thumped as the black figure moved and stood in front of him. In her right hand, she held a wand.

'You don't answer boy!'

Fear flowed through every artery and vein in Mailliw's body and with the witch's wand pointing directly at his head, he was at her mercy.

Mailliw bowed his head and said, 'I come to you in supplication. I am thirsty and hungry, and you have valuable information I need.'

'Hah! The rules of supplication don't apply here and any information has a high price!'

'I have means to pay.'

'Boy, you have nothing I could possibly want. Maybe I ought to steal your flying carpet and leave you stranded, or make you a slave… or even kill you if I so choose!'

Mailliw's brow broke out in a clammy sweat from nervous tension and fear. But why was he still on his knees? The witch had already told him the rules of supplication did not apply, so there was no need for him to remain kneeling before her. His mind flashed over the situation. Should he let her enslave or kill him without a fight? He had nothing to lose and everything to gain.

This simple truth drove Mailliw's fear away, so he rose from his knees and drew himself up to his full height. He was slightly taller and this gave him an advantage.

'I'm not afraid of you!' Mailliw said and drew out his wand.

'Hah! What's your knowledge compared to mine you foolish boy!'

Mailliw coloured slightly and turned his head. The sun's rays struck the locket hanging around his neck. It glinted and reflected the light back at the witch standing in front of him.

'Agh!' she screamed and dropped her wand in the dust. Then her bony hands clawed at her chest. Her nails flailed against her black cloak as if she was trying to cut out her own heart before she finally sank to her knees and doubled over. Mailliw stopped dead. What had he done to cause such a reaction? He watched dumbfounded until the huddled figure lay still.

'Get up!' Mailliw commanded as sternly as he could and watched with amazement as the witch slowly lifted her head and obeyed.

'Throw your wand over there,' he said waving at a nearby rock and the witch discarded it in the direction indicated. This reversal of power was staggering, but Mailliw was suspicious. What if the witch's performance was a trick?

The witch stood before Mailliw with her head inclined and her chest heaving silently.

'Please… tell me… where did you get that?' the witch said, her voice cracking with emotion and her fingers pointing at the locket.

'Why should I tell you? Didn't you say any information has a high price?' Mailliw replied, suddenly realising the locket was responsible for his change in fortune. He remembered Aunt Foggerty had told him to use it wisely and now he fully intended to do so.

'Let's start again, shall we? I'm thirsty and hungry and require a more hospitable welcome,' Mailliw said, fetching the wand from the rock and putting it into his own pocket.

'Of course, of course,' the witch replied inclining her head once more, 'come this way.'

'You go first,' he said, not convinced she was trustworthy. He wasn't going to be taken in by some ruse so she gained the locket and he lost his advantage. Without the locket, he had nothing, nothing at all with which to save his sister.

As the witch walked ahead of Mailliw, he paid more attention to his surroundings. He was curious as to why the air was so thickly fragranced with honey and how she managed to live here for so long on her own. What did she eat and drink? Where did she sleep? Yet, although he desired to know the answers to these questions, he resisted from asking.

Soon, Mailliw noticed a garden with rows of vegetable beds filled with carrots, onions, potatoes, peas, beans, lettuces, radishes, tomatoes and pumpkins. Mailliw also became aware of a musical sound so refreshing to his ears, it was as though the detestable buzzing from the flies had been cleansed away and never existed. He looked around and saw the tinkling and splashing playing upon some rocks. It was water, fresh spring water! The ground changed from being dusty and arid to one rich in grasses, mosses and clovers growing around the rocks where the water sprinkled and quenched the soil. At the end of the vegetable garden, stood a small dwelling constructed of dried mud. The roof was made of woven reeds that looked like they had been harvested from the edges of the swamp.

'Come this way. My home is very humble, just the one room,' the witch said pushing aside a door, also woven from reeds. It was cool inside with a table, two chairs, two small cupboards along one wall, and a bed against the other. At the far end, there was a fireplace where a cauldron waited to be used, and on the table rested a matching goblet and clay pitcher. The witch hobbled to the table, lifted the pitcher and poured water into the goblet.

'You said you were thirsty, here… drink this,' she said offering it to Mailliw.

'How do I know it doesn't contain poison?'

'It's only water, pure water from the spring.'

'You drink first.'

'To do as you ask, I will have to remove the veil. You will not like what you see.'

'I'll take the risk,' replied Mailliw, thinking nothing was worse than some of the gruesome scenes he had witnessed flying over the swamp. The witch removed the veil from her face and bowed her head.

'Look at me!' Mailliw instructed. He took a deep breath ready. When the witch looked up, Mailliw reeled with shock. There he was, gazing at the most sorrowful face he had ever seen. The pain and grief were like an open wound and his heart contracted in an effort to protect itself from being pierced with sympathy. How would he describe such a face to Forthright? He could describe ugly, old and evil, but this… what words described this pitiful creature before him? Every wrinkle was carved with wretchedness.

'I warned you, but you didn't listen!' she mumbled, 'And now you see me as I am… a hideous old creature with a face scarred by the most terrible crime.'

'No… you're wrong… you're not hideous! You're old, yes, but not hideous…'

The witch raised her scrawny hands to replace the veil, but Mailliw put out his hand and stopped her.

'Don't put it back. I'd rather see your face. You're less…' he thought for the right words to use, 'scary without it!'

The witch raised her head and cackled. It was an unpleasant noise rising from her throat and gurgling as if somebody was strangling her. A sneer flickered over her lips.

'So, you were afraid!'

Mailliw stopped talking. His mind whirled. Had he just made an error by almost admitting he had been afraid? No, he might have been afraid at first, but strangely, he wasn't now.

'I want to trust you,' he said, 'I want to exchange this locket in a fair deal. I have something you want and you have something I want. Merry Willows, are you agreeable to an honest trade?'

The witch looked as if Mailliw had slapped her face.

'My name!' she wailed, 'You used my name! I haven't heard my name for so long that I became a nobody, a nothing, a forgotten nothing, but you... you have called me by my name. I'm not forgotten, I'm not nothing... I'm something... I'm someone! I'm Merry Willows!'

Merry Willows shuffled to her bed and fell onto the hard reed mattress. She coughed and wheezed where she lay. Mailliw looked around in bewilderment. What should he do now? She hadn't agreed to the exchange and he wasn't sure whether trust was a word in her vocabulary. His mouth was parched and he took up the goblet of spring water but before he took a sip, a large grey pigeon flapped in through the door and landed on the table. Merry Willows glanced up and chortled, long and hard. The sound rebounded off the dried mud walls and Mailliw put the goblet back down. What was so funny? Was he about to drink poison after all?

'I go for years seeing nobody apart from this pigeon once in a while and today I see a vampire cat, a boy and the pigeon all in the same day! This place is starting to get a bit too crowded for my liking,' she said, and coughed up spittle from deep within her throat. Mailliw watched the pigeon's head bobbing up and down as it paced around on the table. What was a pigeon doing here? He moved closer and inspected the bird. Tied to one leg with a thin thread, was a small roll of parchment.

'The bird's got a message,' declared Mailliw.

'It's from the only person in the whole of Samborca I could even remotely call a friend,' said Merry Willows, 'it's from someone called Mother McGinty.'

'Mother McGinty? Why does her name keep cropping up lately?' asked Mailliw giving her a curious look.

'Do you know her?'

'No, yes... no, well sort of...' replied Mailliw.

Merry Willows rose from the bed and removed the message before taking the bird to the door and thrusting it skyward. She watched it fly away.

'Mother McGinty stays far away from the swamp, but the bird usually arrives to let me know she is about,' she said and unrolled the message to read the contents. Then she put the parchment on the table and watched as it curled back into a small roll. The mystery deepens, thought Mailliw. Merry Willows faced him, picked up the goblet, and drank the water. Then she replenished the goblet with more water and offered it to Mailliw.

'Trust works both ways,' she said, 'and the pigeon is a timely reminder of that. If you help me to prepare a meal by digging the required vegetables and light the fire for the cauldron, I'll tell you about Mother McGinty.'

'So this is not part of the deal for the locket then?'

Merry Willows shrugged, 'Trust,' she repeated, 'works both ways. It's your choice. You can choose to eat and accept my hospitality or you can go hungry.'

Mailliw understood trust had to work both ways, but how far could he extend that trust?

***

After taking the goblet and quenching his thirst, Mailliw hurried after Merry Willows to the vegetable plot. He rapidly pulled onions, carrots and potatoes and then he picked beans and tomatoes. Merry Willows prepared them for the cauldron and soon the vegetables simmered, sending curls of steam up the chimney.

'What I don't understand is why the air smells of honey around here. It's so strong it masks the smell from the swamp,' said Mailliw.

Merry Willows gave the cauldron a stir before replying, 'The fragrance comes from the swamp. Hard to believe, but it's because we're in the centre. The plants at the edge of the swamp don't bear flowers because their scent is incredibly sweet and they need to avoid attracting predators. For self-preservation, only the inner plants have flowers and they also happen to be the youngest plants,' Merry Willows said, and hacked unpleasantly to clear her crackly throat before continuing, 'when the plants age, they become barren. So they naturally progress towards the outer circle where their role becomes one of protection. To prevent the theft of their precious flowers they devour anything living or dead entering the swamp. The honey scent is from the millions of flowers surrounding the island at any one time.'

She stopped and shot Mailliw a grave look before saying, 'But, what many people don't know is this… if criminals die in prison and they are not claimed by their relatives within forty-eight hours, the bodies are disposed of in the swamp. It's the prison authorities' Health and Safety policy!'

Merry Willows opened one of the small cupboards, pulled out a couple of clay dishes with spoons and placed them on the table. On seeing Mailliw's distraught face as he thought about what she had just said, a stab of pity ran through her, so she bent down and opened the second cupboard. Her bowed figure creaked as her joints moved. She reached inside the cupboard, took out a small clay bottle and put it in the centre of the table. Mailliw didn't even notice.

'Now our meal is cooking, I'll tell you how I came to know Mother McGinty.'

At the mention of Mother McGinty, Mailliw's attention refocussed on why he was there. Forthright needed help. His anxiety about returning home increased, but he resisted the urge to rush Merry Willows. The situation hung in a delicate balance.

Merry Willows sat on one of the chairs by the table and offered for Mailliw to take the other. He sat down and listened.

'One night, about ten or eleven years ago, I was awoken by a strange crashing noise. I rushed to the door to see what had happened. There was a full moon and so it was possible to make out something lying not far from the house, but near to the edge of the swamp. It emitted a terrible noise which made my blood curdle. Was it here to kill me? Instinct to survive, yes, survive even in this awful place, became my chief ambition. Kill it before it killed me. I crept through the moonlight, treading stealthily and never taking my eyes off its presence. When I neared the creature, it stopped moving and became quiet. I crept nearer still, then on closer inspection, I found it was a body. I was astounded. What was a person doing here, on my island in the swamp? Although it was a person, I didn't know if it was a witch or wizard. My anger surfaced at this intrusion and I got close enough to push the body over with my foot. I held out my wand with the intention of killing it. Then the face lolled towards me in the moonlight. I saw a witch whose face was bloodied and swollen. Her nose was broken and her lips could barely move. Even so, when she tried to open her bruised eyes, I heard her whimper "Do it!" Well... I couldn't... it didn't seem honourable when the pathetic bag of bones lying before me was no threat. Instead, I dragged her back here and put her in my own bed. But, because I didn't have my usual remedies to help with the healing, it took many weeks before she recovered. During the time she was here, she never spoke, she just watched me and, for the first time in many years, I felt useful... my life had a purpose once more. Her only possessions were the broomstick when she crash-landed, and the rags on her back. One morning, she waited at the edge of the swamp with her broomstick and when she turned around, I understood it was time for her to leave. I nodded, even though I desperately wanted her to stay. She spoke for the first time since I found her. "I'm Mother McGinty" she said, then mounted her broomstick and left. I believed I would never see anyone else ever again and grieved for many months. But, eventually, I grew accustomed to my solitary existence once more. Then, one day, a pigeon flew in with a message tied to its leg. Mother McGinty was now a travelling pedlar and wanted to repay me for the kindness I'd shown her by sending a carrier pigeon with a few gifts, such as small packets of seeds. Now, whenever she passes near here, she sends her pigeon with a message to let me know she has returned. I take the message and send the pigeon back. Removing the message lets her know I'm still alive for her to send more small gifts.'

Merry Willows stopped talking, rose from the chair, and stirred the cauldron again. She collected the bowls from the table and spooned out the potage.

'Boy, you are the first person I've dealt with since she left.'

'You dealt with my cat earlier today,' replied Mailliw, thinking about the hole Merry Willows had blasted in the carpet.

'A vampire cat is not a person and I don't deal with vampire cats!'

Mailliw looked up suddenly at the vehemence in her voice. She slammed the bowls down on the table.

'Don't push your luck boy!'

'Don't forget I have the locket!'

Merry Willows' eyes flashed at the locket around Mailliw's neck. Instinctively, his hand covered the locket. Mailliw had relaxed too much and let his guard slip while he listened to Mother McGinty's tale. Was he a fool to trust this person? Trust! A small word and yet so much depended on it. Somebody had to make the first move, but at what risk? He needed to keep the upper hand and that meant bargaining hard before exchanging the locket. They glared at each other, neither willing to back down.

'Eat your food,' Merry Willows snapped. She clacked her spoon against the sides of her bowl and ignored Mailliw as she spooned her own food into her mouth. Mailliw picked up the spoon and, whilst eating, he thought about Aunt Foggerty and compared her to this thing, this creature, and he became overwhelmed with the urge to dash out of the door, jump on the carpet and get home as quickly as possible.

'Soooo…' the witch rasped, 'how did you come by the locket, boy?'

This interruption on his thoughts brought him up sharply. He must not fail. He must concentrate!

'I was given it by my aunt, specifically for the purpose of my mission.'

'Did she say how she came by the locket?'

Mailliw shook his head and she watched carefully, trying to ascertain whether he was telling the truth or not. Maybe this aunt hadn't told him, but certainly, she was familiar with the importance of the locket and what it contained… why else was it here?

'No? Well then, if you're quite finished, I suggest we get down to business,' Merry Willows said.

'The deal is this, I require information and when I have the answers and I'm ready to fly back on the carpet, I'll give you the locket,' said Mailliw rising from the table.

'Fair enough, but what if I can't give you the answers you need? I might tell you anything just to get the locket. You wouldn't know until it was too late!'

Mailliw spun round, 'Do I have any choice but to trust you? I assume because you have alerted me to the fact you could deceive me, means that you won't.'

Merry Willows gave a guffaw, 'You're a tricky one... for a boy. Well then, what do you want to know?'

Mailliw faced her and let his fingers trail through the locket chain, 'My sister is suffering from silver moonbeam sickness. I understand you were cured of this illness and I'd like to know how.'

Merry Willows sucked her lips, 'My, my! You're talking of something from decades ago, a long time before my husband... but never mind about that. What did you say your aunt's name was?'

'I didn't,' replied Mailliw.

'Hmm...'

Mailliw wasn't sure what to make of the 'hmm' and wondered if she was stalling. He watched Merry Willows cautiously. Her face registered a range of emotions. First, it softened and then it became serious, then angry, and lastly there was the deep sorrow he had witnessed earlier. She hobbled to the door, turned and hobbled back.

'How much do you know about me?'

'Enough'

'Not much of an answer, boy.'

'You haven't exactly answered my question yet!'

Merry Willows chuckled, 'I'm beginning to like you, boy.'

She hesitated and studied him, looking at his blond hair and deep ocean-blue eyes.

'The cure for silver moonbeam sickness is simple enough. The difficulty will be in obtaining it. I'll tell you the cure in exchange for the locket and then I'll give you the information of how I came by it, but only if you give me details as to how your aunt came by the locket, her name and who you are.'

'It sounds like a fair deal, but I'd prefer to do this when I'm back on the carpet and ready to go. I've got friends waiting for me and I've been here long enough,' said Mailliw and headed for the door. He didn't see Merry Willows pick up the small bottle from the table before she followed him out.

He hurried to the carpet and waited for the witch to catch him up. He held the trousers in his hands, ready to wrap around his nose for the dreaded return journey over the stench of rotting, half-eaten flesh.

When Merry Willows stood by the carpet she said, 'Are you ready for the answer then?'

Mailliw nodded and she continued, 'The cure for silver moonbeam sickness is quite simple. You need to find a golden moonbeam.'

'A what?'

'A golden moonbeam… it's the only cure and when you find one, your sister has to swallow it. Now, give me the locket, and then I'll tell you how I managed to get one.'

Mailliw lifted the locket over his head and warily handed it to Merry Willows. She held out her hands and took it very gently. Her face softened as she held it up to her cheek and gave a deep sigh, 'Thank you,' she whispered, 'I never thought I'd see this again,' and opened the locket. Merry Willows crooned as she cradled the contents in her hand. Mailliw was incredulous at the change in Merry Willows. The fact she had thanked him had taken him by surprise and now here she was, humming quietly to her closed palm with pure joy illuminating her face.

'So, how do I get a golden moonbeam?' he said, reminding Merry Willows the deal was only half done.

She looked up at Mailliw with a crooked smile, 'I was very fortunate. When I was young, I saved the life of a unicorn and the creature owed me a life debt. When I became ill with silver moonbeam sickness, I called in that debt. The unicorn told me I needed a golden moonbeam. Alas, they are only available in the Lands of the North where the Aurora Borealis occur. Seeing I was unable to go for myself, the unicorn went to the Guardian of the Winter Mountains. The Guardian helped the unicorn, but how they obtained a golden moonbeam, I'm unable to say. The unicorn returned with it in a block of ice. The ice was thawing rapidly, so to prevent the golden moonbeam from escaping once it became released in the water, we put the ice into a dark container. Then I drank the water and swallowed the golden moonbeam. The cure was successful and has given me lifelong immunity to the illness.' She stopped talking when she noticed the despair on Mailliw's face. An awkward hush fell between them and Merry Willows turned her attention back to the locket.

'I have no chance of finding a golden moonbeam. My sister's going to die!' he said, jumping off the carpet and kicking the stones in frustration.

'Boy! You must go to the Guardian of the Winter Mountains like the unicorn did, and ask for his help. You must try! If you don't, your sister will die and you'll never know whether you could have saved her.'

Mailliw surveyed the swamp and thought of Forthright with her disappearing outline. Of course he had to try and the sooner he got going the better, but first he had to complete the deal and give Merry Willows the information she wanted.

'I don't know how or why my aunt came by the locket. It's something she's always owned. She said that it contained a lock of hair and you would desire it.'

'Only one person could have had the locket all this time and she's not your aunt!'

'No, she's my father's aunt,' replied Mailliw, 'her name is Foggerty Berry and mine is Mailliw Berry.'

The colour drained from Merry Willows' face and as she staggered towards Mailliw, her arms tried to grab him. He quickly stepped aside and jumped onto the carpet, giving it instructions to rise into the air.

'Wait!' shouted Merry Willows, 'Take this,' and she threw the small bottle she had taken from the table. It landed on the edge of the carpet but Mailliw was too busy trying to wrap the trousers over his nose to worry about picking it up.

'You won't need those if you use the bottle! It contains concentrated flower essence from the swamp. Trust me!' she shrieked as the carpet rose into the air. Mailliw glanced over the side at the black figure of Merry Willows and saw her arms flapping wildly. Did she say 'Trust her'? Once more, Mailliw decided he had nothing to lose, so he removed the stopper and sniffed the contents. It was true! The bottle contained the strongest smelling perfume Mailliw had ever come across.

'Come back! Come back...' she said still shrieking, 'and tell me if your sister's cured!'

Merry Willows' voice was soon drowned out by the buzzing flies and Mailliw was grateful not to hear her voice saying, 'Come back!'

He shuddered at the thought. Go back! It was pure insanity... especially now she realised that Aunt Foggerty had sent him! Mailliw thought there wasn't anything that would induce him to return. He lay back on the carpet and his eyes looked intently at the deep blue sky. Concentrate on the sky and don't look down, he thought, anything to avoid seeing those plants again, waiting and watching as he flew overhead.

Mailliw remained still and soon became drowsy from the sun's warmth, helped along by the essence of flower concentrate masking the smell from the swamp. He asked himself, who was the Guardian of the Winter Mountains? What was the best way of getting there... carpet, dragon or broomstick?

He fumbled with the stopper on the bottle and put it in his pocket. It was then that he remembered he still had Merry Willows' wand.

Dingle sat munching some roots. He had no idea what kind of roots they were, apart from them being dry and tough. He chomped a bit longer and then spat the residue out. Peculiar hadn't seen any rats and, out of boredom, had resorted to chewing roots with Dingle. Now they sat together by the ashes of last night's fire, waiting and looking in the direction of the swamp. A movement in the sky drew their attention. A pigeon, high up, was flying away from the swamp in their direction.

'A pigeon,' said Peculiar, 'odd. I'm sure I've seen it before.'

'Don't be daft. When you think about all the pigeons there are, how can you think you've seen that particular one before?' Dingle asked looking skywards.

'Just a feeling,' replied Peculiar. Her eyes observed the pigeon with its wings flapping in the circular motion so characteristic of those birds. She was certain it was the pigeon from the previous day and was curious to know what it was doing around here. Her head curved round as her eyes followed the pigeon. It was flying in the same direction they would use on their return.

The searing heat made Dingle sleepy and he struggled to keep his eyes open. He gave a large yawn, followed by another and then another.

'Can't you stop yawning?' asked Peculiar, turning on him sharply.

'It's the heat,' replied Dingle with his eyelids hanging over his eyes.

'For goodness sake, go and sleep then. I'll keep watch.'

'Thanks,' mumbled Dingle and he padded away to lie down under the frame where the carpet had been supported last night. There wasn't any shelter, but Dingle wanted to lie down in the small hollow where Mailliw had lain asleep. It made him feel closer to the boy, knowing he was curling up in the same spot.

While Dingle slept, Peculiar kept watch. Her eyes remained fixed in the direction of the swamp for any signs of Mailliw and as she sat, she became aware of the sun burning her tail. So, to pass the time, she whisked it back and forth until enough dusty soil buried it. Afterwards, she remained as still as a statue, apart from the occasional blink of her eyes. Even when Dingle emerged from his snooze, Peculiar remained on duty, so he sat down quietly beside her and waited.

Dingle noticed Peculiar's fur rising along the length of her back. He looked about quickly and then spotted what she had seen. In the distance was the carpet, but there was no sign of Mailliw.

'Here he is. He's coming,' murmured Dingle with a quiet note of excitement.

'It might be her!' replied Peculiar, 'She might have stolen it and is lying low so we can't see her.'

'I never thought of that,' said Dingle, 'what do we do if it is the witch?'

'We'll fly up there and bring her down, then I'll take the carpet and go back for Mailliw.'

Dingle looked astonished. Bring down the witch! How exactly? As he pondered this dilemma and the carpet drew nearer. Peculiar saw a head and shoulders rise into view and a hand began waving.

'Yes! Yes! Yes!' shrilled Peculiar. She jumped to her feet and started freaking about. Her bare tail whizzed round as she bounded over stones, zipped under the tent frame and caused clouds of dusty soil to fly everywhere.

'The heat… finally got to her,' Dingle said sadly.

'It's Mailliw!' Peculiar yowled as she came to a complete halt in front of Dingle. Her grin was so wide, he swore it went from ear to ear.

The carpet descended and headed towards them. Just before it touched the ground, Peculiar leapt onto it and bowled Mailliw over the side in her enthusiasm. Dingle grinned almost as wide as Peculiar.

'You've no idea how pleased I am to be back from there!' he said trying to heave Peculiar off his chest.

'You've no idea how pleased we are to see you back!' said Dingle still grinning, while Peculiar rubbed her chin against Mailliw's cheek with a deep rumbling purring.

After spending a few moments scratching Peculiar's ears, Mailliw said, 'She told me the cure for Forthright, but I don't know how we'll find it. We need to hurry because we have another journey to make,' he said climbing back onto the carpet. He moved over to make room for Peculiar. She stepped on and resumed her usual stance, claws gripping on and looking straight ahead.

'Are you okay to fly Dingle?' Mailliw asked, 'I know you were exhausted after yesterday, so you can join us on the carpet if you prefer.'

Dingle gave the carpet a suspicious glance. It seemed rather flimsy to him.

'It's okay! I'd rather fly,' he said unfolding his wings, ready to follow the carpet.

They flew over the makeshift camp and headed for home, travelling above the dry parched countryside towards the lush vegetation of their own region.

***

Nearing Lake Gillyfrec, there was a small fire burning on the ground below. The wispy smoke rose upwards and carried the aroma of cooked meat. Peculiar's mouth watered. So it was cooked meat, but she was hungry and anything was better than those dried roots she had tried eating earlier.

'Look!' she said to Mailliw and tilted her head in the direction of the fire, 'It's the horse and caravan we saw yesterday.'

The tethered horse grazed on a grassy patch next to the caravan, where a woman wearing a red and white checked shawl, sat outside.

'I want to see her!' shouted Mailliw, 'Let's go down.'

'I'm glad you said that,' replied Peculiar, 'I can smell meat and I'm ravenous!'

Mailliw suddenly remembered he hadn't asked if his companions were hungry or thirsty when he had returned. Having eaten and drunk with Merry Willows, the urgency of his own hunger and thirst had diminished and he was annoyed at his own insensitivity to their needs. He signalled to Dingle to descend. They drew nearer to the caravan and it wasn't long before they heard a dog barking and saw Mother McGinty waving. Mailliw felt so relieved at recognising a familiar face. Admittedly, he had only met Mother McGinty and Gypsy for a few minutes the other evening, but after what he had been through, they were like long-lost friends.

'Hallo!' she shouted as the carpet whisked close to the horse's ears and landed a few metres from the campfire, 'You're just in time to join us for a meal. It's spit-roasted chicken, dressed with wild herbs and drizzled with lavender honey.'

Peculiar sighed. Why did people have to keep fiddling with their food? What was wrong with simply cooking it without any added trimmings? Meat! Plain and simple!

'I've got a jar of braised carrots and fennel with dandelion roots we can have as well,' Mother McGinty continued and she laughed as Dingle rolled his eyes heavenwards in delight. Peculiar looked about, trying to locate the pigeon she had seen earlier, but there was no sign of it. She bared her sharp fangs at Gypsy, but the dog ignored her and went over to the fire. Gypsy was more concerned with resting after a long day's walking, not chasing cats and certainly not a vampire cat.

'I thought you had a grey pigeon?' Peculiar asked.

'My pigeon is not on the menu,' Mother McGinty chuckled.

'So you have got one?'

'Yes. It's my homing pigeon.'

'I've seen it!' said Mailliw interrupting the conversation, 'I was there when it landed at Merry Willows' place.'

He heard Mother McGinty's sharp intake of breath. He also noticed a gleam in Peculiar's eyes. She must also have seen the pigeon or else why the questions.

'You've been where? Why... what have you been doing at Merry Willows' place?' asked Mother McGinty, looking confused and taking Mailliw by the shoulders.

'It's a long story and one related to the other night when we first met,' Mailliw said, taking comfort from her concern. He tried to think of all the events that had happened. There was so much and it seemed incredulous. Would Mother McGinty believe him? Mailliw remembered the bottle with perfumed flower essence and with Merry Willows' wand in his pocket, at least he had physical proof of his visit to the witch.

'Then I suggest you tell me all about it over a hot meal. Take a seat and I'll get you some food. Your dragon will have the braised vegetables I suppose and your cat, the chicken?' said Mother McGinty as she indicated a wooden carved stool in front of the fire. It was an unusual stool and Mailliw examined the carvings. His father, Philleas, would be interested in a stool like this. The age, the history, the stories it had heard over the years as people sat on it and told their tale. And now, here he was, just about to recount his own story and add it to the stool's long history. Gypsy rose from the fire and wagged her tail.

'Hello girl. How are you?' he said and stroked her long fur. Her amber eyes studied Mailliw and then she raised her paw and placed it in his hand.

'When are the pups due?' he asked, as Mother McGinty carved some succulent slices of roasted chicken.

'Sometime in the next week, I think,' she said.

'You'll be far away by then so I really can't see why she thought Drabder was ideal to have one of the puppies.'

'Gypsy works in mysterious ways. If she has chosen your friend, then I for one believe her.'

They ate their meal and Mailliw told his story while Mother McGinty listened. The atmosphere was a complete contrast to the one he had shared with Merry Willows. Peculiar ate her fill of chicken, although she left the herby lavender flavoured skin, and Dingle lay curled up with Gypsy, snoozing contentedly after his portion of braised roots. Mailliw put his plate aside and watched the fire. Having told Mother McGinty about his visit to the swamp, he became calmer and, as he relaxed, his eyes became heavy with sleep.

'You'll never make it home before dark and it won't be safe to cross Lake Gillyfrec until daylight. I suggest you camp here for the night and set off at first light,' said Mother McGinty as she bustled about and put more wood on the fire, 'besides, you all look in need of a rest,' she said looking at Mailliw, but before he could insist on leaving she added, 'you won't save your sister if you meet with some incident preventing you from getting home safely.'

Mailliw nodded wearily. Impatience to get home to Forthright was worn down by exhaustion.

'We could do with a rest, especially Dingle. I mean, look at him… fast asleep. It was a long flight yesterday and he was pretty shaken up by the storm over the lake. We can use the carpet again to make a tent, but if you've got a spare blanket, it would be more comfortable.'

Mother McGinty disappeared inside the caravan. She rooted around before reappearing and handing a blanket to Mailliw.

'Feel this,' she said, 'I bet you'll never guess what it's made from.'

'Um, let me think about this,' he said with a playful smile, 'I suspect this is llama wool!'

Mother McGinty's mouth opened with surprise, 'Now how did you know that?'

'Because my aunt has one and she told me she got it from you. She said she hadn't seen you about for some time.'

'I only had two of these blankets, this one and the one you say your aunt has. What a coincidence!' she paused and looked reflectively at the blanket, 'I'm beginning to believe our paths were meant to cross Mailliw, but for what reason has yet to be revealed. Anyway, did Merry Willows mention me?'

'Yes. She explained how she made you better after you crash-landed one night, but said you never spoke until you left.'

Mother McGinty looked up at the sky to examine the red streaks forming in the clouds as sunset approached.

'I can't fathom it out… it was all very mysterious. I don't know why I was speechless, but maybe it had something to do with having no memory of who I was or where I'd come from. It was only as I was leaving that I told her my name. I can't explain where the name came from or why, whether it's what I was called before or not,' she stopped talking because she was still no nearer to having any answers. 'Well, that's all in the past and we need to look to the future, a future with your sister in it. Do you know, the first time I met the Guardian of the Winter Mountains was a few years ago at the feast day of Winter Solstice, when he purchased some gingerbread from me. He wanted to see what it tasted like as he'd heard a folk tale about a witch who lived in a house made of gingerbread, topped with sugar icing to look like snow and icicles. When he tasted it, he almost fainted with pleasure. If Merry Willows says you must go to him, then to gain his help in seeking a golden moonbeam, you will need to take a very special gift. I suggest it should be a gingerbread house. I can't make it for you, as I don't have the right ingredients with me. But I can give you the recipe. What do you think?'

Mailliw considered the idea of presenting the Guardian of the Winter Mountains with such a gift. He had no idea what gingerbread tasted like or how to go about making it into a house, so he hoped Aunt Foggerty would know.

'A house would be far too large to transport on a flying carpet or a broomstick,' he replied.

'Ah! But a gingerbread house is like a model of a house. It would easily sit on a plate.'

'So how could a witch live in something so small?'

'By magic of course!' said Mother McGinty smiling, 'Come on. Let's get this tent sorted. Night will soon be here and we won't be able to see what we're doing.'

Mailliw left the stool to set up a structure ready for the tent and then he placed the blanket underneath. Peculiar had been washing her paws and removing chicken grease from her fur and whiskers. When she saw the tent, she tottered over, sank into the llama wool blanket and purred contentedly. Mailliw decided to leave Dingle where he was, as he looked comfortable with Gypsy. He crawled under the tent and snuggled up with Peculiar.

'I'll stay up for a while,' said Mother McGinty, 'I'm waiting for the stars so I can plot my next journey when we leave here.'

A solitary owl hooted in a tree not far away. Mailliw thought about home and about Forthright. Then he thought about his parents and an odd sensation of loneliness enveloped him. It was as if he lay inside a glass tunnel and they were on the outside, unable to communicate with or touch him. Where were they? At night, did they see the same stars as he did? Moreover, what would they say if he failed to save his sister? He rolled over and lay on Merry Willows' wand. He sat upright and leaned out of the tent.

'Mother McGinty. May I ask a favour please?'

'If I can do something to help, I will,' she replied.

'I've got Merry Willows' wand here. I forgot to give it back when I left. Can your homing pigeon return it to her?'

'Yes. Of course… now go to sleep and dream about making a house of gingerbread,' said Mother McGinty, as she sat watching the first stars of the evening beginning to twinkle in the deepening dusk.

Chapter 10
*P*reparations *F*or *T*he *W*inter *M*ountains

Drabder lifted his head from the desk, yawned, and stared at the closed books lying everywhere in the library. Yesterday and the day before they had continued with their silver moonbeam research, but by late evening, Aunt Foggerty was worn out and even eating did not restore her powers sufficiently to help with the speed-reading incantation. It was something only she could do, as the spell required a level of advanced magic. So she, Forthright and Monity had retired. Drabder had remained in the library waiting for all the books that were still open to complete their search. If a book's pages stopped and the alarm sounded, then he wanted to be there and see if this time it was the real thing. There had been so many disappointments, including the double alarm they had heard from the kitchen when Monity had been slurping her tea. Every time a whistle blew and a book stopped turning its pages, their hearts leapt with nervous excitement. But every occurrence so far had been a false hope and each one so distressing for Forthright.

The library clock ticked away and Drabder noticed it was nearly seven o'clock in the morning. He didn't remember falling asleep, but the fact his neck was stiff told him he had slept over the book in front of him. Drabder rose from the desk and stretched his legs. His normally neat appearance was now more like Mailliw's, with creased trousers and his shirt hanging out. Drabder yawned again, then sauntered to the window to open the curtains when something whizzed over his head. He swivelled round. Monity grinned as she stood in the doorway.

'Look up!' she said.

Drabder looked and smiled when Bit dipped and swerved as she flew around the room.

'She's b-better!' he said.

'She's as good as new! The potion my dad gave her and all the sleep she's had since has healed her. She arrived this morning and I'm just so relieved,' she said and then noticed all the closed volumes, 'I don't suppose you found anything last night or else you'd have been pounding on our doors. Anyway, I came to tell you breakfast is ready. Aunt Foggerty thought an early start a good idea.'

***

Drabder bit into a crispy slice of bacon and looked about the dining hall. The morning sunshine was creeping along the floor. Just now, it had touched the feet of a suit of armour standing to the right of the tall window, but now the toes were in shadow once more. Monity poured the tea as Aunt Foggerty brought in a rack of warm toast and placed it on the table. Forthright entered the dining room and sat down.

'I didn't hear you come in,' said Monity.

'No. I guess I'm not as heavy as I was. I'm not sure I want to go to sleep anymore. Every time I wake up, some more of me has disappeared,' Forthright replied miserably.

Aunt Foggerty piled a plate with bacon, eggs and mushrooms and handed it to Forthright. Monity noticed the increased silvery sheen in Forthright's hair since last night, and how sad she now looked as she tried to eat some breakfast.

'Bit is better. Drabder saw her flying around the library earlier,' she said to Forthright in an attempt to cheer her up. Forthright gave a weak smile, but not before Monity noticed her eyes brimming.

'Come on, let's hurry up with breakfast and then we can get back to the library,' Monity said and reached out to take Forthright's hand. But, as she took it, her own fingers failed to tell where Forthright's began.

***

At two thirty in the afternoon, Mailliw burst in through the library door, followed by Peculiar and Dingle.

'We've got it!' he shouted above the noise of whirring pages.

Forthright leapt up from the sofa and hugged Mailliw so tight he couldn't breathe. Drabder beamed. He was overjoyed at seeing his best friend back safe and well. Aunt Foggerty looked at him desperately.

'You've got it?' she asked, hardly daring to hope.

'Got the answer… yes,' Mailliw replied excitedly, trying to get his breath back after Forthright let him go, 'but not the actual cure. I've got to go to the Guardian of the Winter Mountains and ask his help.'

'What do you mean "I"?' growled Peculiar, 'You're not going anywhere without me!'

Dingle stood near the door, unable to take his troubled expression off Forthright. Aunt Foggerty stepped forward and embraced Mailliw. He felt the relief in her arms as she held him.

'It's just so, so good to see you my boy,' she said.

'Don't!' he replied and pushed Aunt Foggerty away. She recoiled.

'What have I done?' she asked, stricken by his reaction.

'I'm sorry! You haven't done anything… it's… it's what you said… you called me "boy" and that's what she kept calling me. I had to tell her my name as I was leaving and then she tried to attack me. I think if she had caught me, I'd still be there now, her prisoner. I heard her begging me to go back. It was horrible and I just wanted to get away from the place.' Mailliw continued babbling about events, but everything came out jumbled.

'Stop!' Forthright cried and placed her fingers over his mouth. Mailliw was stunned to find he felt no pressure from them.

'Hush!' she said, 'It's okay, you're home now. Come and sit down and tell us everything,' she said and led him to the sofa.

Norgruk strolled into the library and slapped Dingle on the back. Cleopatra spied round the door, watched the commotion and then headed back to the dragons' kitchen for some peace and quiet.

Aunt Foggerty, Forthright, Drabder and Monity sat around Mailliw while he recounted everything about Merry Willows the Widow, as well as how he met up with Mother McGinty again and stayed at her camp last night. He unfolded the gingerbread recipe and gave it to Aunt Foggerty.

'Mother McGinty suggested we take this as a gift to the Guardian of the Winter Mountains. Do we have all the ingredients?' he asked.

'You'll have to check in the kitchen. Why don't you all go down and make a start. I'll come shortly,' said Aunt Foggerty, 'Norgruk, I'd like you to wait here. I have a job for you.'

Norgruk grunted. He wasn't happy knowing the others were going to the kitchen to make food without him. He watched them leave the library and sulked. Aunt Foggerty sat at Philleas' desk. Taking out some parchment, ink and a quill pen, she wrote some letters. When she finished, she sealed them with wax.

'Thank you for waiting Norgruk,' she said looking at the dragon, 'please deliver these immediately and bring me the responses.'

***

When Norgruk returned with the replies, he followed Aunt Foggerty to the kitchen where they were greeted by the delicious aroma of gingerbread. Mailliw, Drabder and Monity were cutting the freshly baked gingerbread and constructing it into a house. Dingle and Cleopatra drooled, watching intently for the slightest crumb accidentally falling in their direction. Forthright was mixing white icing and Peculiar was searching in one of the drawers in the dresser. She fished out a small tube and placed it on the table.

'What have you got there?' asked Forthright.

'Stardust! When the house is iced you can sprinkle it around the edges so when it's dark the house will twinkle,' replied Peculiar.

'It's going to look so beautiful at night time,' breathed Monity.

Aunt Foggerty cleared her throat and they all spun around to look at her. 'I have formulated a plan for the journey to the Guardian of the Winter Mountains, so I sent letters asking permission for Monity and Drabder to accompany Mailliw this time. Drabder, your father has agreed but expects you to stay out of mischief, and Monity... your mother says you must do what you can to help your friends.'

Mailliw threw his arm around Drabder's shoulders and chuckled, and Monity gave an unsure smile at Forthright. She was remembering how she hadn't wanted to come and help but Roo had said, 'How would you feel if your friends deserted you in your time of need?' and she was ashamed at the memory.

'Now, before you get too excited, I have also promised you will be chaperoned by Mr Trotter...'

'What! Sturvald Trotter! The gardener come handyman!' protested Mailliw.

Aunt Foggerty frowned at him and he fell silent.

'Mailliw, I will feel much happier knowing you have your friends with you, but for them to be able to go and for their parents to feel reassured about their safety, you must have an adult with you. Sturvald Trotter is available and someone I trust. He will be going with the three of you along with Peculiar, Dingle and Bit. I will remain here to look after Forthright.'

'But…' Mailliw began. He stopped when Aunt Foggerty held up her hand.

'This is not open to discussion. This is how it's going to be,' she said firmly and they all knew Aunt Foggerty had made her decision. It was with Sturvald Trotter or not at all, and there was no question of not going. Forthright's life depended on them.

'We'll make preparations tonight for you all to set off early tomorrow morning and by then the icing on the gingerbread house will have set,' said Aunt Foggerty, 'I'll go and start preparing. Mr Trotter will be arriving soon to help out.'

When Aunt Foggerty left, Forthright surveyed Mailliw and said, 'You won't do anything stupid will you?'

'Like what?' grumbled Mailliw.

'Well, I know you, and it's quite likely you'd cook up some half-baked idea like leaving tonight without the Trotter.'

'Sounds like a good idea. Perhaps we should,' he said.

'Promise me, all of you, that you won't leave tonight without him,' said Forthright. Mailliw's eyes met Forthright's and he saw the grief. Hadn't he already done enough? This whole business was because of him.

'Okay! We promise not to leave tonight without him,' he agreed, 'in the meantime, can we get this house finished?'

They put the gingerbread pieces together to make the walls of the house and then finally put the roof on the top. Small windows had been cut out and the front door opened and closed. Forthright took the white icing and spread it over the roof. When the icing drizzled over the edges, it formed natural hanging shapes resembling icicles. She fluffed up the remaining icing like mounds of snow around the bottom of the house. For the final touch, Monity took the stardust and sprinkled it around the edges of the roof. They would have to wait until dark to see it twinkle.

***

After clearing up the kitchen and mopping the floor where two dragons had left a large pool of saliva, the children returned to the library. Aunt Foggerty and Sturvald Trotter were studying a map. The library books were now all back on the shelves and the room seemed eerily still.

'This pass is quite narrow, but, with care, I'm hoping you will be able to get the carriage through,' said Aunt Foggerty pointing at the map, 'it'll be much quicker than going around the far side.'

They both looked up when the children entered.

'I can show you the journey,' said Aunt Foggerty and indicated for them to come over, 'the best way for all of you is by carriage. Norgruk will be reined up. To save weight, Dingle will have to fly. As the carriage hasn't been used for some time, it requires a thorough safety check. Mr Trotter will do it tonight. In the meantime, I suggest each of you pack a few items of warm clothing and anything else you think you might need. But please… travel lightly; speed is of the essence tomorrow.'

Mailliw, Drabder and Monity examined the map. Only Forthright sat down on the sofa. She was dozy but determined not to fall asleep. If she slept, who knows how much more of her would have disappeared by the time she awoke. She listened to the low voices discussing the route and then thought about her sickness. So, she needed a golden moonbeam. She had never heard of such a thing and what were the chances of obtaining one before she disappeared? Her eyes drifted over the books. Was there a reference to a golden moonbeam anywhere in those pages? Forthright didn't know, but she did know she was feeling depressed. She was going to miss the others when they left in the morning. What if she disappeared before they got back and she never saw them again? What if she never saw her parents again? If only she knew where the archaeological site was situated, at least then she could try and get a message to them. Where were they? She wanted her mother so much and she also desperately wanted to live!

***

Later, in Mailliw's bedroom, Drabder and Monity sat on his bed. He could tell by the looks on their faces, his words had stunned them and Monity's hand stopped caressing Bit.

'Look, the Trotter is just so slow. I mean… have you seen him pruning the roses? He stands there dithering for about twenty minutes just trying to decide if he's cutting the right bit of twig… then he takes forever to put on his gardening boots and an eternity to take them off again! You heard what Aunt Foggerty said, "speed is of the essence", but if the Trotter drives the carriage, by the time we get to the Winter Mountains, Forthright could have disappeared!' he paused and then added, 'It's a risk I'm not prepared to take.'

Drabder glanced nervously at Monity and said, 'I-I'm with M-Mailliw. I don't th-think Mr Trotter is going to be f-fast enough.'

'But you promised Forthright you wouldn't do anything stupid,' Monity argued.

Mailliw smiled sweetly as if trying to appease her, 'Yes, yes… I know I promised Forthright not to leave without the old Trotter tonight, but I didn't promise her we wouldn't do it tomorrow…'

Monity stood up from the bed and inspected the items which Mailliw had laid out on the dresser. There was a pair of thick socks, a compass, his wand, a notebook on basic spells, gloves and a strange black object.

'What's this?' she asked picking it up.

'My parents sent it back as a gift. It's a sort of apology for not being back on time. Forthright thinks it's a black diamond,' said Mailliw.

'So what's it used for?'

'I couldn't even begin to guess, but I wanted to take something to remind me of Mum and Dad and as it's pocket-sized, it seemed the ideal thing to pack.'

To one side of the dresser, Monity noticed a small flask emitting a powerful honey fragrance and asked, 'What's in the small bottle?'

'It's what Merry Willows the Widow gave me to mask the smell from the swamp,' he said and paused, 'I think she threw it to me in the hope I'd use it to return.'

'And will you?'

'Not likely!'

Monity moved away from the dresser and fiddled with her plaits. She was playing for time but the boys were waiting for her reply to Mailliw's suggestion. Was she really going to go against both of them?

She faced them and declared, 'Mailliw, if you have a plan, I'll go along with it, if and when it happens, but I don't want to know any details. I'd find it too difficult to face your Aunt in the morning if I knew what was going to happen. So, I think I'd better go now so you can discuss your plan. I'll see you in the morning. I'm going to keep Forthright company.'

Monity closed the oak door behind her as she left and it was Mailliw's turn to look stunned. He hadn't expected Monity to stand up to him like this. She had been like their shadow, going where they went, doing what they did. Girls were so unpredictable!

Chapter 11
The Guardian

The next morning, Mailliw packed his items in a small rucksack and put it on board the carriage. He admired the black bodywork of the carriage gleaming in the early morning sunshine, and thought with the pace at which Mr Trotter normally worked, he must have been polishing all night to get the carriage looking so immaculate.

Sturvald Trotter was just finishing harnessing up Norgruk and he could tell by Norgruk's stubbornness that the dragon was sulky. Then he examined the carriage and rechecked the wheels and spokes, the suspension springs and the reins; he opened and closed the doors to ensure the handles were secure and made sure all the nuts and bolts remained tightened. Monity slowly approached the carriage with Aunt Foggerty and looked back over her shoulder to wave at Forthright standing in the shadow of her bedroom curtains. Aunt Foggerty had been quiet this morning and Monity wondered if she suspected some sort of plan to get rid of Sturvald Trotter. It was best to keep smiling because if she didn't, Aunt Foggerty might ask if everything was alright. She wasn't prepared to say, 'Well, not really, you see… Mailliw and Drabder are plotting to lose Mr Trotter, but I'm not supposed to tell you…'

Instead, she remarked on what a beautiful day it was to travel. Aunt Foggerty glanced up at the cloudless sky and then over to Forthright, standing alone in her room.

'I'll have to think of something to keep Forthright busy. She's fretting already.'

'I know. I went to see her before I went to bed last night. I didn't know what to say,' said Monity taking Aunt Foggerty's hand.

'I understand, it's such a difficult situation, but thank you for trying Monity. Have you seen the gingerbread house? I've wrapped it in magic paper. It shimmers with the colours of the rainbow, a bit like mother of pearl and the bow on top is made of golden mist. I'm hoping the presentation will help to enhance the unique gift being offered. Anything to try and improve Forthright's chances.'

When everything was ready, Mailliw and Peculiar waited inside the carriage.

Roo had arrived early to say goodbye to Monity and Bit, but there was no sign of Turnbull Fink to say farewell or good luck to Drabder. Roo's generous body hugged Monity and Drabder in turn as they climbed into the carriage and sat down with Mailliw on the buffed leather seats. 'I'm proud of you both for being such loyal friends,' she told them and her eyes went all misty as she closed the carriage door. Dingle remained outside. He was ready to fly alongside the carriage led by Norgruk and driven by Sturvald Trotter.

'Goodbye my dears and have a quick and safe return,' said Aunt Foggerty. She tried to smile encouragingly, but she was near to tears.

She and Roo waved as Norgruk hauled the carriage through the gates. He wouldn't fly with the carriage until they had left the narrow streets of Feyngrey.

The carriage bounced along the town's cobbled streets and Monity looked out of the window at the geraniums cascading from window boxes. Without warning, Drabder rolled forward and clasped his stomach.

'What's the matter?' Monity asked leaning towards him. She was concerned. Surely, this must be genuine. The boys were too close to home to try out something now… weren't they?

'F-feel sick,' he moaned, 'c-carriage too bouncy.'

'But we're not going very fast!' said Monity.

'Can't h-help it! Going to be s-sick.'

'I'll bang on the hatch and tell the Trotter,' said Mailliw and started to hit the hatch with his fist. The carriage stopped and Sturvald Trotter looked in.

'Problem?' he asked.

'The carriage is too bouncy for my cousin. I think he's going to be sick,' said Monity looking up at him.

'N-need some ginger barley sugar,' moaned Drabder, 'usually h-helps.'

With the last two words, Monity became suspicious. What did Drabder mean, 'usually helps'? When did he ever travel in a carriage to know ginger barley sugar usually helps?

'Can you stop at Madam Bonbons please?' asked Mailliw, 'She stocks ginger barley sugar. I can't ride in a carriage with someone being sick all over the place.'

Mailliw pulled a disgusted face. Sturvald Trotter looked alarmed, nodded his agreement and guided Norgruk towards Madam Bonbons. The carriage pulled up outside the shop, and Norgruk and Dingle examined the mouth-watering window display. They smacked their lips and dribbled at the candy canes hanging from silver stars; miniature trees looked like they were growing sherbet pips and pear drops, and a chocolate fountain gushed into a molten chocolate lake. At the side of the lake, there was a grotto made of crystal white peppermints, and behind this stood a pink castle made of strawberry ice cream and decorated with jellybeans.

'The castle never melts,' breathed Monity, 'it must have a freezing spell surrounding it.'

Sturvald Trotter opened the hatch and informed them they were outside Madam Bonbons.

'I'd offer to go,' said Mailliw, 'but by the time I remove this stuff off my lap, get you to open the door, climb out of the carriage and go in the shop, you could've been in and out. It would save time if you went instead.'

He said it with such an innocent expression, that Sturvald Trotter was easily convinced and quite willing to oblige. Besides, if the children waited in the carriage, at least he knew where they were. Mistress Foggerty had stressed the importance of making sure the children remained safe.

Mailliw waited until Sturvald was inside the shop before climbing up through the hatch and taking the reins. He quickly took up the slack and slapped the reins together. Norgruk looked back and with surprise, he found Mailliw sitting in the driver's seat.

'Yah!' yelled Mailliw and Norgruk responded. He lumbered away from the cobbled streets towards the open countryside. Inside the carriage, the sudden jarring and bumping threw Monity, Drabder and Peculiar all over the place and if Drabder hadn't been feeling sick before, he was now. This time, he was moaning for real.

Norgruk reached the outskirts of Feyngrey, unfurled his wings and rose into the sky. The bumping ceased and was replaced by a rhythmic flying, as the carriage gently dipped and rose in time with the dragon's beating wings. Dingle flew synchronised with Norgruk and in the air they appeared graceful. They were nothing like the creatures who shambled clumsily on their feet at home.

Drabder observed Dingle flying alongside, but Monity looked down at Feyngrey and saw a small Mr Trotter waving a bag of ginger barley sugar. She groaned, unable to believe that the boys dared to lose him so close to home. Monity hoped Mailliw knew what he was doing.

***

Mailliw guided Norgruk over the River Feyn and followed its winding route towards the Winter Mountains. He had never thought about it before, but all the water flowing in the River Feyn was melted snow and ice from these mountains. Now here he was, heading for the river's source.

They travelled over fields and isolated cottages, small orchards and hay meadows. The countryside looked warm and tranquil, not like Feyngrey with its hubbub of market town noises and smells.

The carriage progressed and Mailliw saw a large wood looming in the distance. The canopy of leaves looked too dense to see the river below, so Mailliw decided they needed to descend if they were to continue following the river. He hoped for sufficient space to navigate through the trees without landing, otherwise, travelling with Norgruk pulling through rough terrain would dramatically slow their progress.

Close to the woodland, Norgruk decreased his speed. Only fools entered a wood at top speed, for all kinds of danger might be lurking in the murky darkness. Norgruk scanned the area. His eyes searched for the telltale signs of wood dwarves. These beings might be small, but they more than made up for it with their unpleasant nature. After the initial survey, Norgruk sniffed the air. He couldn't smell wood dwarves in the vicinity and if they could be avoided, so much the better!

'Any signs of wood dwarves?' yelled Dingle at Norgruk.

He yelled back, 'NO!'

Dingle looked over at Mailliw, 'No signs of wood dwarves!' he bawled.

Dingle noticed the slightly alarmed look on Mailliw's face. So, he hadn't been expecting a confrontation with wood dwarves then! For a moment, Dingle wondered whether Mailliw's naivety about such things was a good or a bad thing. Does not knowing about something make you braver or more foolhardy? He glanced sideways and was disturbed to find Peculiar staring at him from the carriage window.

'What?' he mouthed at the vampire cat. The lack of response made him realise she was not looking at him but just over his head. What had she seen? Dingle inclined his head to follow her line of sight. Flying on his left, he saw a grey pigeon.

After they entered the wood, Dingle noticed the pigeon stayed on its own course. It was flying over the wood, whereas they were going through it. Was Peculiar thinking it was Mother McGinty's pigeon again? And, if so, what was it doing here?

Soon Dingle forgot about the pigeon. He had to concentrate on flying around tree trunks rather than into them. Norgruk weaved in and out of the trees and the carriage swung left and right as it trailed after him.

Inside the carriage, Drabder felt sick again. He closed his eyes tight and tried to shut out the sensation of sliding from side to side on the seat. Monity stretched her body across the width of her seat. She pressed her back against one side of the carriage and her feet against the other. This stopped her from sliding around, but it was an unusual sensation having her spine compressed and stretched like a piece of elastic. On her lap was the gingerbread house. She was terrified of it falling and breaking. If it did, they would have no gift for the Guardian of the Winter Mountains. She considered having to return and explain to Forthright that everything failed because of her. She nearly burst into tears at the thought. Peculiar sat huddled under Monity's seat with her claws hooked into the red carpet, and so it was only Bit who was not suffering. She hung upside down from the ceiling and swayed like being in a tree on a windy night.

They continued through the woodland and Mailliw noticed the river becoming narrower until it was no more than a stream. If they had flown over the wood, they would have missed locating the river on the other side.

After a while, Mailliw detected an increase in Norgruk's speed and they were gaining height. He glanced at Dingle and noticed his wings beating faster.

'Slow down! We might crash!' he yelled.

'Need to move fast… can smell wood smoke… wood dwarves in the area, trust Norgruk… he knows what he's doing,' Dingle replied, puffing as he spoke. He fell silent and concentrated on keeping up with the carriage.

The trees were thinning out and they were almost through the wood when an arrow whizzed upwards, then another and another. A searing pain shot through Dingle's left wing. An arrow had pierced it and he struggled to maintain his flying balance. More arrows bounced off the carriage and Mailliw heard Monity scream.

'Get your head down!' Dingle yelled at Mailliw, when he saw the boy looking around. Mailliw ducked and heard the swish of an arrow as it zipped by his ear. Norgruk zigzagged through the wider spaced trees to confuse the aim of the wood dwarves below. Dingle nearly collided with the carriage several times. With his injured wing, he was completely out of synchronisation with Norgruk.

When, at last, the carriage left the woodland behind, Norgruk looked back and was relieved the arrows were falling short of their target. It had been an arduous flight through the wood and if he was breathless, then Dingle would be too. He slowed down and when Dingle caught up, Norgruk noticed the wobble in his flight.

'My wing… hole… from arrow…' Dingle panted, 'going to be hard… work… to keep up.'

'We will stay at this pace. I need to get my breath back too. Are they okay back there?' asked Norgruk.

'Look... a bit green,' said Dingle and discerned a small twitch at the corners of Norgruk's mouth.

'Green is better than being full of arrows,' he said with a grin.

Inside the carriage, Peculiar crawled out from under the seat and joined Monity in looking out of the window. Now that they had left the woodland, Monity hoped the journey was nearly over. Drabder had finally been sick and lay motionless on the seat. He gazed blankly at the ceiling and the smell was making Monity feel queasy.

'I need some fresh air,' she said and banged on the hatch. Mailliw opened it and looked down. Monity noticed he was very pale.

'Drabder's been sick. Can you leave the hatch open or can I open the windows?'

'I'll leave the hatch open. If you open the windows, it might cause a through draft in the carriage. Norgruk is tired and I don't want any drag to make it more difficult for him,' he replied and paused before adding, 'the Winter Mountains are straight ahead, so our flight should be fairly smooth until we reach the pass.'

Monity settled back onto her seat and looked at the gingerbread house. Inside the magic wrapping lay a small pile of crumbs where a roof corner was damaged. Although it didn't look too noticeable in daylight, it would show up at night where the flow of twinkling stardust was broken. She was mortified.

With the fresh air filtering into the carriage, Drabder felt better and fell asleep, and whilst sleeping he missed the breathtaking approach to the Winter Mountains. Small slushy streams of melted snow became a frozen blue lake and out of the ice rose the towering craggy slopes. Boulders and rocks poked out through the ice and the mountains were blinding white against the azure sky.

In order to find the pass, Mailliw needed to land the carriage. He tugged the reins to tell Norgruk to descend. It was only as they neared a flat area of ice, Mailliw questioned if the ice was thick enough to take the weight of the carriage. However, there was no choice, he had to land.

Norgruk raised his head and chest, then turned the undersides of his wings towards the mountains to create a braking effect. The carriage slowed but when the wheels hit the ice, they didn't turn. Instead, the carriage slid forwards at an alarming rate. It screeched over the ice. Norgruk was unprepared for a sliding carriage, and the next thing he knew, it had slammed into him and was shoving him across the surface. Both he and the carriage accelerated towards a pile of boulders at the foot of a mountain. Norgruk slid along, belly down, and the only chance he had to save himself and the carriage, was to use his wings like a parachute and hope it was enough to avert a disaster. He opened his wings and felt the resistance as the air stretched them to their limits. Norgruk's chest muscles ached and burned as he desperately held his wings open. Despite his valiant effort, the carriage swerved and began rotating. It dragged Norgruk, and he instantly folded his wings to prevent them from being ripped off as he spiralled round. Through a window, he saw Monity's terrified mouth open with a soundless scream. The carriage spun him round several times and, before he had time to think, Norgruk found he was still heading nose-first for the boulders. He closed his eyes and waited for the crunch.

After a few seconds when nothing had happened, he opened his eyes. To Norgruk's amazement, his nose was about three centimetres away from the nearest boulder. It was so close he stared at it cross-eyed. Norgruk lifted his weary head to look at the carriage where Dingle was fiddling with something.

'Dingle! What are you doing?' he yelled.

'I'm releasing Mailliw,' he replied, 'he's dangling over the side with the reins wrapped around his wrists.'

As Dingle spoke, a carriage door opened and Monity and Drabder staggered out. Monity was shivering, half with shock and half with cold. With trembling hands, Drabder handed her a large coat, put one around his own shoulders and then took one for Mailliw.

'Are y-you okay?' he asked as Mailliw stretched his fingers and gently rubbed his wrists to ease the friction burns. He helped Mailliw with the coat.

'I think I was very lucky my wrists didn't snap!' groaned Mailliw and then looked towards Norgruk, 'Can you make sure his harness is untangled. Thanks.'

Mailliw continued massaging his wrists as he stumbled over to Monity.

'Sorry about the landing. It was a pretty spectacular... but one I don't want to repeat in a hurry,' he said trying to smile reassuringly at her, but Monity's face was almost as white as the ice.

'I've lost it,' she whispered, 'the gingerbread house...'

Peculiar, who had been clinging to the ceiling of the carriage, at last climbed down and emerged with her fur standing on end.

'The bat took it,' she said, 'when you had your eyes shut, the bat flew up through the hatch.'

Monity's face drained so much she looked deathly. How did Bit fly with something so much bigger than herself? She couldn't have gone very far, but the carriage had slid a long way and Monity had no way of knowing when Bit left the carriage.

'I'll go and look for her,' said Dingle and took off in the direction they had just come from, but he had difficulty flying straight with his injured wing. He was fed up of wobbly flying, first it was seasickness and now this!

Drabder returned and confirmed Norgruk's harness was sorted.

'Best get in the carriage until Dingle gets back,' said Mailliw, 'at least it'll be slightly warmer inside.'

They weren't used to this sudden change of temperature. Back home, it was midsummer with deep blue skies and hot sun. Here there were blue skies but the air was ice-cold.

Monity sat in silence and kept scouring the area for signs of Dingle. Mailliw and Drabder were studying the map, trying to decide how far they were from the pass.

'I think if we go this side of the boulders, it shouldn't be too far from this point here,' said Mailliw.

'I can see him,' said Monity in a voice so quiet, it took a moment before it registered with Mailliw and Drabder. They looked up to see Dingle's uneven flight. He landed and slid along the ice before he stopped outside the carriage. On his head was Bit and in his front claws was the gingerbread house. They gaped at the house. Half the roof had come off and was hanging down and lopsided.

'What are we going to do?' Monity cried, nervously taking the house from Dingle.

'Does anybody know a spell for repairing a gingerbread roof?' asked Mailliw.

'I know one to m-m-make things hover above a surface,' volunteered Drabder, 'b-but I don't know if it's suitable,' he said looking at the house with dismay.

'I'm not sure we've got much choice. It's that or nothing,' said Mailliw, 'and I don't fancy offering it as a gift like this.'

'I totally agree,' said Monity.

Drabder got out his wand. It was smaller than Mailliw's wand, but there was a sheen and quality about it. Drabder's mother had left it behind and when Roo chanced upon it, the wand was wrapped in silk inside an ebony chest. Although Turnbull Fink objected, Roo insisted it was Drabder's right to inherit it.

Drabder stood poised, raised his wand over the gingerbread house and cast the spell. The dangling gingerbread roof moved slowly from its precarious position and rose upwards. Drabder's face grew pink with concentration but there was still a large gap where the roof hovered over the walls. Drabder needed to lower it, so he continued with the energy pouring from his wand, until he barely saw the gap.

'That's the b-best I can do,' he said, 'it's not p-perfect, but it's better than it was.'

Monity looked at him with admiration. No. It wasn't perfect, but considering the circumstances, it was the best any of them could have done. Next year in school, she would start learning spells like this.

'Well done!' said Mailliw giving Drabder a pat on the shoulder. He was rewarded with a big smile from Drabder, but Mailliw knew if he had worked better at school, then he could have been in a position to do this spell at least as well as Drabder.

Mailliw hastened over to Dingle, 'Let me see your wing.'

Dingle held out the damaged wing.

'Is it painful?' asked Mailliw as he inspected the wing, double-checking for any broken arrow pieces.

'No, not now. It's just annoying because the wind whistles through the hole and unbalances me when I'm flying.'

Mailliw gently allowed the wing to fold and said, 'Let me know if it becomes a problem, okay...' and then he went to Norgruk and gave him a final check for any injuries. He was grateful to find Norgruk's pride was injured more than his body.

Reassured, he said, 'Let's get moving then.'

***

When everyone was back in the carriage, Mailliw took his seat on the top and picked up the reins. Norgruk pulled the carriage wide of the boulders and headed for the direction of the pass. There were more rocks and loose stones than they realised as they trundled over the bumpy surface.

They arrived at the pass and Norgruk looked at it. The entrance was very narrow. He would be able to get through, but he wasn't sure about the carriage.

'What's the matter?' shouted Mailliw.

'Too narrow!' replied Norgruk.

'Are you sure?'

'No! But it isn't sensible to risk getting the carriage stuck.'

'Bother!' muttered Mailliw and sprang down from the carriage to inspect the pass. He eyed up the entrance and compared it to the width of the carriage. Norgruk was right. It was too risky. They would have to leave the carriage behind and walk the rest of the way.

Mailliw's stomach cramped with frustration at so many things hindering their progress. It seemed as if everything was trying to slow them down.

When Monity and Drabder joined him, they agreed the risk was too great. They swiftly unharnessed Norgruk, allowing him to remain and guard the carriage ready for the journey home. Mailliw, Drabder, and Monity took what they required from the carriage and for safekeeping, Monity placed the gingerbread house under her coat. It bulged, making her look like a walking tent.

They headed for the pass and saw it had vertical sides of solid ice as smooth as glass. Their footsteps echoed as though a monstrous troll was following them and even whispers echoed back like a pit of hissing snakes.

Trudging on, they wondered if this was the shortcut, then what was the long way round like? With Dingle's damaged wing, Mailliw wasn't sure about asking him to go ahead as a scout. Visions of him bouncing off the narrow walls of the pass came into his mind. Besides, Mailliw didn't want the party to be split up, he preferred the idea of safety in numbers. Even so, a small voice nagged him, 'A scout might spot an ambush and be able to give warning.'

While he was having these internal arguments, Drabder stopped and pointed ahead.

'Look! I think there are some g-gates!' he said.

He was right, but they weren't obvious because they were the same colour as their surroundings. They were also the only visible entrance within a high security wall constructed of ice.

The children stood before the gates as they slowly opened with a deafening noise of ice grating on ice, then a loud voice boomed out, 'Welcome! I've been expecting you!'

A giant of a man appeared before them. He had a long white beard, snowy-white hair and wore a white robe. Everything about him blended into the background. Mailliw looked baffled, 'How could he have been expecting us?'

It was Peculiar who answered his question, 'Mother McGinty's pigeon… it flew over the wood in this direction. It must have taken him a message.'

Mailliw nodded, 'It's a logical explanation, but I wonder why?'

'Can't imagine,' said Dingle, 'but… if we're expected, they might have some food for us. I'm starving.'

'Come this way,' the white man said and extended his arm indicating where they were to go. The man towered over them, and Mailliw saw his beard was tucked into the belt tied around his waist. He was also astonished to see, despite the snow and ice, the man was wearing leather sandals and had exceptionally long toenails and they were painted gold!

The children were herded to a large door made of ice, adorned with carvings of people and strange creatures. Once inside, the man led them to a huge ice cavern. To their amazement, it was filled with people. Some were standing around and others were moving, but they all had something in common. Everyone had suitcases and trunks.

'Welcome again!' boomed the loud voice, 'And let me introduce myself. I am the Guardian of the Winter Mountains and this...' he paused and waved his hand in a circular motion to draw their attention to the vastness before them, 'is Central Junction.' He smiled, revealing a gold tooth nestled between two neat rows of white teeth.

'It's a very big place,' said Monity with awe, 'but why does everyone have luggage with them?'

'Hah! Because Central Junction is the place where everyone from the Northern Winter Lands travels through to the Southern Winter Lands, and vice versa...'

'Oh! You mean for holidays and business...' she said.

'Yes, that's right. Central Junction houses the gateways which enable everyone to reach their destinations quickly and easily. It's a lucrative business all this travelling. Look at all the shops selling travel maps, gifts, luxury foods, specialised travel bags, books and magazines. We have cafés and restaurants...'

'But do you have anywhere selling peppermint and parsley patties?' interrupted Dingle, 'I'm famished!'

The Guardian of the Winter Mountains looked slightly uncomfortable at this question and then replied, 'I've never heard of them, but then I don't know all of the products sold in the shops.'

Peculiar nudged Dingle in the ribs, so he stopped talking. All of them watched the hubbub of activity: the clamouring voices, the scraping of luggage towed across the ice, doors opening and shutting with a constant flow of people on the move.

'So, if you were expecting us, does it mean you also know why we are here?' asked Mailliw, his attention back on the Guardian.

'Ah! An old friend sent a message saying you were on your way. Said you were special friends of hers and asked me to take care of you.'

'I take it our mutual friend is Mother McGinty. My vampire cat saw her pigeon heading in this direction,' said Mailliw. They waited as a dreamy glaze appeared on the Guardian's face.

'Yes…' he said absent-mindedly, 'finest gingerbread I purchased from her… never tasted anything like it since…' he paused and licked his lips at the memory. A loud clanging brought him out of his reverie, 'But why you're here? No, I don't know that. If you come with me to my chambers, you can tell me there.'

He led the way and the children could see everything was made of ice: the arches, the doorways, the pillars and the shop fronts. It was no surprise when they saw ice benches, chairs and desks in the Guardian's chambers. The Guardian clapped his hands and a small man appeared. In his arms, he carried thick furs and proceeded to spread them on the benches.

'Please, take a seat,' said the Guardian. He sat down behind a large desk and waited until everyone was comfortable. Monity took the longest because she didn't want to squash their gift underneath her coat.

'I'm ready when you are,' the Guardian said and smiled encouragingly, the gold tooth flashed in the light. Mailliw commenced and the Guardian listened. Every now and then, the Guardian raised a bushy eyebrow and then lowered it again.

When Mailliw finished talking, the Guardian sighed deeply with a troubled expression.

'I do remember a unicorn coming and asking for help in locating a golden moonbeam because it was such an unusual request. However, it was a long time ago and back then, the political situation meant it was not too much trouble bargaining for one. But…' he let out a deep breath, shook his head and got up from behind the desk. Mailliw, Drabder and Monity waited anxiously for him to continue.

'Times have changed. I'll have to negotiate and ask for help, and these days, it will be a very difficult undertaking.'

Monity saw the Guardian hesitating. She looked at Mailliw and then pointed to the large lump underneath her coat. Mailliw cleared his throat and decided now was the time to barter.

'Well, of course, we didn't expect your help for nothing. We have something you might consider to be of value. It's rather unusual and as far as we know… quite a unique item.'

Mailliw paused for effect, but he also wanted to see if the Guardian was interested in what they had to offer. He didn't want to present the gingerbread house too quickly, especially as it was not in mint condition anymore. His aim was to persuade the Guardian this was a most desirable object, a priceless gift.

'You don't understand how complicated locating a golden moonbeam will be,' continued the Guardian, 'and you have seen for yourselves the wealth the travellers bring. I have more gold, silver and jewels than you can imagine. I have furs, silks, velvets and tonnes of cloth of gold. My mountain cellars are filled to the brim with unique treasures and gifts. You are simply children… what can you offer that I don't already have?'

Drabder gave an involuntary shiver. Both Mailliw and Monity felt it. Disappointment was cutting deep. Even Dingle and Peculiar were hanging their heads.

'But…' said the Guardian when he observed the children's despondent faces, 'I'm not an unkind man. Continue with what you were saying.'

Mailliw swallowed and forced himself to speak, 'It was childish of us not to understand you have such magnificent treasures, and our own offering is insignificant compared to such wealth as you possess, but what we have to offer is truly special. It is not jewels or gold and it is not a luxurious fabric or cloth of gold. Yet, I know it is one of its kind because it was handmade to a particular specification. A one-off order individually decorated and finished with a rare substance...'

Mailliw watched the Guardian as he spoke. When he caught sight of the glint in the Guardian's green eyes, Mailliw took his opportunity. It was now or never.

'Yes... finished with a rare substance,' he repeated and then he whispered, 'stardust that twinkles in the dark!' so quietly, the Guardian had to bend forward to hear the words before they vanished forever.

'Show me! Show me this special gift you have,' he urged.

Monity, Drabder, Dingle and Peculiar stopped breathing. Monity waited for Mailliw to look at her and tell her to reveal the gingerbread house, but he didn't.

'First, we must know if you agree that what we have to offer is a worthy gift in exchange for locating a golden moonbeam,' Mailliw persisted. He was desperately hoping the Guardian's curiosity would get the better of him. It did!

'Yes! Yes! I agree. I will help you to locate a golden moonbeam, but you must show me this wondrous gift!'

The Guardian was like an excited child, one who guessed his parents were hiding a toy with the promise of being rewarded with it for good behaviour. Mailliw gave Monity a nod. Slowly, Monity opened her coat and withdrew the gingerbread house. In her hands, she held the rainbow coloured wrapping with the golden mist bow and inside was the gingerbread house with its white icing and stardust trimmings.

The Guardian stared and stared. 'My! Oh my! Oh my!' was all he uttered. His hands shook and then he sat down, still unable to take his eyes off the gingerbread house. Monity stepped forward and offered to place it on the desk.

The Guardian gulped, 'Is it... is it what I think it is?'

'Yes,' said Mailliw, 'it's a gingerbread house!'

Chapter 12
The Search Begins

'Have you any idea how wondrous this item is? Do you know how long I've desired a gingerbread house?' the Guardian's voice wavered as he spoke, 'It's truly magnificent!'

Mailliw, Drabder and Monity were relieved he hadn't noticed anything wrong with the roof.

'So what's the procedure for locating a golden moonbeam?' asked Mailliw as the Guardian continued gazing at the gingerbread house. This reminder brought the Guardian back from his trance and he summoned the little man who had brought the furs in earlier.

'I need the keys to the war chamber,' he commanded briskly.

The little man looked as shaken as Mailliw, Drabder and Monity.

'But my lord…' he spluttered.

'Silence!' boomed the Guardian, 'These children need my help and they've paid a handsome price. My part of the bargain must now be honoured.'

'Very well my lord,' replied the little man and he scurried off to fetch the keys.

The Guardian turned back to the children and noted their worried expressions.

'The likeliest chance of finding a golden moonbeam lies in the Land of the Ice Pixies. We haven't been on good terms with them for some time due to our differences of opinion on certain business matters. But I'm prepared to contact them and negotiate terms for you. I expect King Pomidor to be rather difficult about this, so I'm afraid you won't be able to attend the discussions in the war chamber. But I'll organise a meal to be prepared so you can eat and rest while you wait.'

The little man returned with a set of keys. They looked as if they were made of ice, like everything else, but the Guardian explained they had been cut from one large diamond. In fact, the whole war chamber was made of cut diamonds. It was such an important room that it had to be far more secure than ice. Diamond had been chosen because it blended in with the rest of Central Junction. The Guardian left the room after giving instructions for food and drink to be brought.

After he left, Drabder said, 'I think I must b-be dreaming. He has a war chamber made of cut d-d-diamonds! He has so much unbelievable wealth and yet he went gaga over our gingerbread house. You'd have thought he'd be able to buy m-millions of gingerbread houses!'

'Bizarre isn't it,' agreed Mailliw.

'I can sort of understand why he doesn't,' said Monity looking at them. They regarded her with puzzled expressions and then raised their eyes to the ceiling as if to say, 'And what would a ten year old know about it?'

'If he did buy millions of gingerbread houses, he would lose his dream because it wouldn't be a dream any longer. The uniqueness of a gingerbread house would disappear and become a commonplace thing. Because he has so much wealth, I think he needs to desire something he can't have or won't permit himself to have. It works not only as a discipline but also as a way of holding onto his dream.'

During Monity's explanation, none of them heard the little man return. When he spoke, all three of them jumped.

'For a girl, you are pretty smart,' he said and proceeded to lay up the Guardian's desk with a tablecloth, soup plates and cutlery. While he was busy, Mailliw and Drabder grinned at Monity for being right but Monity felt riled. What did the little man mean, 'For a girl, you are pretty smart'? Did he mean girls were not supposed to be intelligent? She scowled.

Dingle lay curled up asleep on one of the furs, or so everyone thought, but his eyes opened at the mention of food. Peculiar washed her paws as if totally bored by the whole process. She wished her tail had fur. It was very cold in this place and there was a risk of it getting chilblains.

The little man clapped his hands and several servants entered. They brought a large tureen of soup, a platter of assorted cheeses and an enormous basket of freshly baked bread.

'The soup is fresh mushroom and wild garlic, the bread has been flavoured with caraway seeds and...' but before the little man finished, Dingle zoomed to one of the benches and sat down in front of the large breadbasket.

'And for the dragon and cat,' the little man continued, 'if they follow me, I'll show them where they can eat.'

Dingle slipped down from the bench and meekly followed the man. He tried to ignore the half-smile Peculiar had on her lips as he padded by. It was the twitching whiskers that gave her away.

***

Hours after the meal finished, the children stifled yawns and wrapped themselves in the furs. The warmth the soup had given them was wearing off. Conversation was fizzling out, they were tired and there was still no sign of the Guardian.

'I hope Norgruk will be okay. He's going to have to spend the night on his own,' said Monity as she checked underneath her furs to see if Bit was all right. The cold was sending the bat into hibernation and although it was getting dark, Bit was not showing any sign of wanting to wake up and search for food.

'We left him plenty of roots and some peppermint and parsley patties, so he should be fine,' said Mailliw absently, his mind now focussing on how long the Guardian was going to take. He wanted to be making some sort of progress instead of sitting around.

'But it's so cold out there and there may be strange beasts lurking,' Monity replied.

'He'll probably breathe fire onto a few rocks or boulders and huddle around them for warmth, besides, it would be a stupid beast to take too much interest in a guarding dragon!' he said, his thoughts were now on Forthright. What had she been doing today? Was she all right?

Monity leaned her head against Drabder's shoulder and closed her eyes, and Mailliw began pacing the room. When he turned around, the little man had reappeared.

'Negotiations are continuing, so I've prepared rooms for you to retire. If you come this way I'll take you to them.'

They followed him into a long ice corridor and, as they marched along, they noticed the ice became solid walls of rock.

'I-I think we're inside the mountain,' said Drabder and Mailliw nodded in agreement.

Embedded in the rock were large wooden doors with the same type of carvings as the ice doors they had seen earlier. The little man opened a door and showed them into a large hexagonal room. Tapestries adorned the walls and there were five other internal doors, each leading to a small bedroom. The main room had a pile of hot rocks in the centre and resting in front of these lay Dingle and Peculiar. Inside the bedrooms, a similar pile of hot rocks gave out warmth and on the beds were mounds of golden furs.

'I'm so tired,' said Monity, 'I bagsy this room,' and she fell towards the bed, lay down, and pulled the soft furs up to her chin. Mailliw and Drabder left her in peace and in moments, she was asleep. A few minutes later, she did not hear the Guardian enter the main room. She did not hear the discussions and she never heard the boys leave.

***

'This has been rather difficult and it took hours just trying to access the right people,' the Guardian told Mailliw and Drabder as he warmed his hands over the hot rocks, 'King Pomidor is suspicious of me making contact, so for security reasons only two of you can go. I told his Chief of Staff that the matter was top secret and you had not disclosed any details to me. I thought it for the best not to mention you required a golden moonbeam. You have a tough task ahead and once you leave here to find the gateway, you will be on your own. I've given my word you will not be followed.'

'Find the gateway?' queried Mailliw, 'Aren't they all here?'

'Only the ones by agreement… due to the bad relations between us, King Pomidor refuses to allow any gateways here that might enable us to penetrate their security. All I can give you is a piece of magnetised rock. This will guide you to the chosen coordinate. I have no idea how far you will have to go… oh… and of course you'll need to carry the jewels as payment.'

'Jewels?' asked Mailliw.

'Yes. The price was a rucksack full of diamonds. They are forever wanting diamonds. At least a rucksack is easy enough for one of you to carry.'

'When do we go?' asked Mailliw.

'King Pomidor insists you go immediately. He wants the business concluded and you sent back as soon as possible. So it means no sleep for you tonight,' the Guardian said and then looked at them both, 'I'm sorry I couldn't do any better for you but King Pomidor can be very stubborn. Come...' he said, and waved his hand indicating they were to follow.

Mailliw and Drabder obeyed and, as they went through the door, Peculiar and Dingle rose from lying in front of the warm rocks and followed.

'No!' said Mailliw, 'You must stay and look after Monity.'

Dingle stopped in his tracks. Peculiar gave a low growl of disapproval but halted at the doorway.

'I c-c-can't believe we're leaving Monity behind,' said Drabder, 'or Dingle and Peculiar for that m-matter.'

'You heard as well as I did what the Guardian said,' Mailliw replied, 'we don't have any choice.'

'But to go and n-not tell her, it-it's wrong Mailliw!'

Mailliw's astonishment at the tone in Drabder's voice was clear.

'You know how tired she was... she was falling asleep before her head touched the bed. She's younger than we are and not up to it. Besides, she'll slow us down,' he said, trying to justify the situation.

Drabder admitted part of it was true. Monity had been almost asleep on her feet. Maybe it was for the best because if she knew they were leaving, she would probably stay awake all night worrying. Even so, his conscience remained unhappy at not telling her. Drabder watched a disgruntled Peculiar and Dingle turn around and then skulk into the room where Monity lay sound asleep.

***

In addition to their own items the boys wished to take, the Guardian had given them hats and furs, spiked boots, two lanterns, emergency rations, a rucksack of diamonds and a magnetised rock on a golden chain. He led them to a small set of gates opening out onto the side of the mountain and bade them farewell.

'P-please take care of Monity. She'll be furious when she knows we've gone,' said Drabder to the Guardian as he proceeded through the gate with Mailliw.

'I'll explain everything. I understand she's quite an intellectual so I'll give her plenty to think about,' replied the Guardian.

He stood and waited as the boys climbed the snowy slopes with their spiked boots. When the light from their lanterns disappeared, he ordered the gates to be closed.

***

The icy air hit their lungs as they breathed, and again Mailliw and Drabder wondered how it was so cold here and yet summer back at home. They were grateful for the spiked boots, the furs and the lanterns. Underneath their boots was a mixture of loose stones, rocks and compacted snow but the spikes held them firm so they could ascend the mountain. Drabder carried the rucksack of diamonds on his shoulders and Mailliw held the magnetised rock. It hung from the golden chain and, from time to time, he had to stop and see how it was behaving. If the rock gave a clockwise rotation, they had to keep going forwards. If it went from side to side as in east to west, they had to turn left. A north to south movement indicated to turn right and an anticlockwise movement meant they had to retrace their steps until it changed and gave them another direction to follow.

As they climbed higher, large fluffy snowflakes floated down. Whenever they stopped trudging to check the magnetised rock, they became aware of the night being so quiet, they heard the snowflakes making small fizzes and crackles, as they landed on their hats and furs.

'Everything is so p-peaceful,' whispered Drabder as he stuck out his tongue and caught a snowflake. There was a sharp twinge of cold before the sensation melted away.

They continued their strenuous climb for several hours, only stopping to check they were still travelling on the correct path. The snow finished falling and the only sound was the crunching of their boots on the ice and snow. Neither of them felt cold, the exertion of walking kept them glowing beneath the Guardian's furs, but Drabder was worn out. The rucksack was biting into his shoulders. His back ached and cramp in his neck muscles was threatening with every step he took. It had been a long day and normally by this time, he'd be asleep in bed.

'C-can't we rest for a few minutes?' he said the next time Mailliw stopped to check the magnetised rock. Mailliw held his lantern to Drabder's face and saw his eyelids were heavy with exhaustion.

'No,' he said softly, 'if we stop moving I'm not sure we'll be able to get going again. We're both too tired and I reckon if we stop, we'll fall asleep... and once asleep the cold might penetrate even these thick furs and then...' Mailliw hoped Drabder understood what he was trying to say.

'You're afraid we might n-never wake up again. Freeze to death out here, alone, on the side of a mountain. Th-that's what you mean isn't it?' Drabder said, feeling the sleep tugging his eyes. 'C-c-can't we find some sort of shelter, a hollow or something and get some wood to make a fire to keep us warm while we rested?'

Mailliw imagined lying in front of a fire, but in reality, the fire had to be kept alive with a constant source of fuel, so someone needed to stay awake. He understood Drabder was exhausted, but so was he and he couldn't guarantee not falling asleep himself.

'It's not only being afraid of freezing to death,' he said, 'it's also the unknown. It might be quiet now, but who knows what wild animals live in these mountains. There might be bears or wolves. What if they follow our scent and find us asleep? I don't want to be a meal just waiting for them. Besides, Forthright doesn't have the luxury of time and so neither do we… we must keep moving!'

Drabder trembled and nodded wearily and Mailliw knew exactly how Drabder was feeling. Until someone experiences a lack of sleep, it's difficult to understand just how demoralising a situation can be. Everything looks too arduous, too demanding, too wearisome. How easy it is to sit down and say just a few minutes wouldn't hurt. The temptation of just a few minutes… it was a delicious thought stealing into Mailliw's mind… the cosiness of deep and welcome sleep!

The roar quickly brought them to their senses. Drabder's eyes opened wide as if his face had just been slapped with a wet fish.

'I-I'm not ready to be w-wolf fodder,' he stuttered.

'Might be a bear!' muttered Mailliw.

'Do b-bears eat meat?'

'I don't know and we're not hanging around to find out,' said Mailliw, 'let's go…'

He grabbed the rucksack off Drabder's shoulders and pulled him along, praying the magnetised rock was leading them away from the clutches of whatever it was that just roared. They headed upwards in the darkness with the cold becoming more penetrating. Each pulled their furs around them to keep out the cold but the wind was rising and beginning to drive into their faces. They checked the magnetised rock, but were unable to tell which direction to go. The wind blew the rock and their lanterns in all directions. Shadows flashed around them as the lanterns swung backwards, forwards, left and right. The wind howled around the rock faces, spinning snow particles into and around Mailliw and Drabder.

'This is useless!' shouted Mailliw above the wailing wind, 'I can't tell which direction to go!'

Mailliw held his swinging lantern above his head. The swirling snow was blinding against the dark shadows.

'We need to find somewhere sheltered from the wind,' he said and tugged on Drabder's sleeve to get him to follow. They bent forwards against the wind and shuffled towards a narrow pass. Drawing closer, they observed a large opening to one side. They approached cautiously and discovered it was large enough to walk into.

'Do you want to g-go in there?' asked Drabder, 'There might be something... waiting.'

Mailliw heard the uncertainty in Drabder's voice. The same thought had occurred to him. Was it the roaring beast's den? He handed the rucksack back to Drabder, put the magnetised rock into a pocket and fumbled underneath his fur coat. He drew out his wand.

'Get your wand ready Drabder,' he whispered.

If something jumped up on them, hopefully they would be able to cast a defence spell with enough speed to protect themselves. Mailliw held his wand out in front of him.

'Stay behind me but watch our backs,' he instructed quietly and slowly moved forwards. They crept together, holding their lanterns up for as much light as possible and soon they discovered the opening was an entrance to a cave. Compared to outside, the interior of the cave was warm. There was no wind and it was a relief to be inside. However, Mailliw was still tense and moved slowly. Drabder tiptoed close behind, trying to limit the noise of his spiked boots. They examined the cave and continued to hold their wands. They stopped and listened, but all was quiet. There was no sound of movement or breathing.

'Can you smell anything?' Mailliw whispered.

Drabder inhaled and then shook his head.

'No. Me neither. I think if any sort of animal lived in an enclosed space like this, we'd be able to smell it.'

Drabder's eyes searched around and saw Mailliw's doing the same. They needed a position where they were not too far from the entrance, in case they had to make a speedy escape, but on the other hand, they didn't want to be in the path of any returning creature.

'Look! There's a good place,' said Mailliw indicating a raised area, 'it would give us an advantage to be higher up with the bonus of being above the entrance. If anything came in we could jump down and escape if necessary.'

They climbed up and sat down. Mailliw took out the magnetised rock but, to his dismay, nothing happened.

'It's not working!' he said disappointed, 'Well, I suppose we may as well have a rest after all. Let's eat and drink and then I'll try again.'

After their rations, Mailliw tried the rock once more. Again, nothing happened and he nearly threw it against the wall in frustration. For the time being, they could only wait and hope, so they turned down the lanterns to preserve the oil. Although exhausted, Mailliw was now unable to relax, so he opted for the first watch while Drabder slept. Every now and again he tried the magnetised rock, but without success.

***

It was during Drabder's watch something strange started happening in the cave. Drabder was trying to keep his eyes open as he peered above the dimmed lanterns and into the darkness of the cave. A light blue dot was shimmering on the opposite wall. Drabder blinked. He looked again. It was still there. He repeatedly looked away from the blue dot and then back at it. Surely, it was bigger now, yes, it was bigger. The dot was definitely growing.

Drabder shook Mailliw.

'Mailliw,' he whispered, 'look over there! C-can you see a blue light?'

Mailliw rubbed his eyes and tried to fix his gaze on where Drabder was pointing.

'How long has it been there?' asked Mailliw suddenly sitting upright.

'About a m-minute and it's getting larger, I'm sure it is.'

They watched as the blue light doubled in size.

'I don't like the look of this,' said Mailliw, 'we'd better get out of here... NOW!'

They scrambled to their feet and Mailliw slung the rucksack of diamonds over his shoulders. The blue light grew rapidly and by the time they slid down from where they had rested, it was like a bright hole that appeared to be gobbling up the cave. Mailliw headed for the cave entrance and dragged Drabder along by the arm. Suddenly, Drabder tripped over a rock and went sprawling. His arm wrenched out of Mailliw's grip.

'Mailliw!' he yelled and Mailliw wheeled round to grab hold of Drabder's wrist. He was alarmed to see the blue light spreading out. It was almost touching Drabder's feet. Drabder struggled to get up. The light was now touching his spiked boots. Mailliw watched with fear as the boots vanished. Then Drabder's legs disappeared.

'Give me your hands!' shouted Mailliw as he watched Drabder being sucked into the blue hole. Drabder thrust his hands forward and Mailliw grabbed them. He heaved with all his strength but, to his horror, Drabder was still being sucked in. Mailliw dug his spiked boots into the ground and leaned backwards. The light was spreading. Drabder was only visible from his waist upwards. Mailliw tugged. He read the panic in Drabder's face.

'Help me!' he gasped.

Mailliw pulled again and again. The light grew and the agonising strain in Mailliw's muscles, made him groan with pain. His hands and arms ached, but he had to hold on. Drabder tried to push his body towards Mailliw.

'Help me! Help me!' Drabder screamed.

'I'm trying,' Mailliw yelled through gritted teeth.

Mailliw looked into Drabder's terrified eyes. Beads of perspiration on his forehead rolled into his own eyes and he closed them for a couple of seconds to relieve the stinging. When he looked again, Drabder's face had disappeared. All Mailliw could see were his arms. He was holding onto a pair of arms and nothing else. Then it was just a pair of hands. Mailliw frantically heaved again, but then he felt Drabder's fingers go limp. Every finger slid from his grasp and disappeared.

'NO!' screamed Mailliw, 'DRABDER!'

But Drabder was gone.

Chapter 13
The Mystic Of The Ice Cavern

Mailliw fell backwards with the release in tension once Drabder's fingers let go. The diamonds in the rucksack dug into his back. He attempted to get up but the blue light was already fixed on his own feet. The tugging sensation increased. Mailliw rolled over and grabbed hold of a rock near the cave entrance. The blue light was now on his legs and was swallowing him up just like Drabder. He clung to the rock and tried to drag his body forwards.

A snarling noise at the entrance made Mailliw look up and, for a brief moment, he thought his heart had stopped. In front of him stood three snow wolves. With drawn back lips, they showed bared teeth and saliva dripped from their jaws.

The blue light pulled Mailliw relentlessly. His mind raced with two options, snow wolves or blue light? What a choice! Go forwards to the snow wolves and face certain death or let go of the rock and be swallowed into the unknown!

A snow wolf lunged forward and hot breath brushed Mailliw's hand. He let go of the rock and allowed the blue light to envelop him as the cave rapidly disappeared. His eyes saw the other two snow wolves pounce and his ears heard their jaws snap on empty space.

A floating feeling swept over Mailliw. His body was rotated before something shoved against his feet. Instantly, Mailliw was thrust like a speeding bullet through a long blue tunnel. Images of zigzagging shades of blue whizzed by as he travelled. It was over almost before it began and the floating feeling returned. His body rotated once more and when his eyes refocussed, he could see a body lying on the ground and someone bending over it. The person straightened up.

'I can't wake him,' she said in a soft voice like a muffled bell.

Mailliw looked down at the floor again. It was Drabder lying there.

'Is...' Mailliw's voice choked. After a few moments, he tried again. 'Is... is he dead?'

'No,' replied the woman.

'Then what's wrong with him?'

'Was he prepared for the gateway?'

'Is that what it was?'

'You didn't know?'

'We were looking for it, but we didn't know what to expect or when. The weather deteriorated so we took shelter in a cave. I tried the magnetised rock inside but it didn't work,' explained Mailliw.

'Ah, I see. It appeared not to work, because you were already at your destination. So, being unprepared means it's a case of your friend's mind shutting down when he travelled through the gateway,' said the woman, 'it's a common occurrence under these circumstances. The person resists the power and everything becomes too much of a struggle. The mind shuts down to protect itself.'

The woman surveyed Mailliw and then said, 'You made it through safely, so I presume you did not resist.'

'I did at first, but then I had to choose between facing three snow wolves or the blue light.'

'You made the correct choice,' said the woman.

Mailliw knelt down by Drabder. He touched Drabder's ashen face and then felt his cold hands.

'Drabder,' Mailliw said, gently shaking him, 'it's me… Mailliw.' There was no response. He tried again, but Drabder was as lifeless as before.

The woman knelt beside Mailliw. She was dressed in a long grey gown where the hem, the sleeves and the neckline glittered with tiny diamonds and on her forehead, she wore an ornamental diamond headband. Her hair was bound high above her head and miniature diamonds were woven between strands of hair so that whenever she moved her head, her hair sparkled with miniscule flashes of light.

'You said you couldn't wake my friend,' said Mailliw, 'but do you know how long he will stay like this?'

The woman leaned over Drabder and concentrated on him for a minute before saying, 'It all depends.'

'On what?'

'On whatever is required to make his mind wake up again.'

Mailliw's head hammered with frustration. This woman, whoever she was, was not being particularly helpful. He had just escaped from being eaten alive, he had no idea where he was, or whether he was anywhere near locating a golden moonbeam, and Drabder was in a very sorry state.

'Look,' he said, 'I don't mean to be rude, but it would be helpful if you answered some questions.'

'But of course. What do you wish to know?'

'Was this the gateway organised by King Pomidor?'

'Yes.'

'So where is he?'

'In his palace.'

'And where's the palace?'

135

'Not too far from here.'

'Is my friend, Drabder, going to be alright?'

'If you are prepared to help him, then yes, I believe your friend will be alright.'

The frustrated hammering in his head eased slightly and Mailliw asked, 'What do I need to do?'

'Fetch some water from the crystal lake. I need it to help Drabder, but you will have to exchange something for the water. It must be all of whatever you have on you which you truly believe as having the most value.'

Mailliw removed the rucksack. The diamonds were undoubtedly the most valued item he had on him. He frowned at the thought of having to exchange all of them. They were supposed to be for King Pomidor for the golden moonbeam. Without the diamonds, the chances of finding Forthright's cure were zero. What should he do? Use the diamonds to save Drabder or Forthright?

Mailliw rolled his eyes in desperation. He was tired of all this. If he hadn't knocked over and damaged Forthright's moondial, none of this would be happening.

'You have a difficult decision to make?' asked the woman.

'Yes, I have to choose between saving my friend or my sister.'

'I see…'

'No you don't! You have no idea of the torment I'm going through,' snapped Mailliw. He got to his feet and kicked the rucksack. The diamonds chinked against each other as the bag slid a few feet away.

'Let me finish. It's you who doesn't understand,' she said gently, 'I am the Mystic of the Ice Cavern and have a certain amount of foresight. So I can see things. Sometimes the images are very clear, but at other times, they are misty. When I look at Drabder, my mind is picking up images of a dog with long black and tan fur and amber eyes. The images are very clear. When I look at you, everything is clouded. I cannot see your sister

136

clearly. She seems insubstantial, a bit like a ghost. Therefore, I can help Drabder but I cannot help your sister.'

'My sister is like a ghost! She has silver moonbeam sickness and will disappear by the next new moon unless I can get the cure.'

Mailliw sat down and cradled Drabder's head. He removed Drabder's hat and lifted his dishevelled hair away from his forehead. As he nursed his friend, Mailliw thought about Forthright. How much more had she disappeared? Was there any certainty about even finding a golden moonbeam for her? At least Drabder was here and, at this moment, Mailliw could do something to help him. He would have to face King Pomidor without the diamonds and find some other method of payment.

'Where's the crystal lake?' he asked.

***

Mailliw took the crystal flask from the Mystic and tucked it inside his fur coat. He slung the rucksack of diamonds over his arm and headed in the direction of the lake. His spiked boots gripped on the ice in the tunnel and he remembered the Mystic explaining why she couldn't take the water from the lake. She had taken an oath to be the singer of the crystal waters to help heal others and must never take the water for her own purposes, or her curing powers would cease to exist.

He traipsed along and puffed. He hadn't realised the tunnel was on an upward gradient. His arms swung and the diamonds jostled in the rucksack. It wouldn't be long before he offered them to the lake and took back the precious water for Drabder.

Mailliw reached some steps carved out of the ice and ascended into another cavern. On the last step, Mailliw stopped. He looked around and viewed the cavern lit up with candles. The scene was breathtaking. The walls and ceiling were encrusted with turquoise crystals glittering in the candlelight. The crystal lake was like a mirror and reflected both the turquoise crystals and the light from the candles. It gave the impression of being deep underwater with rays of sunlight flickering through aqua-green depths.

Positioned close to the lake was a large set of scales carved out of white crystal. Mailliw's instructions were to place the diamonds on one side of the scales then collect the water in the flask and place it on the opposite side. When the scales balanced, he could leave with the flask of crystal water. But if the scales dipped in favour of the water, then he had taken too much and had to return some to the lake and weigh the flask again. Alternatively, if the scales dipped in favour of the diamonds, then Mailliw was entitled to take more water until the balance was correct.

'Be warned!' the Mystic had said, 'Don't try and cheat the scales.'

'Why? What will happen?' Mailliw had asked.

'I won't be able to make the water work and you will forfeit your offering and your right to any further water from the lake.'

Mailliw hastened towards the scales. His boots crunched on the crystals and the sound echoed around the walls. The vibrations travelled to the lake and Mailliw saw small ripples disturbing the surface. He opened the rucksack, carefully poured the diamonds onto the scales and inspected the interior to make sure none remained inside. When it was empty, he took out the flask from inside his coat and went to the water's edge. To his amazement, the water was warm to his fingers as he sunk the flask. Mailliw had expected the lake to be ice-cold. The water glugged into the container and Mailliw filled it to just below the neck. He lifted the flask up to inspect the level of water. It wasn't overflowing and he prayed he hadn't taken too much.

He returned to the scales and placed the flask on the opposite side to the diamonds. Slowly the scale with the diamonds rose and the scale with the water dropped until they balanced perfectly.

'Thank you, thank you,' he whispered, removing the flask. He expected the scales to tip back again with the weight of the diamonds, but they didn't. They remained balanced because the diamonds were no longer there. Mailliw didn't know how or where they had disappeared. All he was interested in was getting the crystal water back to Drabder.

Mailliw strode briskly, but as he went along, he speculated on how he was going to pay King Pomidor now he didn't have the diamonds. Could he strike a bargain of some sort? He had to… it was his only chance to save Forthright.

On his return, the Mystic was sitting with Drabder and when she took the flask, she smiled.

'Excellent. Can you hold Drabder's hands for me? He needs to be in contact with somebody he knows.'

The Mystic moved gracefully and knelt beside Drabder. She sprinkled a few drops of water on his forehead and then bathed his face. She poured the remaining crystal water into a turquoise bowl, then stirred the water with one finger and began singing. At first it was quiet, but as her voice grew stronger, she withdrew her finger and placed her hands in her lap. Mailliw soon sensed that her voice was causing the water to continue swirling in the bowl. The Mystic's voice was pure, like a lark singing high in the sky, like water trickling down a mountainside, like wind chimes softly moving in a breath of air. It was a sound of everything beautiful, something where pain and sorrow were stolen away, then hidden where nobody could find them.

'Mailliw, Mailliw, wake up,' said the Mystic giving him a gentle shake. 'I need you to help me raise your friend into a sitting position.'

Mailliw had no recollection of falling asleep, only aware of having lost something precious now the singing had stopped.

They supported Drabder and as they lifted him, his eyelids flickered and opened.

'Quickly,' said the Mystic, 'he needs to drink the water. You hold him while I get him to drink.'

She lifted the bowl to Drabder's lips, 'Drink this. It will make you sleep and when you awake you will be well again.'

'D-d-don't want to,' murmured Drabder and moved his head to the side.

'Drabder, it's Mailliw. You must drink!'

Recognition flashed through Drabder's eyes. He opened his mouth and the Mystic gently poured in a few drops. He swallowed and opened his mouth for more. When he finished the crystal water, his eyes probed Mailliw's and he smiled weakly.

'I can see her,' he said.

'Yes, she's the Mystic. She's saved you,' said Mailliw.

'No, no,' whispered Drabder, 'not her… she's got one puppy and I'm going to call him Max…' and then he fell into a deep sleep.

'What's he talking about?' asked Mailliw looking at the Mystic.

'He's found what he needs to make him well. He'll sleep for some time now.'

'Do you know how long?'

'No.'

'I must hurry and go to King Pomidor's palace, even though I have nothing left to bargain with, so can I leave Drabder here with you until I return?'

'Yes, I'll look after him until then. I'll also give you the directions to the palace and Mailliw…'

'Yes?'

'I wish you luck and safekeeping.'

Chapter 14
The Palace Of King Pomidor

It was with reluctance that Mailliw left Drabder in the ice cavern, but there was no alternative, he had to go on alone, and Mailliw was grateful for the directions the Mystic had given him for the palace.

He slogged through the ice cavern and reflected on how much had happened in such a short period. The boy who, just a few days ago, had kicked the kerb and tempted Fate, felt like a younger part of himself had been left behind sitting on a milestone. A milestone where childhood ended and the blurred edges of adolescence arrived, where the reality of the adult world revealed that actions and decisions might have life and death consequences. Mailliw was uncertain about how to approach King Pomidor and courage seemed like it had been left on the milestone with his younger self. He dug his nails into his palms. Fear crawled up through his feet and settled at the nape of his neck. He had to do this. He had to do this for Forthright! Could he honestly say his fear was greater than his sister's? She was depending on him to live!

An image of Merry Willows the Widow flashed into his mind... and he remembered he had succeeded then, so surely he was capable of seeing a King by himself... but what about not having the diamonds to exchange for a golden moonbeam? Wouldn't a King would be magnanimous enough to understand the importance of what he had done? He imagined himself saying, 'Your Highness... I truly regret not having the gift of diamonds... but they were required to save a life,' or 'Your Highness... when a life was at stake, I exchanged the diamonds...' and the King would reply, 'Think no more of the matter, you acted out of loyalty and concern for your friend,' or 'Bravo! Such a noble gesture. What are diamonds compared to a life?' and buoyed by the optimism of these thoughts, Mailliw's inner strength revived and he hurried more confidently towards his destination.

On exiting the cavern, Mailliw came face to face with an ice forest. It wasn't a forest of trees, but one made up of large tree-like ice structures. They were like leafless trees. They had ice trunks and frozen branches at the top which created a lacy canopy overhead. Mailliw scrutinized a blue sky peeping through and, although he had lost track of time overnight, he guessed it was early morning.

Eventually, the ice forest thinned and Mailliw trekked up an avenue flanked by ice pillars leading towards the palace gates. Behind the gates, four round towers dominated the scene, and King Pomidor's palace reminded Mailliw of ones he had seen in Forthright's fairytale books.

'You're late!' said a guard. Another stood to attention, but glared at Mailliw.

They were shorter than he was and had long pointed ears sticking outside their helmets. They must be ice pixies.

'You have kept King Pomidor waiting and he is not pleased. When you go through the gates, you are to be escorted to the King and explain yourself.'

Mailliw's newfound confidence evaporated but, before he could retreat, the guards opened the gates and pushed him through. On the other side waited a line of soldiers, who also had pointed ears and were standing to attention. A soldier stepped forward, took Mailliw's arm and steered him towards the palace. The other soldiers marched behind. If Mailliw had any thoughts of trying to escape, he soon forgot them.

Once inside the palace, they walked through what seemed like an endless number of corridors before the soldier led Mailliw into a large hall. It was a cloakroom and numerous ice pixies were either taking off or putting on outdoor clothes.

'You must wear slippers in the throne room,' said the soldier. 'Here, put these on,' he said handing a pair to Mailliw, 'and give me your coat.'

Mailliw put the slippers on and was taken to the grand throne room. At the far end were two thrones, one made of gold and the other of silver. A man with black slicked hair stood to one side of the golden throne and his hawk-like eyes studied Mailliw. A chill ran through Mailliw and he averted his gaze. Instead, he looked at the near end of the room where an enormous fireplace was stacked with logs and a large fire crackled.

'You are to wait here,' said the soldier. He moved back and stood at ease. A trumpet sounded and Mailliw heard the soldier's feet shuffle to attention.

'His Majesty is coming. You are expected to drop down on one knee and keep your head bowed once he is seated on the throne,' the soldier commanded.

The King entered from a large door on the right and was about the same height as Mailliw. Underneath his bejewelled crown, the King's bald head gleamed like it had been polished with a mirror cloth. To prevent the crown from slipping on such a shiny surface, the King's long pointy ears were positioned to keep it perched in a dignified manner. In the centre of the crown rested the largest diamond Mailliw had ever seen. It was the size of an egg and flashed colours of fire as the King proceeded in a stately manner towards his throne. Mailliw also saw the King's downturned mouth. It didn't need words to know his Highness was displeased. The King continued with his royal progression and Mailliw became aware of the grandeur of his clothes and the striking contrast between the full-length ermine lined purple cloak and the red carpet. Four bearers trailed after the King and lifted the cloak hem off the floor. Underneath the cloak, the King wore a gown made of cloth of gold embroidered with seed pearls and silver thread, and he wore matching slippers on his feet.

Behind the bearers followed a girl about the same height as Monity. She wore a white gown adorned with diamonds in a similar style to the Mystic of the Ice Cavern. Her skin was pale and her white hair hung in a long plait down her back. A small diamond tiara sparkled when she bowed her head at Mailliw, but on lifting her head, she gave him a mischievous grin before resuming a serious expression.

The King and the young girl sat on the thrones. The man with black slicked hair continued to examine Mailliw.

'The King and the Princess are now seated,' announced a loud voice and the King looked haughtily down his hooked nose and acknowledged his subjects.

Mailliw dropped to one knee and bowed his head as instructed.

'You're late,' scolded King Pomidor as he brushed a bearer's hand away from fussing with his cloak, 'I was told to expect two of you. You have not kept to the bargain that was agreed. Breaking the agreement indicates you have come here as a spy. What do you have to say for yourself?'

'I come with apologies your Highness. There are two of us, but I had to leave my friend with the Mystic of the Ice Cavern. He wasn't prepared for the gateway experience...'

The King exploded with an interruption, 'Wasn't prepared? What a preposterous claim, not prepared… of course you were prepared! You were told to search for the gateway and were given a magnetised rock to find it! What feeble story is this? You are trying to deceive us… you are a spy!'

'No! No!' cried Mailliw leaping to his feet, 'I'm not a spy! I came here seeking something to save my sister's life. She has silver moonbeam sickness…'

'Enough!' bellowed the King, 'You impertinent boy! Who gave you permission to stand in our presence? I certainly didn't!'

Mailliw dropped to one knee and bowed his head once more. His hopes of striking a bargain with King Pomidor were dashed like pebbles thrown onto a beach in a storm. Everything seemed lost.

The Princess put out her hand and touched the King's sleeve.

'Father,' she said quietly, 'he doesn't look much of a spy to me. He's just a boy.'

The King looked at her. His frosty face melted, he hummed and hawed, then patted her hand and looked back at Mailliw.

'So, if you're not a spy, prove it by presenting us with the diamonds that the Guardian of the Winter Mountains promised.'

Mailliw's heart sank lower than it was already. The Princess had just spoken up for him and now he was going to prove to be another disappointment.

'I don't have them,' he said in a small voice and bowed his head so low, his forehead almost touched the floor.

'I THOUGHT AS MUCH!' bellowed the King, 'HE IS A SPY!'

'Father, let him explain.'

'No! He does not have the promised diamonds. He has broken the agreement not once but twice. This is a trick! Put him in prison! I'll deal with him later!'

The soldier stepped forward and lifted Mailliw to his feet. Mailliw had just enough time to look at the Princess and witness the alarm in her face, before he was removed and taken to the prison.

'Not prepared for the gateway,' muttered the King, 'never heard such nonsense. How can you be deliberately guided to one and not be prepared?'

'You might have asked him,' replied the Princess softly.

***

Mailliw sat on the hard bed in the prison and kept asking himself how much worse things could get. He had to do something. If he could escape, he would return to Drabder and then ask the Mystic for help to get back to the Winter Mountains. There was no chance of finding a golden moonbeam for Forthright now, and he just wanted to go back home and be with her before she disappeared completely. The thought of having to explain how he failed to find her a cure was unbearable, but it would be even worse if he wasn't there at all.

Mailliw hunted through his pockets. He drew out the compass and the magnetised rock. He would need the compass if he escaped. Then he pulled out his rolled up notebook of basic spells and flicked through the pages. He was disappointed to find there was nothing on how to unlock a padlock or bend metal bars. Lastly, he took out the gift from his parents, the black diamond. When he examined the shape, Mailliw remembered it was harder than rock, harder than ice and harder than the bars of the prison. He paused and listened to see if anyone was about. It was quiet.

Mailliw moved from the bed, took a seated position by the prison bars and started filing. He stopped from time to time just to make sure nobody was coming. The black diamond slowly cut through the first bar and Mailliw commenced on the next one. The filing was hot work and Mailliw's thirst raged. He hadn't drunk anything since being in the cave with Drabder before they were sucked into the gateway. Once he escaped and was outside the palace, he would suck several large chunks of ice.

'Are you trying to escape?' said a voice.

Mailliw looked up, startled. The Princess was standing a few metres away from him. He sat up with the black diamond dangling from his fingers.

'I didn't mean to make you jump, but obviously you were too busy trying to escape to hear me. That is what you're doing isn't it?'

When Mailliw remained silent, she continued, 'I don't believe you're a spy and I came to tell you so. I also came to ask if you needed some food. Do you?'

When Mailliw still refused to speak, she advanced towards him and knelt down on the other side of the bars.

'I'm Frija. What's your name?'

'Mailliw.'

'Nice to know you, Mailliw. I don't meet many boys as my father considers them unfit for my company. Now I mention it, I don't get to meet many girls either. It gets very lonely being a Princess...' she paused and gazed at the black diamond in Mailliw's fingers.

'May I see?' she asked, pointing at it.

Mailliw hurriedly put the black diamond into his pocket and said, 'No. I'm not going to give you the only thing I have that will get me out of this place!'

'Listen to me. If what you have is what I think it is, then it is definitely the thing to get you out of here.'

Mailliw glared at Frija and she saw the stubborn look in his eyes.

'Fine! Don't let me see it, but I'm going to guess it's a black diamond. Am I right?'

She was met with a stony silence.

'I'm trying to help you, you idiot. If you have a black diamond, then I will help you to escape and find what it is you came here for, and then I'll make sure you return to your friend and where you came from. The only condition is… when we find what you came for, before you go home you must present the black diamond to my father.'

'I can't.'

'Why not?'

'It was a gift from my parents.'

'A gift from your parents! How rich are your parents? As a King my father is wealthy, but not so wealthy he could give me a black diamond!'

'Is it very valuable then?' Mailliw asked and pulled the black diamond from his pocket, inspecting it with new interest. So much had happened since his parents sent it to him, that he hadn't given the black diamond much consideration. It never occurred to him that it might be something more than just another artefact for his bedroom collection.

'Valuable? Yes! It's valuable! My father has been searching all his life for a black diamond and never found one. What you have there is worth more than a thousand rucksacks of white diamonds. It's priceless!'

With shock, Mailliw almost dropped the black diamond. How could it be worth so much? If it was, then why had the crystal scales only accepted the rucksack of diamonds to save Drabder? His mind raced back over the Mystic's words, '… you will have to exchange something for the water. It must be all of whatever you have on you which you truly believe as having the most value.'

Then he understood. The scales worked on belief, not fact, and he had truly believed in the rucksack of diamonds. Even if Mailliw had only offered a small coin, so long as he truly believed it was the most valuable thing he had on him, it would still have been accepted by the scales.

Mailliw felt like someone had punched him. Why did everything keep going wrong? If he had known about the black diamond, he could have exchanged it to save Drabder and still had the rucksack of diamonds to offer King Pomidor for a golden moonbeam. Well, if the black diamond was now the only way he could get out of prison, then he intended to use it!

Mailliw looked into Frija's eyes. He saw a pair the colour of deep ocean-blue similar to his own, but hers were fringed with white lashes.

'So, this is my passport out of here,' he said sharply.

'Maybe, but I thought you didn't want to part with it.'

Mailliw regarded Frija's face. He could have sworn she was mocking him.

'Look, if this gets me out of here and can help me save my sister, I'm quite willing to give it to your father. But, I need your solemn promise you're not tricking me.'

Frija's face froze, 'I'm a Princess! Who are you to demand a solemn promise from me? I offered to help you and that should be good enough. Take my offer or stay here.'

She got up and flounced off.

'Wait!' shouted Mailliw. She stopped. When she twirled round, she had the same mischievous grin on her face as when she had viewed him in the throne room.

'Okay. We have a deal, but I want to do this my way, not my father's. I'll come back with some food and drink in a few minutes and when you've eaten, I'll tell the guard at the entrance you're asleep, so he can go off duty for a while. When he's gone, I'll come and get you out of here. Then you can tell me your story... I want to know why you're here. Then we can plan what we are going to do about it. By the way... what do you like to eat?'

'I'm so hungry and thirsty, I'll eat anything you bring!' replied Mailliw, as hope surfaced once more.

'Will fried slugs with a chilli dip be alright then?'

Mailliw heard her chuckling as she went up the corridor. He sincerely hoped she was joking.

***

Mailliw sat in Frija's personal chambers. So far, everything had gone according to her plan. She had returned to the prison with a tray of savoury pancakes, a dish of baked apples drizzled with honey and raisins, and a jug of pink lemonade. Whilst he was eating, she convinced the guard everything was well enough for him to go off duty and, once he was out of sight, she removed the prison key from its hook and let Mailliw out.

She told Mailliw that the corridors were quiet because all the courtiers were in the main hall for court business and the guards were on parade duty, so it was unlikely anyone would spot her taking Mailliw to her rooms. On the way, he had thought the corridors of the palace austere after the sumptuous elegance of the throne room, but now as he glanced around Frija's room, he could see she lived in splendid luxury.

Frija waved at an overflowing bowl of fruit on a carved white stone table, 'Help yourself if you're still hungry. I'm just going to get changed,' she said and opened the door to what appeared to be a dressing room filled with rows and rows of clothes. She disappeared inside and shut the door.

Mailliw peeled a banana and admired the room. The air was perfumed from several large vases of white lilies and silk rugs were scattered over the marble floors. Everything was elegant and refined, unlike his own room with his unmade bed, cluttered floor and desk strewn with dog-eared homework books. Like Mailliw, Frija had a four-poster bed, but whereas his had thick embroidered tapestries, hers had silver satin drapes edged with the finest lace. Three walls were painted with a pattern of golden swirls and the centre of every swirl was studded with gems, such as rubies, sapphires and emeralds. The fourth wall had a life-size painting of a unicorn. It was so realistic, Mailliw expected it to walk off the wall.

'Beautiful isn't it.'

Mailliw was as startled as he had been when Frija spoke to him in the prison.

'I wish you'd stop creeping up on me,' he said as Frija stood behind him.

'My mother painted this creature before she died,' she said, and her voice took on a wistful quality, 'she told me this story about how she only ever saw it once many years ago but fell in love with its beauty and grace. Although she was a small girl at the time, she couldn't forget the noble features and the wisdom in its eyes. Everyone had always believed unicorns to be mythical creatures, not real. It seemed a miracle to everyone when it turned up. Anyway, she told me it was sent here by the Guardian of the Winter Mountains to find a golden moonbeam. She always hoped to see it return one day, but it never came.'

With Frija's explanation, Mailliw's hairs on the back of his neck stood on end. This was uncanny. Frija was telling him the other end of the story Merry Willows the Widow had told him. She moved away quietly and leaned against the bed. Mailliw noticed she had changed from her white gown into a pair of trousers and wore a shirt underneath a fur waistcoat.

'Right!' said Frija picking an apple from the fruit bowl, 'Let's get down to business. I want you to tell me everything so I can formulate a plan.' The wistfulness in her voice vanished and was replaced by a 'well, let's get on with it' type of attitude that reminded him of Forthright.

She sat on the bed cross-legged and bit into the apple, 'Well… I'm waiting!'

Mailliw clenched his fists. Working with a Princess who was used to giving orders, and getting her own way, was not going to be easy!

Chapter 15
Locating The Golden Moonbeam

'Wow!' said Frija, 'You've had a really exciting adventure. Well, it hasn't finished yet,' she said grinning at Mailliw. He noticed how grinning affected her pointed ears. They went up when she grinned and down when she didn't. Even if Frija had her back to him, he could tell whether she was grinning or not.

'It's an amazing coincidence that you're here for the same reason as the unicorn... for a golden moonbeam,' she said, pausing and scratching her chin, 'they are rare but the occurrence does happen. You see, in our country, at certain times of the year, there is a phenomenon called the Aurora Borealis, commonly known as the Northern Lights. When there is a full moon at the same time as the Northern Lights, some ordinary silver moonbeams travel through them and are converted into golden moonbeams. They are only preserved if they hit the ice. Then they become frozen into a line of golden particles running through a block of ice. If the ice should thaw, the golden moonbeam escapes and disappears.'

Mailliw was captivated and listened attentively.

Frija continued, 'We've got dozens of experimentalists trying to understand these events, so we have a special security room monitoring all golden moonbeam activity in our area. What they are trying to discover is how silver moonbeams convert into golden moonbeams. The experimentalists also want to know if it's possible to harness the power of the conversion. If so, we would have a new type of energy for cooking our food and heating our homes. Currently, we have to buy our fuel from other countries and it's getting very expensive… that's why we need diamonds…' she paused as if realising she had said too much. The trials of moonbeam conversion were top secret and the reason why her father was paranoid about spies. King Pomidor didn't want anyone finding out about their experiments.

After hearing Frija's explanation about golden moonbeams, Mailliw realised everything was more complicated than he had imagined when he made the promise to save Forthright. Aunt Foggerty's words repeated in his brain, 'You have no idea of what's involved in such a promise…' and he wondered if Aunt Foggerty had known more than she let on. For all his life she had just been plain Aunt Foggerty, but recent events were revealing another side to her character, especially all the business with Merry Willows the Widow.

'Right,' said Frija, 'the first thing I need to do is to access the details of any golden moonbeams. You'll have to go back to the prison while I get things organised. I don't know how long this will take and if anyone finds you missing, the alarm will be raised before I'm ready.'

Mailliw grew hot with irritation. Frija was taking control and he was powerless to stop her. He needed her more than she needed him. It was a new experience and he didn't like it. It wasn't even worth arguing that he ought to help, because of course… she was right. They couldn't afford somebody raising the alarm.

'Well then, I'd better get back to where I belong,' he said with a sniff of indignation.

Frija put her hands on her hips, threw back her head and laughed.

'What's so funny?' he asked.

'You!'

'Explain!'

'Haven't got time,' she said and glanced around the door to make sure the coast was clear.

***

When Frija left Mailliw at the prison, she knew he was miffed. At this stage, it was for the best that he remained there.

Her first job meant accessing the golden moonbeam security room. All the other planning depended on the location of a golden moonbeam. If they had to travel far, she needed to organise some reindeer, a sleigh, furs and a special container for the golden moonbeam, and – for the worst-case scenario – some weapons. If she succeeded in getting her plan that far, then the best time to depart would be later, under the cover of darkness. With Mailliw not being in the best of moods, she decided it was better not to mention that he might have a lengthy wait, just in case he decided not to return to the prison.

With being the Princess and heir to the throne, Frija was entitled to know the codes to the security areas of the palace. She could gain entry to the golden moonbeam security room by using the codes, but if anyone caught her, they'd probably report it to her father and she didn't want to raise his curiosity. The peak time for the experimentalists using the room was around the full moon, when there was a chance of a golden moonbeam being created, but the moon was now waning, and the possibilities of someone working in the security room were significantly reduced. They would be occupied with carrying out their research and writing reports in their offices down in the palace cellars. Even so, she remained cautious. Everything needed secrecy because she didn't want anything to spoil this chance for an adventure.

Frija strode towards the golden moonbeam security room and then walked straight on, her eyes searching around to see if anyone was about. When she was certain it was safe, she darted back and placed her forefinger on the golden ball situated outside the door. The ball rotated and stopped. A flap opened and she keyed in a sequence of numbers and symbols. The flap closed and the ball rotated back to its original position. A door slid open and Frija slipped inside. She breathed with relief when she saw that nobody was there.

The room was small but filled with dials and clocks. All of them were linked to a map on the wall showing The Northern World. The dials and clocks monitored the Northern Lights on full moons and detected the number of golden moonbeams occurring at any one time. Frija didn't understand how the equipment collated the information, it was far too technical, but she did know how to switch on the map showing the locations.

The map lit up and Frija was disheartened. Only one marking showed up. If there had been several, then locating one golden moonbeam and extracting it may not have been so bad, but to take the only one would greatly displease her father.

'This is not good!' she murmured to herself, 'I only hope the black diamond will outweigh his anger.'

Frija noted the coordinates and groaned silently. The golden moonbeam couldn't have been in a worse place. Its position was probably the only reason why it was still there. It meant having to cross the ice and travel into the sea monster zone, where the terrifying creatures called the Scribb, lived under the ice. It was the worst-case scenario and they would have to take ice bombs and ice fire.

If the golden moonbeam had been in a safer location, Frija may have taken the risk to steer the reindeer and sleigh herself. But, as vibrations were just the thing to attract the Scribb, she needed someone more experienced to outrun the monsters if necessary. The only person Frija trusted was Snaf, an ancient ice pixie who had been devoted to her mother.

Frija flicked off the switch to the map and put her eye to the spyhole looking out into the corridor. She couldn't see anyone, so she quietly opened the door and exited the security room. She moved swiftly and collided with someone coming around the corner.

'Princess, his Highness has been asking after you,' said Slymus, the King's Chief of Staff, 'are you going out, you've changed your clothes?' His voice was smooth and quiet as if he'd drunk liquid silk and the effect was to make it appear that he was asking out of concern for her. However, Frija personally believed it was disguised interrogation.

'I thought I'd visit the reindeer stables and see whether the baby reindeer has been born yet. I changed because a gown is not suitable for crawling about in the straw and reindeer moss,' replied Frija, trying not to show her dislike of the man. There was something unnerving about his black slicked hair and calculating hawk eyes.

'Ha! Ha! Of course... of course...' he murmured rubbing his forefinger over his thin lower lip. Frija recognised this as a nervous trait when he was uncomfortable in someone's presence, especially hers. She also often thought he spied on her and she had the feeling now.

'Would you care to accompany me?' she asked, smiling politely.

'I'd be delighted to your Highness, but I have to attend to some business for the King. I'll let him know I've seen you,' he said in his liquid silk voice before continuing briskly down the corridor.

Frija headed for the reindeer stables. If Slymus doubled back to spy on her, then she was going exactly where she had said. She needed to avoid arousing his suspicions, so she would have to ask Snaf to organise the reindeer, the sleigh and the weapons.

***

In the reindeer stables, Snaf was surly as usual. He grunted his acknowledgement of Frija when she entered. He never spoke more than necessary, instead he watched, listened and recognised who was to be trusted and who wasn't. Frija saw his small bent body hovering around a bed of straw.

'Not here yet?' she asked, looking for signs of a newborn reindeer.

Snaf shook his head and stroked a reindeer's ears before trying to straighten up.

'Actually, now I'm here, there's something I need to discuss with you,' Frija said and when Snaf looked up, she winked at him. A gleam entered his eyes and he pointed to his office. Frija understood nothing was to be said until they were inside and the door was shut.

'So,' said Snaf perching on his desk, 'what's the deal?'

As Frija recounted the story of Mailliw and the golden moonbeam, the gleam in Snaf's eyes grew brighter and by the end, his dangling feet were twitching. Got him! Frija thought, those feet were such a giveaway.

'Scribb country eh?' he crowed, 'Leave everything to me.'

He jumped off the desk, 'I'll also deliver the evening meal to the guard on duty with a touch of something to make him sleep well! As for you, behave normally and attend your afternoon lessons as usual. I'll send a message when the time is right,' he said and then opened the office door. Frija stepped out and caught a glimpse of Slymus's shadow retreating behind a stable door. So, he was spying on her! Her mind raced. How could she mislead him?

'There's no need to be so grumpy about me asking after the reindeer. I am the Princess!' Frija said in as haughty a tone as she could muster. She heard the office door slam behind her and she stomped off in the direction she had seen Slymus disappear.

'Shall I have a word with him your Highness?' said a liquid silk voice behind her. With deliberate calm, Frija turned and acknowledged Slymus.

'Good gracious no!' she said cheerfully, 'He isn't worth the effort. Besides, I thought you had some business to attend to for my father. I don't want to waste your time on something so trivial,' she paused and waited for his explanation.

'Ah yes! I wanted to find you because I forgot to mention something earlier. The King has asked for you to attend and judge the annual musical icicles competition next week. He thinks it an excellent opportunity for you to exercise your royal duties.'

'I'd be delighted,' said Frija in an agreeable tone, 'was there anything else?'

Slymus shook his head and bowed. Frija took the opportunity to leave but felt as if his eyes were burning into her as she walked away. Stay calm, she thought as she headed towards the tutorial room. It was with dismay that Frija remembered she had not done her homework on the structure of ice crystals.

***

That evening, Frija paced up and down in her chamber. It had been a long afternoon pretending nothing was going on and now all this waiting was frustrating. She had no idea how Mailliw was and hoped he had not done something stupid like try to escape on his own. He had a personality like hers, impatient and headstrong.

A knock at the door made her jump. Frija opened it and found a young stable lad holding out a note. She took the note and closed the door. The note read, 'Imminent. Come now.'

It was a typical Snaf message, brief and to the point. Even if Slymus managed to get hold of it, there was little detail to give anything away, he would just assume Snaf meant the birth of the reindeer.

Frija strode down the corridors towards the stables. She smiled at a few courtiers, nodded at servants and continued with normal behaviour, but it was difficult because her stomach fluttered with nervous excitement. She didn't hesitate or look over her shoulder as she entered the stable. Don't do anything considered suspicious, she thought.

Snaf was waiting for her in the dimly lit stable. 'This way,' he said and led her to a small enclosure, 'it's female.'

He moved aside for Frija to see the newborn reindeer.

Frija smiled, 'She's beautiful,' she said, and crouched beside the mother and her baby.

'You have the privilege of naming her, so you may stay here until you've thought up a name,' Snaf said and gave her a swift nod, but at the same time his eyes shifted towards the pile of hay in the enclosure. Frija looked across, and there was Mailliw's tousled head peeping out. She grinned and was relieved when he smiled.

'I'll check everything is ready and then we can go,' Snaf said quietly and left the stables.

'Did you get a fright when he came for you?' whispered Frija to Mailliw.

'I thought he was the executioner, he had such a black look on his face,' he whispered back.

'Oh that's quite normal!' she said and giggled but quickly put her hand over her mouth.

Snaf returned and beckoned Frija and Mailliw to follow. Mailliw clambered out of the hay and brushed it from his clothes. He smelt like a summer meadow.

The old pixie led them into his office, where he rolled up a rug positioned underneath his desk and lifted a trapdoor.

'Go! Keep following the tunnel. It will bring you out where the sleigh is waiting. I've lit a few candles to provide some light. I'll meet you there,' Snaf said as he helped them descend. When they were in the tunnel, Snaf closed the trapdoor and replaced the rug.

Inside the tunnel, the air was cold and Mailliw shivered as his eyes adjusted to the candlelight.

'This way,' said Frija and took Mailliw's arm, 'I'm sorry you were left so long in the prison, but I had to rely on Snaf to organise everything. I had to behave as if it was a normal afternoon. I've never known time to pass by so slowly,' she said.

'I have to admit, I was beginning to think you'd changed your mind or else been caught out. I was just about to start trying to escape again when your man arrived, and after the initial scare of thinking I was for the chop, he told me the guard was fast asleep and it was time to go. He didn't hang about... I had a job to keep up with him!'

At the end of the tunnel, icy air blew in and, waiting by the entrance, they saw the sleigh and four reindeer. Snaf was coming towards them with some snow boots and fur coats.

'Put these on and climb on board,' he said crisply, before slipping his arms through his own coat.

Mailliw was still wearing the slippers he'd put on before visiting the throne room. His feet were numb and he was more than happy to exchange the flimsy slippers for proper snow boots.

When they were seated, Snaf put on a pair of snow goggles, tucked his ears underneath his hat, took the reins, and gently urged the reindeer forwards.

'Normally the reindeer wear bells on their necks to let people know they are coming, but tonight we need to be as quiet as possible,' Frija said and snuggled down into her fur coat. A thick hood framed her face and, as the sleigh picked up speed, strands of fur quivered in the breeze.

'How much has Snaf told you about our plan?' she asked.

'Not very much. He's not the most communicative of fellows,' said Mailliw.

Frija told him how she accessed the security room for the golden moonbeam location and how there was only one available. Then she told him about the danger of the location, the risk of the Scribb hearing them in the sea monster zone and the weapons.

'And what exactly is a Scribb?' asked Mailliw.

'A Scribb is an enormous jelly bodied, multi-tentacled creature. The tentacles spread out underneath the ice feeling vibrations. The creature tracks the vibrations and catches its prey by spearing the ice with a poisonous lance from its rear. The poison paralyses the prey and the lance sucks out the body fluids.'

'How horrible!' Mailliw said and squirmed in his seat, 'Are we likely to attract one?'

'I'd like to say no, but to be honest I think it's more likely we will. That's why Snaf is driving. He's the fastest driver I know and the only one I can trust.'

When Mailliw had been sitting in the prison, he thought his day could not get much worse. Now it just had. The Scribb sounded like a nightmare, the sort where something terrifying is chasing you and, hard as you try, you cannot escape. He thought about his journey over the Carnivorous Swamp. It was a gruesome experience, but at least the plants were well below the flying carpet and he was out of reach. With the Scribb, it was only the ice separating them and they were able to pierce it. Mailliw shuddered and pulled his coat tighter around him.

As for the weapons of ice bombs and ice fire Frija mentioned, Mailliw had no idea of what they were let alone how useful they were in the face of a Scribb.

Snaf expertly drove the sleigh through the dark. Mailliw tried to keep his eyes open but the icy air made them water. With panic, he discovered that the tears leaking out from the corners of his eyes were beginning to freeze. What would he do if he fell asleep and found his eyes frozen shut when he awoke?

'I think my eyes are freezing up,' he said grabbing Frija's arm.

'Mine too! Look in the coat pockets and see if Snaf's put in some snow goggles,' Frija replied and thrust her hands into her own furry pockets. She pulled out a pair at the same time as Mailliw and pushed back her hood to put them on. Mailliw did not want to admit wearing goggles was a new experience, so he waited to watch Frija. With the movement of the sleigh, it was difficult for Frija to get the headband over her head, but when the goggles were in place she heard Mailliw snorting with laughter.

'What's so hilarious?' she demanded.

'You resemble a frog!' he said, doubling over with mirth.

'I'd rather look like a frog than have my eyeballs freeze up! So if I were you, I'd get a move on and wear those goggles!'

She spoke sharply and Mailliw blinked. There were now ice particles on his eyelids! He hastily put on the goggles and stopped laughing.

The sleigh sped along and Mailliw could just make out the landscape. It was a clear night and although the moon was waning, it gave enough light to show they were travelling across a vast stretch of flat ice. Snaf bent over the reins and drove the reindeer on. All Mailliw heard was the swish of the sleigh as it cut through a thin layer of snow to the ice below.

Now that Mailliw's eyes were protected he became aware of the warmth generated by his body under the furry coat and it was increasingly difficult to keep his eyes open. The swishing sleigh was soothing and Mailliw was almost asleep. His mind drifted and he dreamt about being at home in his four-poster bed with a smouldering log fire in the grate. Everything was peaceful and relaxed.

The jolt, when it came, shook Mailliw out of his cosy dream world and back into reality. It took a few seconds for him to remember where he was. By the second jolt, Mailliw knew exactly where he was.

'What's happening?' he yelled at Frija.

'Hold on Mailliw!' she yelled back, 'We've got a Scribb hunting us!'

The third jolt rocked the sleigh sideways and ice exploded all around them.

'Run!' shouted Snaf at the reindeer, 'Run! All our lives depend on it!'

Mailliw's jaw tightened as he fought against the inner turmoil in his own mind. Fear! It crawled over his skin and lay like a fat snake coiled around his throat trying to squeeze the life out of him.

The fourth jolt slammed underneath the sleigh and threw it almost a metre in the air. The sleigh bounced down. Mailliw heard Frija scream.

'Eject the ice bombs!' Snaf bellowed over his shoulder.

Frija reached for a lever on the side of the sleigh and pulled. A lid flipped open on a container attached to the outside of the sleigh, and small blue fireballs were launched into the air all around them. When the balls landed and bounced across the ice, they flared into a storm of blue lightning, forking across and through the ice. The reindeer sped on with their feet skimming the surface. Mailliw glanced over his shoulder and saw the lightning flash like a manic storm in the distance.

'Those should keep it off our track long enough to put some distance between us,' said Frija leaning back against the seat.

'How?' was all Mailliw managed to whisper. It still felt like a fat snake lay coiled around his throat. Now he identified with what Monity and Drabder had gone through when he was driving the carriage to the Winter Mountains. They had depended on him to keep them safe. This time, it was his turn to depend on someone else for his safety and he did not like the experience.

'The ice bombs send out a frequency interrupting the vibration sensor in the Scribb. It'll be confused for an hour or so.'

'So we'll be okay then?' he asked.

'Depends!'

'On what?'

'On whether we pick up another Scribb ahead!'

Mailliw sat in his seat and tried to release the tension in all his muscles, but the thought of another Scribb ahead made it impossible. He intended to stay alert and ready for action, but Frija snuggled back into her seat.

'How can you relax when there might be another Scribb lurking beneath us?' he demanded.

'It's no good me worrying about something that might not be there. I'll just end up wasting useful energy stores. If I rest now, I'll be prepared for later. Now, if you'll excuse me, I'm going to meditate!'

'Meditate!'

'Yes, meditate, you know… chill out, make my mind blank, switch off from you…'

'I get the message,' Mailliw grunted, and pulled his coat up around his mouth so she couldn't see him muttering to himself.

***

The landscape began to change. With the flat ice behind them, the sleigh rose and descended as it slid over what appeared to be frozen waves. Snaf pulled up the reindeer and, when the sleigh stopped moving, he looked over his shoulder.

'We're not far from those coordinates you obtained. Get the black box ready,' he said to Frija and pointed under the seat. She bent over and unbuckled two leather straps before pulling a black container forwards in front of their feet.

'This is for the golden moonbeam when we retrieve it from the ice,' she said, 'it is watertight, so even if the ice melts, the moonbeam will still be secure.'

Excitement flooded through Mailliw's body. Finally, there was a real chance to save Forthright.

'What will the golden moonbeam look like?' he asked.

'They vary, depending on the angle that the moonbeam hits the ice. They might be long, short, wavy or curved. I can't say what ours will look like. I only know we will see a small golden glow above the ice. It's a good job it's dark because they're difficult to locate in daylight. Start looking. I'll look to the left and you look to the right,' she said and then instructed Snaf, 'don't go too fast or we might miss it.'

'Respecting your wishes Princess, but we need to be back before dawn. If you're not back in your bed by then and the King finds out what we've been up to… I won't be the only one losing his head!'

Mailliw gave an appalled glance at Snaf and saw he was looking directly at him. Frija cleared her throat nervously, 'Okay, let's get started then.'

Snaf clicked his tongue and the reindeer paced forward.

'He was joking, right?' whispered Mailliw.

'Start looking!'

Frija did not answer Mailliw's question, so he grimly assumed Snaf was telling the truth.

'I'm going to take the reindeer into a wide circle around the coordinates and keep moving inwards on a spiral. It will be easier and quicker to walk them in a circular path, rather than going up and down a square area and having to turn them at each end,' Snaf said as he guided the sleigh on a wide curving sweep.

Frija and Mailliw scanned the icy scenery. The reindeer plodded forward as they pulled the sleigh over the frozen waves. The sleigh went up and downhill and Mailliw's exasperation grew when he found the waves prevented them from seeing much more than their immediate area.

Snaf guided the sleigh and at first Mailliw couldn't see if they were making any headway. But as the spiral became tighter, he observed they were indeed making progress.

'Anything?' Frija shouted to Mailliw. She shouted because she wanted him to hear without having to take her eyes off the landscape.

'No!' he yelled back, half wondering why she had bothered to ask. If he had seen anything, he was unlikely to keep quiet about it.

The reindeer tramped on and on and Mailliw's eyes ached from searching. He hardly dared to blink in case he missed the vital glow, the clue to declaring that here, at last, was the golden moonbeam waiting for them to collect and take back to Forthright.

'Are you sure it's here?' Mailliw yelled with a distinct note of doubt in his voice.

'Of course it's here!' Frija answered back angrily. She was a Princess. He was just a boy. He certainly had the knack of knowing how to make her temper flare.

'How dare you question my judgement!' she yelled and whipped round, 'It's about time you learned some patience and stopped being so aggravating…'

'And it's about time you stopped bossing me about. I've done nothing but do as you tell me ever since I got here… you're worse than my sister!'

'I'm a Princess… I'm allowed to tell you what to do!'

166

Snaf brought the sleigh to an abrupt halt.

'Are you two paying attention?'

'YES!' Frija and Mailliw hollered together and glared at each other through their goggles.

'Well, if that's so, how come I can see the glow and neither of you have mentioned it?'

Chapter 16
*D*iscovered

Mailliw and Frija leapt out of the sleigh and scrutinized where Snaf was pointing. Just a few metres away was a soft golden glow coming from the ice and it was on the side Mailliw had been looking. He experienced a feeling of bitter disappointment with himself… after all he had been through to get this cure for Forthright, only to find he nearly bodged it at the last moment! If Snaf had not seen the glow, Mailliw would surely have missed it because he was too occupied in trying to make his point with Frija.

Snaf lit some lanterns and unloaded a long box from underneath the sleigh. He carried it towards the glow. Then he returned for the black box.

'Come along,' he snapped, 'we don't have much time. The sun will rise in four hours. I don't know how long it will take to cut out the golden moonbeam and I must return the Princess before dawn.'

Frija took Mailliw's hand, 'I'm really sorry if I annoyed you. It should have been your victory to have spotted the golden moonbeam and I spoiled it for you.'

Mailliw looked at her. The hood around her head had fallen onto her shoulders and he watched her pointy ears drooping.

'It's not your fault,' he said, 'it's mine. I shouldn't have doubted you...'

'Apology accepted. Let's go, we've got work to do!' she said grinning and headed towards Snaf.

Mailliw stared after her. She was down one moment and up the next. How infuriating! He followed and stood by her side as Snaf opened the long box. The old ice pixie spun round aghast.

'Look!' he groaned and held up something in each hand. Frija jumped forward and took the items from Snaf.

'How?'

'What's the matter?' Mailliw asked, not understanding what was happening.

'Must have occurred when the sleigh bounced on the ice when we were escaping the Scribb,' Snaf answered to Frija's question.

'Will someone tell me what's wrong?' demanded Mailliw.

'It's the ice cutter... it's broken,' Frija said and held out the two pieces for Mailliw to inspect, 'we can't get the golden moonbeam without anything to cut the ice! Oh, this is terrible. To get so far and then fail now!' She stamped her foot and thrust the broken cutter into Mailliw's hands. He stared at two pieces of tubing. When Frija had said 'cutter' he had expected to see something with blades, but there wasn't a sign of anything sharp to cut through ice.

'How does it work?' he asked mystified.

'The tubing was filled with substances that when combined, create a chemical reaction giving off heat. The heat is internally pressurised and when forced through the fine nozzle it cuts like a red-hot knife,' Frija answered angrily.

'Nothing can be done now,' said Snaf, 'we'll have to return. If we leave now you'll be back before dawn and nobody will be any the wiser about this.'

Snaf picked up the long box to take back to the sleigh. Mailliw stood dumbfounded. It couldn't be true. To get this far and have no way of getting the golden moonbeam. No… not true! His heart shrivelled. He tried to speak but despair overwhelmed him.

Frija grabbed Snaf's sleeve, 'There must be something, surely? We can't leave just like this! Isn't there anything on the sleigh suitable for cutting the ice?'

'What do you suggest? I rip off one of the metal runners and use that or perhaps start scraping away with my nails?' he replied.

'I could command you to do it!'

'You could.'

Frija heard the knife-edge in his tone and begged, 'Snaf… please help us.'

Snaf shook his head and said, 'I can't remove a runner without damaging the sleigh and then we'll be stuck here. I'm not signing the death warrant for all of us, besides, if you think fingernails are hard enough to cut through ice then think again. You'd need something like a diamond to make any headway in cutting through this stuff.'

'That's it!' Frija shrieked, 'Diamond! Snaf you're brilliant!'

'What are you talking about? I don't carry diamonds on me!'

'No! But Mailliw does! Mailliw… show him!'

'What?' said Mailliw faintly.

'Haven't you been listening? Your diamond! Now!'

Mailliw pulled the black diamond from his pocket and offered it to Frija. She snatched it from his fingers and waved it under Snaf's nose.

'This, Snaf, is a diamond. It's a black diamond. When the sun rises I'll show you properly, but now we need to start digging.'

'I'll start,' said Snaf, 'when I get tired, Mailliw can take over. When he tires, you can take over… but hopefully we'll have retrieved it by then.'

They advanced towards the golden glow and Snaf set about cutting the ice with the black diamond. Frija positioned the black box and Mailliw inspected the glow emanating from the moonbeam. Here he was, standing very close to the only cure for Forthright. Although Mailliw was weary, he wanted to memorise every detail and be able to explain to her what it was like.

The golden glow shimmered in the dark and Mailliw put out his hand towards it. His hand went into the glow and he saw the golden colour bathing his fingers. He moved them as if trying to catch the colour.

'It's stunning isn't it?' said Frija quietly.

'Yes,' he said, 'but although I can see it, I can't feel anything… it's just there.'

Mailliw suddenly had an idea and took out his wand, 'I can generate some heat with this. If it can melt some ice, would it help?'

Snaf gave a quirky smile and said, 'At this stage, anything will help.'

Mailliw pointed his wand at the ice and said the appropriate spell. Soon sparks were generated on the end of the wand and, when he drew the wand across the ice, they heard it sizzle. Steam rose from the surface. Snaf resumed cutting with the black diamond, but now followed the melted lines and quickly scraped at the ice with the black diamond before it had time to refreeze. Frija watched with fascination. She had never seen wand magic before. In her kingdom, this kind of magic was no longer taught. Over the last hundred years or so, the experimentalists had created other ways of achieving the same results based on scientific theories, the old ways mostly belonged to history. Even so, Frija had heard rumours that some people still practised in secret.

After half an hour, Mailliw's already low energy levels were too depleted for this kind of continual magic and his wand was failing to respond.

'I'm sorry,' he mumbled, 'I can't do any more.'

Frija heard the disappointment in his voice. She knew Mailliw wanted to contribute something important towards the collection of the golden moonbeam for his sister. Mailliw put his wand away. Snaf grunted and continued to cut and scrape away at the ice. Frija and Mailliw remained silent, taking it in turns to remove the scraped ice out of Snaf's way. He worked for two hours before stopping to stretch his fingers.

'Almost there,' he said, 'but there's something rather odd about this golden moonbeam.'

'Explain!' Frija said, gripping Mailliw's arm tightly.

'Not sure, but I think we have something very unusual here. Look,' Snaf said.

They both leaned forward as Snaf pointed at one end of the area he had been working on.

'See here… there is a small gap in the golden line… and yet… it continues further down. Examine it and see if you agree with me.'

Frija looked first and said, 'Yes. It is a small gap, but it's definitely there. What does it mean?'

Mailliw agreed with both of them.

'I think we have the golden moonbeam of a lifetime. I believe this is a twin!' Snaf said.

'A twin! Are you serious?' Frija shrieked, half with astonishment and half with excitement.

'Will somebody please explain,' begged Mailliw. His stomach was churning with nerves. Was it no good after all?

'Sorry Mailliw. Snaf, tell him,' said Frija nudging Snaf.

'If we have a twin golden moonbeam, it means we can remove one of them and leave the other here…'

'And it means nobody needs to find out we've taken one,' Frija continued, 'because the one left behind will still register. Nobody will suspect anything! This is such good luck. I can't believe it. Everything's going to be okay!' Frija said and did a little jig up and down the ice.

'No it isn't!' replied Snaf, 'We're not going to be back by dawn and once it's discovered you and the prisoner are missing, your father will send the army out to find you. How are you going to explain where you've been, especially with me?'

Frija became thoughtful, 'I don't know, but I'll think up something on the way back.'

'How much longer will this take?' asked Mailliw.

'About fifteen minutes. I'll cut through the ice at the gap and continue cutting across the ice below the first one, then I should be able to lift it out without exposing the second one. I'll backfill and leave the other one safely covered,' Snaf said and got down on his hands and knees. He carefully lined up the black diamond with the gap between the golden moonbeams and commenced cutting.

'Two of them… this is remarkable,' said Frija watching Snaf's hands moving back and forth.

'Doesn't happen often then?' asked Mailliw.

'I should say not! It's extremely rare, almost unheard of and even more of a mystery why it happens.'

Snaf shifted his body towards the end of the ice block and then moments later, the black diamond broke through. The golden moonbeams were now apart forever. Snaf lifted the block of ice and pushed it gently over the snowy surface towards Frija and Mailliw.

'It's a semicircle,' said Mailliw as he gazed at the thin golden line frozen in time and place, 'perhaps the other one is its mirror image… an attempt to create the perfect shape… a circle.'

'Or to represent the moon… its place of origin,' said Frija interrupting him.

'I think we have something indicating the relationship between the moon and the sun,' said Snaf quietly, 'there's an old legend about how the sun god and the moon goddess were lovers and were as one, but another jealous god played a hoax on them. He sent a message to the moon goddess, saying an arrow had killed her daughter when they were out hunting. The moon goddess was so stricken with grief that she blotted out the light from the sun god. It became permanently night. The other gods forced the moon goddess to separate from the sun god and move across the skies away from him, to enable light to return to their world. When they found out everything had been a hoax and the daughter was still alive, it was too late to reunite the moon goddess and the sun god. They were too far apart. The moon and the sun have been apart ever since.'

Mailliw looked stunned at this lengthy speech from Snaf.

'Yes! Yes!' cried Frija excitedly, 'Look at how the story might be represented here… this was originally a silver moonbeam. It became a golden moonbeam forming a circle like the sun, but… it is still essentially the same moonbeam. They are one, as was the moon goddess and the sun god. But this golden circle is separated by a gap. Perhaps this indicates the fact they can never truly be together again,' Frija sighed and said slowly, 'somehow, I feel we shouldn't take this one away, but I don't know what else we can do. If we don't, Mailliw's sister will die.'

'Make an offering,' suggested Snaf.

'What about asking permission and explain we are taking it to save another's life?' said Mailliw.

'How about both?' said Frija.

'Agreed,' said Mailliw, 'and I'll do it because if it wasn't for me, we wouldn't be here now.'

He left Frija and Snaf and walked several metres away before kneeling on the ice and bowing his head in the direction of the waning moon.

'Moon goddess,' Mailliw said respectfully, 'when you were at your highest beauty a few nights ago, I broke my sister's moondial. Now my sister is dying from an overdose of silver moonbeams. Only a golden moonbeam can save her life. I humbly ask permission to take half of the golden moonbeam circle for her, so she can live. My offering to you for your kindness, is to see your fair face on the next full moon. The following day, I promise I will tell the sun god how your beauty is still as lustrous as when you were together.'

Mailliw remained silent for a couple of minutes, then said 'Thank you,' and rose from his knees.

Frija and Snaf lifted the frozen golden moonbeam and placed it inside the black box and Mailliw memorised the promise he had just made as he went over to help.

The ice containing the golden moonbeam was now placed on its side and Mailliw could see the semicircular shape more clearly. He didn't know what happened to the shape once the ice thawed, only that Forthright had to swallow the water containing the golden moonbeam particles.

Snaf closed the lid and fastened the black box, then refilled the ice hole and tamped it down before Mailliw helped him carry the box to the sleigh and put it securely under the seat.

'Come on! Let's go!' Snaf barked and leapt onto his seat and took up the reins. Mailliw and Frija jumped into the sleigh as the reindeer were urged on for the return journey.

Now they were on their way back to the palace, Mailliw tried to fix the moment of seeing the golden moonbeam for the first time in his mind. He remembered the luminosity of the thin gold line, the perfect shape of the curve, the feelings of excitement and hope, the sheer wonder of finding not just one, but two golden moonbeams… a twin, and now he had one, just for Forthright.

***

The sleigh sped along and Snaf drove the reindeer hard. Once they were back on the flat ice, their feet skimmed the surface once more. Frija had snuggled down and was asleep, but Mailliw valiantly fought off the fatigue threatening to overtake him. He wanted the reindeer to wing their way home and get them back to King Pomidor's palace so he could return to Drabder and Forthright.

Through his snow goggles, Mailliw saw the first signs of dawn awakening in the east. On the horizon, a faint pink blush was turning the sky into a soft inky blue colour as the remains of the night faded. In a few minutes, the sunrise had spread across the skies with a magenta red and orange glow. The ice reflected the colour of the sky and both looked like they were on fire. Mailliw had seen many sunrises, but this was truly outstanding.

It was only when the sleigh slowed down that Mailliw turned his attention back to Snaf. The sleigh came to a standstill and the old ice pixie observed the landscape.

'Why have we stopped?' he asked.

'Shush!' hissed Snaf and cocked his head to one side. He remained still, although Mailliw could see his whole body was alert. Mailliw froze and hardly dared to breathe. The hairs on the back of his neck started to tingle and he became aware of small but fast vibrations rising through the sleigh.

Snaf cursed, then whispered, 'Wake up the Princess and ask if we have any ice bombs left. If not, pass the container with the ice fire. Then I want both of you to hold on to the sleigh handles, because this is going to be a very rough ride.'

Mailliw shook Frija awake. Her eyes were heavy with sleep, but they opened wide with fear when she became aware of the vibrations.

'Mailliw... this is serious and I'm really scared,' she whimpered.

'What's causing the vibrations?' he asked, keeping his voice low.

'Scribb! Underneath the ice, there must be so many of them, they keep bumping into each other. That's what we can feel. It must be seething down there!'

'Snaf wants to know if there are any ice bombs left.'

Frija looked inside the container and shook her head.

'He said if not, then to pass over the ice fire,' he whispered.

She pointed to another smaller container. Mailliw took it and stretched forward to hand it over to Snaf.

'Now hold tight!' Mailliw instructed, and he only just had enough time to slip his own fingers through a handle before Snaf slapped the reins with a ferocious crack.

The two reindeer at the front stood on their hind legs and pawed at the air. When they came down, their front legs were ready for action and they took off at high speed. Mailliw and Frija were thrown back into their seat with the first lurch.

The sleigh swished over the ice and Snaf worked the reins to keep encouraging the reindeer to gallop. The scenery was rushing by as the reindeer charged forwards. They seemed to be making good time when the leading reindeer suddenly slewed to the right.

'What the...' yelled Snaf.

The movement was unexpected and Snaf tried to compensate with the reins. The sleigh slid in an arc and followed the reindeer round. Memories of Norgruk and the carriage sliding across the ice at the Winter Mountains flooded into Mailliw's memory. Then, the reindeer began running back in the direction they had just come from.

'Stop!' Snaf shouted and tried to pull the reindeer up. They were beginning to panic and swerved sharply once again. Snaf stood up from his seat and yanked the reins hard. The reindeer slowed from a gallop to a trot, but they insisted on turning in a circle. Snaf kept them at a trotting pace and scanned the ice as the sleigh moved in a circular route. He finished surveying the ice and pulled the reins again. The reindeer walked while Snaf steered them with his right hand and opened the container of ice fire with his left. He threw the ice fire and scattered it across the ice. Bright blue flames flared upwards and enclosed the sleigh in a thirty metre diameter circle of ice fire.

When Snaf was certain there were no gaps in the circle, he said, 'We are surrounded by Scribb, but I expect you're fully aware of the situation by now. They won't penetrate the ice within the ice fire ring, so we're safe for the time being. Princess… there is no way I can return you to the palace in time without your absence being discovered. I'm sorry.'

Snaf bent his head as if ashamed at not being able to complete the task she had asked of him.

'Snaf… it's not your fault. You've done everything I asked and more. Please don't blame yourself…'

An explosive crunching drowned out Frija's speech as the ice outside the ring of ice fire started breaking up.

'What is it?' Frija shouted.

'The Scribb are breaking up the ice… they've cordoned us off,' warned Snaf.

'What are we going to do?' she shrieked.

'There is nothing we can do, but sit here and wait it out,' replied Snaf.

'How long will the ice fire burn?' asked Mailliw.

'About an hour,' he said.

'And then?'

'When it dies down, I'll be searching for any area of unbroken ice and see whether we can make a getaway. In the meantime, I suggest everyone keeps very still and quiet. Maybe we can fool them into thinking nothing is here.'

Mailliw and Frija looked at each other and then Mailliw moved closer to put his arm around her. His heart thumped so hard in his chest that he wondered if the Scribb could detect it.

Everyone sat still and waited. Even the reindeer stood like statues. Mailliw held Frija trying to comfort her but, in his own mind, he was terrified. Under the seat was Forthright's cure, yet at this rate, he was going to disappear from this world before her.

They waited while the blue flames danced and burned bright. It caused Mailliw to think about Dingle's emerald-flamed fire breathing after he had eaten a peppermint and parsley patty. His throat constricted as he remembered Dingle, Peculiar, Drabder, Monity, Forthright, Aunt Foggerty, his Mum and Dad, and how unlikely it seemed that he would ever see them again. His mind mulled over the good times and now, faced with imminent death, he thought how foolish it was to waste time on the trivial things in life when there were so many other important ways to spend time. Time! But how much did he have left?

***

Mailliw felt Frija putting a gentle pressure on his hand. He saw her staring at the ice. It was the area Snaf had first deposited the ice fire. Mailliw's stomach dropped when he realised the ice fire was dying. Before long, the rest died down as well. Time was up!

Snaf was scanning the circle, 'Hold on,' he whispered, but just as he was about to jerk the reins into action, a loud shattering wrenched through the ice, followed by several more. Frija screamed and Mailliw clapped his hand over her mouth.

'It's too late!' yelled Snaf, 'They've broken through!'

Mailliw glanced around desperately and, to his horror, the poisonous lances were spearing the ice. Three became six, then twelve and after that, Mailliw lost count as the Scribb lances punctured the ice, withdrew and tried again to catch their prey. With every stab, the lances moved closer. Mailliw's insides writhed. He didn't want his innards to be sucked down into a Scribb. He was even too petrified to feel sick.

One thought entered his mind and he screamed it out to Snaf, 'Why are we still sitting here? Get out! Run!'

'No!' screamed Snaf in return.

However, every instinct in Mailliw said run. He tried to scramble over the side but his legs remained unresponsive.

Terror had paralysed him. Frija was screaming and clinging to him and Snaf was desperately trying to steady the reindeer. Several lances broke through between the reindeer and one of the leaders jerked aside and fell to its knees. Snaf jumped off the sleigh and ran towards it. He hauled the reindeer to its feet just as a lance shot upwards and pumped poison, just missing both of them. Another lance burst through, centimetres from Snaf's foot. Ice was crunching and exploding all around them.

Without warning, another terrific explosion ruptured the air. Snaf rebounded and fell sprawling on the ice. The reindeer reared and snorted fear into the smoke-filled air. Mailliw and Frija choked as smoke billowed around them. Another explosion left their ears ringing. Mailliw grabbed Frija and thrust her to the floor. Shards of ice showered the sleigh as further blasts surrounded them. Mailliw ducked as a block of ice hit the side of the sleigh and shot it sideways. The motion slammed Mailliw into a corner of the black box holding the golden moonbeam and he yelled as pain shot through his thigh. Frija looked up, her face contorted in fear.

'Down!' screamed Mailliw. He pushed her head down, and threw himself over the top of her. He buried Frija's head under his coat. Mailliw tried to grip the floor with his fingers to pin Frija down but another detonation lifted the sleigh into the air. His nails scraped against the floor as his body rose above Frija. He became weightless for a second before the sleigh smashed down. As the reindeer thrashed against each other, they scrabbled and twisted their bodies, trying to rip free from the reins. The sleigh bucked as Mailliw tried to grab a sleigh handle and missed. Frija remained curled in a tight ball beneath him. He raised his head to locate the sleigh handles as another blast and smoke surrounded them. Mailliw's head jolted back and smacked against one of the seats. He sagged down and tried to raise his hand but it fell limply as his vision became a grey blur… and everything went black.

Chapter 17
*K*ing *P*omidor's *A*nger

Mailliw opened his eyes. The room looked foggy and everything was dim and quiet.

'Hi!' said a familiar voice.

Mailliw moved his head in the direction of the voice.

'Drabder? Is that you?' he croaked and then swallowed. His throat was like sandpaper and his head throbbed. 'Where am I? What happened?' he whispered.

'You're in King Pomidor's palace in a private room. A doctor says you will recover in a day or so… well King Pomidor hopes so, because he wants us out of here. I don't know all of what happened, but I do know that you were escorted back by the King's army on a sleigh with the Princess and a small old man.'

'Where's Frija?'

'She's recovering in her own chamber.'

Mailliw leaned forward and tried to lift the bedcovers, 'Must go and see if she's okay, must try…' he said, then fell back against the pillow, moaned, and put his hands to his head. The throbbing was unbearable.

'It's probably best not to anger the King any more than you've already done. His face has been like thunder every time he's come in to see if you were awake,' Drabder said and stopped talking when he heard the door creak open. An ice pixie nurse came in and examined Mailliw.

'I'll let his Majesty know you're awake,' she said when she finished, and left the room.

Drabder leaned on the bed and said, 'So, can you remember anything?'

Mailliw nodded but didn't want to discuss the horrors of the Scribb just yet so he said, 'Can I tell you later? It was horrifying. I honestly thought I was going to die. I'd rather know how you got here.'

'Okay,' said Drabder and gathered his thoughts, 'I remember panicking when I let go of your fingers and being swallowed by the blue light, but I don't remember anything else until I woke up with a strange woman looking after me. She told me what had happened. It was a relief to understand it had only been the gateway that we had been searching for, and she said you'd saved me by offering the diamonds in exchange for the crystal water. She also explained she was the Mystic of the Ice Cavern and it was her job to heal people. At first it sounded incredible, but she said her singing helped people to think about something important, and this in turn, made them better. In my case, it was Gypsy and her puppy, Max. Then some soldiers came and marched us to the palace. The King questioned the Mystic. She confirmed everything you told him and you weren't a spy. I explained about needing a golden moonbeam and the King ordered your release. He was going to organise a golden moonbeam search, but when he discovered you had escaped and the Princess was also missing, he was furious. He summoned his army and they left in the early hours of the morning.'

Drabder finished, but even through his throbbing head, Mailliw was aware of a significant change in his friend. He was coherent and speaking clearly.

Mailliw shifted position in the bed and stifled a groan. His right thigh was tender and bruised. The door opened again.

This time King Pomidor entered and his face still looked like thunder. The man with black slicked hair and hawk eyes followed the King.

'I understand you're feeling better,' King Pomidor said but the acidic tone was unmistakable.

'Yes, thank you,' said Mailliw quietly.

The King glowered at him and Mailliw saw him swallowing hard as if he had difficulty containing his anger. He was right. King Pomidor was finding it difficult. This boy had endangered his daughter, the only heir to the throne, and he was not in a forgiving mood.

'Do you understand how close you came to being killed?' he questioned, his eyes piercing into Mailliw. 'If we had been seconds later, it would have been all over for you and for my daughter. I had to make the decision to bombard the area with charges to confuse the Scribb, so they didn't know where to spear through the ice. I had to make this decision, knowing I might kill all of you in the rescue attempt. Have you any idea what it was like? Giving a command where I could kill my own child! You...' King Pomidor paused and stifled a sob, 'you are a corrupting influence, a liability and a danger to this court. I will not have you subjecting the Princess to any further peril. Once you are well, you and your friend will return to the Guardian of the Winter Mountains and you are both forbidden to return to this country. You are banished! If you disobey this ruling, you will be locked up and the key will be thrown away!'

A silence followed and a couple of tears rolled down the King's cheek. Slymus, standing at the King's right shoulder, leered at Mailliw, and Mailliw had never known such an intense dislike for anyone like this before.

'Your Highness,' Mailliw said, his voice not much more than a whisper, 'I fully understand your ruling and I give my sincerest apologies for having been the cause of so much grief. I also thank you for saving our lives under such terrible circumstances. I came here to save my sister who has silver moonbeam sickness and instead have caused more trouble than I could have possibly imagined. It was not my intention to disrupt your lives and cause you so much pain. We will leave as soon as you permit us.'

Mailliw stopped speaking and then remembered his promise to Frija. He slid out of the bed and fell towards to a chair where his clothes were laid out. From a trouser pocket, he pulled out the black diamond. Then he knelt down before the King and held out the diamond in his hands.

'I promised the Princess to give you this before I left.'

King Pomidor took the black diamond without looking at it, turned and left the room. When Mailliw glanced up, he saw a flicker in Slymus's eyes. Here was someone who knew exactly what the King held in his hands. Slymus followed the King, but before he closed the door, he looked back and said smoothly, 'I hope you both understand you'll be returning to the Guardian of the Winter Mountains without the golden moonbeam.' Then the door closed with a click. The sound cut through the silence and was like the sound of death stealing Forthright away.

Drabder exhaled deeply and asked, 'What is a Scribb?'

Mailliw crawled back into bed, briefly explained and watched Drabder's eyes grow wider and wider.

'They sound completely terrifying,' he said.

'They are, especially when there are so many of them you can feel them jostling for space under the ice.' Mailliw gave a shudder and lay back against the pillows, 'I can't believe it's all been for nothing. We'll be going home with nothing, Drabder… I can't believe I saw it, helped to bring it back for Forthright and now… nothing… nothing at all to save her…' he fell quiet, unable to speak. Disappointment stuck in his throat like a poisoned arrow.

Drabder picked at the sheets. He remained unsure how to help Mailliw feel better. It was almost impossible to believe he had seen and retrieved a golden moonbeam and been so close to success. After all the struggles, this final failure had knocked everything out of Mailliw.

Mailliw closed his eyes. His head throbbed even more and he felt as helpless as a newborn baby.

Drabder tiptoed from the room. He had never seen Mailliw like this before. He seemed defeated, no fight left. Mailliw, who had always looked out for him, protected him, been strong and helped him so many times, he had lost count. Drabder decided he was not going to stand by and do nothing.

He saw the King disappearing down the corridor and pursued him. The King and Slymus swept into the throne room and King Pomidor took his place on the throne. The smaller silver throne was empty. King Pomidor looked at it and he clasped his hands over his chest for a few moments, before giving his attention to the bowed courtiers. Drabder advanced into the room and sped down the red carpet towards the throne. Courtiers whispered as they moved their bowed heads to follow Drabder's progress. He stopped and knelt before the King.

'Remove him from my sight!' growled King Pomidor. Slymus signalled for the guards. Drabder started to panic. Now! He had to speak now! He had to speak for Mailliw!

'Please your Majesty, my friend is devastated by having caused so much trouble...' he said, the words tumbled out of his mouth, but the guards heaved Drabder to his feet and dragged him backwards.

'Your Royal Highness... please listen,' Drabder begged, but King Pomidor wasn't even looking at him.

The guards reached the door and were just about to throw him out when a voice said, 'Release him!'

Frija stood in the doorway. The guards held Drabder by the scruff of the neck and looked to King Pomidor for guidance.

'Father, please tell the guards to release this boy!'

'Give me one good reason,' replied the King sharply.

'I can give you several reasons,' she said, 'but the main one is because you have accused the wrong person in this matter!'

The courtiers raised their heads and murmurings went around the room. Their eyes shifted backwards and forwards between the Princess and the King. Slymus was frowning.

'Explain!' said the King who stood up from the throne and raised himself to his full height. Frija contemplated her father. She was apprehensive, because what she was going to say next was going to grieve him deeply.

'I planned and executed the locating of the golden moonbeam. I told Mailliw I wanted it done my way, not yours. He only did as I commanded. He didn't like doing what I told him, but I gave him no choice.'

King Pomidor stared at his daughter. Her words were unbelievable and yet he was hearing them. His chest tightened as if someone was crushing the life out of it. His one and only child had betrayed his trust. He did not understand.

Frija read the agony in her father's eyes but continued, 'Not only that, but when you had to rescue us, Mailliw saved my life. He protected me with his own body from the explosions and he became injured as a result. I owe him a debt of gratitude and I can't remain silent, knowing there is a miscarriage of justice taking place.'

The King stumbled to his throne, sat down and covered his face with his hands. Frija heard a strangled moan as her father struggled to control his grief.

When he finally removed his hands, he whispered, 'Why?'

Frija gulped. Her own throat ached with unhappiness, but she had to answer him.

'I discovered Mailliw had something of value. Something you had been searching for all your life, so I saw an opportunity of securing it for you by exchanging it for a golden moonbeam. I wanted to give you something so precious, you would regard it as a measure of my love for you... but it all went horribly wrong,' she explained, trying to fight off the desire to burst into tears in front of the courtiers.

Frija stepped up to King Pomidor and took his hands, 'I made Mailliw promise to give it to you before he left.'

'He has given it to me,' replied the King flatly and dropped her hands. Frija's ears drooped towards her shoulders at this rejection.

Then, the King withdrew the black diamond from his cloak and held it up for Frija and the court to see. The courtiers drew in their breath with amazement.

'And you think this...' he said, giving the black diamond a twirl so it sparkled in the light, 'is worth more to me than your life?'

The courtiers stopped breathing while they waited for her answer. It was deathly quiet.

'No father,' she mumbled and looked at the floor, 'but if you have accepted the gift,' she continued, barely audible, 'then I ask most humbly for my part of the bargain to be honoured, so Mailliw can take the golden moonbeam to save his sister's life.'

Slymus interrupted, 'Your Majesty, I must protest...'

'Be quiet Slymus,' ordered the King.

Underneath her serious face, Frija felt a small spark of relief at hearing Slymus being told to shut up, but she kept looking at the floor.

'And, as for you madam,' King Pomidor said coldly, 'I need time to think about this. Leave the court until further notice.'

Frija was devastated by this dismissal. It was the first time in her life the King had spoken to her like this. She glanced at Slymus. He was observing her and they both knew neither was in a position to influence the King either for or against Mailliw. Frija curtsied and took Drabder's arm as she left.

'What will the King do?' asked Drabder.

Frija could barely speak, 'I really don't know. This is the first time I've broken his trust.'

She led Drabder back to Mailliw's room and knocked on the door. There was no reply.

'I think he needs to be alone right now,' said Drabder, 'I've never known him like this before. Mailliw is not used to failing.'

***

Mailliw had a fitful rest. Images of Forthright being no more than a ghost tormented him. When he heard the knocking at the door, he chose to ignore it. The pain in his head still pounded. Aunt Foggerty had jars of chamomile with crushed willow bark in her store cupboard and he wondered why nobody here had offered him something similar to ease the pain.

When a second knock occurred, Mailliw had no idea how long it had been since the previous one. When he opened his eyes, his head had ceased throbbing. He sat up and said, 'Come in.'

Frija and Drabder entered, followed by King Pomidor, Slymus and a number of other courtiers. When they were all in the room, the King looked around and spoke.

'We all know the circumstances of this unfortunate business, so I'll refrain from repeating them here,' he said and glowered at Mailliw, 'however, you do not know my daughter has confessed to being the perpetrator. I admit to being bitterly disappointed in the Princess in her lack of judgement and trustworthiness.'

Mailliw watched Frija hang her head.

'I have given this matter a great deal of thought, and have decided to honour the Princess' word and allow you to return home with the golden moonbeam. The black diamond given as a gift in exchange, is a fair one and more than worthy of the diamonds you offered to the crystal lake to save your friend. A special place will be built to house the black diamond, so my people can come and see such a rarity for themselves. From today, your gift shall be known as The Black Icicle. I believe this decision is an honourable one considering what has happened. Even so, I do not withdraw my previous decision... quite simply, you are forbidden to return. This is my daughter's punishment for her actions, and she will have to live with the knowledge that you are the ones to suffer as a result,' the King said and frowned at his daughter, 'this is not negotiable. Frija, do you understand?'

Frija looked up. She was crying and sniffed loudly as she accepted her father's ruling. King Pomidor's voice had been cold and aloof throughout and this distancing from her was hard to bear.

'This evening is your last visit Frija, before they return home tomorrow morning. I give you grace to say your farewells after I leave the room, but afterwards you are not permitted to see either boy again,' King Pomidor said and signalled to Slymus and his courtiers to follow him out. He did not wait for any thanks or acknowledgement from Mailliw or Frija.

Mailliw, Drabder and Frija remained silent for a short while. Frija couldn't speak for crying, Mailliw because he was astounded at the sudden turn of events and Drabder because he could not think of anything appropriate to say.

Then Mailliw held out his hand to Frija and said, 'I don't know how to thank you for giving me this opportunity to save my sister.'

She rubbed away the tears with the palms of her hands and said, 'There's nothing to thank me for. I only told him the truth. Mailliw... in the short time you've been here, you have been the best friend I've ever had and now I'll never see you again. Between that and knowing how much I've disappointed my father, my life is going to be pretty miserable.'

'Difficult isn't it,' said Drabder, 'knowing how to say goodbye when you've been commanded to do it. Anyway, I'll go first if you like.'

Drabder bowed deeply before Frija, took her hand and kissed it, 'Goodbye your Highness,' he said quietly and when he reached the door, he looked back, 'just need to fix your face into my memory,' he said, smiled and left the room.

Mailliw glanced at Frija, 'Very considerate of him to allow us to say our goodbyes in private.'

'You're very lucky having a friend like Drabder and he's very lucky having a friend like you,' said Frija, 'I've never known that kind of friendship and probably never will.'

'I wish I had something to give you to remember our friendship by,' said Mailliw.

'You can give me something,' said Frija. She saw the unsure expression on Mailliw's face, 'Tell me all about your life back home, who your friends are, what your sister's like, your parents, your school, your home... I want to see, in my mind, the images you tell me. If you do, it will be the most wonderful gift... and nobody else will know about it, nobody will be able to take it away and whenever I feel lonely, I'll imagine I'm there with you, seeing your family and friends.'

'This is going to make it a very long goodbye,' said Mailliw and noticed a weak smile returning to Frija's face.

She said, 'I don't remember my father telling me it had to be a short goodbye, do you?'

Chapter 18
Return To Forthright

This time Drabder was prepared for the gateway. He stood near the black box containing the golden moonbeam and saw Slymus waiting for them. Mailliw limped up to Drabder. His bruised thigh was already turning deep purple and yellow. He only had a few hours sleep during the night after telling Frija everything she wanted to know about his life, and it seemed unreal that after she closed the door, he would never see her again.

Mailliw saw Snaf step towards them. 'The Princess asked me to make sure you left safely,' he said, giving a stern look at Slymus.

'I'm glad to see you're okay,' said Mailliw shaking Snaf's hand.

'Take more'n one or two Scribb to get rid of me,' he replied.

'Ahem!' coughed Slymus, 'It's time you two departed. We've arranged for you to travel directly to the Guardian of the Winter Mountains at Central Junction. This way, we will know both of you are where you should be.'

Mailliw let go of Snaf's hand and said, 'If you see the Mystic of the Ice Cavern, please thank her from both of us.'

Snaf gave a brief nod as Mailliw and Drabder prepared for the blue light in front of them, to transport them back to the Winter Mountains.

'The gateway is ready. Who's going first?' asked Slymus.

'Drabder,' said Mailliw and gave him a gentle shove towards the blue light. Snaf pushed the black box to Drabder. He placed his hands on the box as he stepped into the gateway and felt the familiar tugging at his legs. Drabder allowed himself to relax, and soon he was accelerating through blue zigzags, as he sped towards Central Junction in the Winter Mountains.

***

When Drabder stepped out of the gateway dragging the black box, the first person he saw was Monity.

'We've got it!' he grinned and pointed to the box.

Monity ran up to him, 'I've been so worried. Thank goodness you're back!'

'You all right lad?'

Drabder was facing Sturvald Trotter! His face grew warm when he thought about how they tricked him outside Madam Bonbons' shop. He didn't dare ask how the Trotter got to the Winter Mountains, so he nudged Monity instead.

'Tell you later,' she whispered.

Mailliw soon followed Drabder. He limped towards Monity with a big smile. She gave a slight inclination of her head and walked away.

'What's up?' he asked Drabder.

'No idea!' he said, 'She was fine with me just now.'

'What's he doing here?' said Mailliw indicating the Trotter. Drabder shrugged his shoulders making it clear he had no idea about that either.

Mailliw looked about Central Junction and could see the Guardian of the Winter Mountains coming to greet him.

'Success! Success!' he boomed at Mailliw, 'Well done! Now we need to get you on your travels again so you can take the golden moonbeam to your sister. I can't tell you what a momentous occasion this is. Not only have you been successful in bringing back the golden moonbeam, but you have also opened up the chance for dialogue with King Pomidor. His command to send you directly here surely indicates you have earned his trust. What an ambassador you are!' he said smiling with his gold tooth gleaming. Somehow, seeing the Guardian's warm and welcoming smile, Mailliw found he was unable to tell him the truth. He dropped his gaze and noticed the Guardian's polished golden toenails. The Guardian clicked his fingers and two porters came forward to carry the black box containing the golden moonbeam.

They left the gateway and Peculiar sidled up to Mailliw, 'If you need to blame anyone, blame him,' she said, and pointed a sharp claw at Dingle who was ambling towards them.

Mailliw asked, 'Blame him for what?'

'For Monity not speaking to you.'

'What's he done this time?'

'He told her we overheard Drabder saying it was wrong to leave without waking her.'

'It was for her own good,' said Mailliw.

'Try explaining to her,' said Dingle, 'you're not the one to suffer the consequences. Have you ever seen Monity lose her temper?'

'No.'

'Believe me, you don't want to,' said Dingle.

'He's right... it was verrrrry scarrrry,' said Peculiar with a quick shudder.

'Really?' said Mailliw with an element of surprise, 'Thanks for the warning!'

'Now everyone,' said the Guardian clapping his hands for attention, 'it's time you were leaving. I've organised some sledges to transport you to your carriage and also some parcels of food, so you don't waste any more time.'

Sturvald Trotter followed the Guardian who was accompanying Monity. Mailliw, Drabder, Peculiar and Dingle bustled behind as a small group.

When they reached the gates, there were snow wolves harnessed in front of the sledges.

'Do we have to use those? I recently had an unpleasant encounter with snow wolves,' Mailliw moaned.

'You'll be quite safe. These wolves are home-bred, so they are tame and can be trained quickly,' replied the Guardian stroking one of the wolves.

The porters secured the black box with the golden moonbeam onto a sledge. Mailliw, Drabder and Peculiar sat together on one sledge and Sturvald Trotter, Monity and Dingle sat on the other with the parcels of food.

'If you're ever this way again,' the Guardian said to Monity, 'we can continue our philosophical talks,' and he smiled kindly at her before asking, 'is everyone ready?'

They nodded. The sledges rumbled forward and they started their journey home. The wolves trotted out of the gates towards the pass. When Monity looked back, she watched the Guardian raise his hand in farewell and she waved in return.

She was grateful to him, for his guidance when she lost her temper after learning Mailliw and Drabder had left without telling her. She had thrown the golden furs all over the floor and was weeping when the Guardian entered the bedroom.

'Anger can be a good thing,' he had told her, 'if it's channelled in the correct way. Use it to focus on your strengths rather than allow it to control and weaken you. Think about it.'

The Guardian had left Monity with this advice and she concentrated on tidying up the mess she had made in the room.

'I am in control,' she told herself, 'nobody else, just me. I am calm. I can deal with this.'

She repeated this mantra as she picked up the furs from the floor and folded them neatly. By the time Monity had finished, she was in charge of herself and her emotions. She remained calm, detached and empowered. She was now able to deal with Mailliw on her terms not his. This understanding made Monity aware she had always been seeking Mailliw's approval, or did things hoping to make him like her better, to accept her more as a friend rather than being Drabder's shadow, his little cousin. The other night when Monity openly declined from knowing about their plan to escape Sturvald Trotter, was the first time she had opposed Mailliw and the situation had left her feeling uncomfortable. Now, Monity realised, she was entitled to her own opinions as much as Mailliw was entitled to his.

Monity sat on the sledge and gave a little smile to herself in the knowledge that Mailliw had expected her to greet him with big smiles, and then tell him how wonderful he'd been in finding the golden moonbeam. It had not happened and Monity congratulated herself on maintaining her cool composure. She was indebted to the Guardian for having shared his wisdom and advice.

***

The sledges soon emerged on the other side of the pass and waiting for them was their carriage and Norgruk... and... another dragon!

'So that's how he got here,' Mailliw said to Drabder and pointed to Cleopatra, 'it also means the Trotter went back home and told Aunt Foggerty we left him behind.'

'I must admit he was the last person I expected to see when I stepped from the gateway,' said Drabder, 'has he said anything to you?'

'Nope!' said Mailliw and waved at Norgruk as the sledges drew up in front of the carriage.

Sturvald Trotter lifted Monity off the sledge and Dingle went over to see Norgruk and Cleopatra.

'How's the wing?' asked Norgruk.

'Mending slowly,' Dingle replied.

'Ho ho,' grinned Norgruk, 'you'll have to ride back on the carriage!'

'Thanks a bunch!' said Dingle and leaned towards Cleopatra, 'Nice to see you,' he said and gave her a pat on the back.

Cleopatra gave a large yawn and smiled, 'Aunt Foggerty promised to bake me some gingerbread if I brought him here,' she said glancing over at Sturvald Trotter.

Mailliw and Drabder placed the golden moonbeam box under a carriage seat and Monity loaded the food parcels. Sturvald Trotter adapted Norgruk's harness and reins to include Cleopatra, and then he hitched both the dragons to the carriage.

'Two dragons will be faster than one,' he said and threaded a rein loop securely. Mailliw was astounded. The man who dithered about where to prune a rose bush was now showing a fair amount of knowledge and speed. Sturvald Trotter squinted at Mailliw.

'I know what yer thinking lad, but I ain't slow at everything… I used t' be a carriage driver,' he said.

Mailliw groaned inwardly. Why hadn't Aunt Foggerty told him? She had chosen Mr Trotter deliberately because of his driving skills! What an idiot he'd been not to trust her judgement! He didn't even want to imagine what her reaction was when Sturvald Trotter had gone back to the chateau without them.

'Right young man,' said Sturvald to Mailliw, 'I'm taking you straight home an' I'm not stoppin' this time. If anyone feels sick you'll just have to put up with it.'

Sturvald helped Monity into the carriage but refused her offer of food, 'No thanks, I just wan' to get you lot back home in one piece, an' get the black box to the little girl who's disappearin'. She didn't look too good when I left.'

Mailliw didn't think Forthright would appreciate the phrase 'little' girl, but the Trotter was correct about getting the golden moonbeam to her.

Once everyone was settled inside the carriage, Sturvald shut the doors. Dingle's job was to sit next to Sturvald and keep a lookout for wood dwarves on the return journey.

At first, the carriage was slow to pick up speed on the ice, but soon Norgruk and Cleopatra opened their wings and the carriage lifted into the air. From inside the carriage, they looked back at the Winter Mountains set against the deep blue sky.

Sturvald Trotter was an excellent driver. The carriage glided under his guidance with Norgruk and Cleopatra responding to the slightest change in tension from the reins.

Monity kept up her appearance of cool composure. Mailliw thought that once they had eaten the food parcels, she would burst with impatience to know everything about finding the golden moonbeam. She conversed normally with Drabder but not with him. She had not said one word to him since they returned to Central Junction.

He listened to their chatter and, as he listened, he was even more positive something had happened to Drabder. His speech still flowed and he radiated confidence.

'Drabder,' he said, when there was a natural pause, 'do you realise, you haven't stammered once since you left the Mystic of the Ice Cavern?'

Drabder beamed, 'I know... isn't it amazing! I think it happened because you really cared enough to save me and somehow when combined with the Mystic singing me better... some sort of magic happened. It went away... just like that,' he said, snapping his fingers. Then he giggled.

'Oh Drabder! I'm so thrilled for you!' shrieked Monity and threw her arms around him.

Mailliw wanted to throw his arms around Drabder as well. It was incredible and he was overjoyed for Drabder, but on seeing them together, Mailliw experienced a sense of exclusion.

'Apologise to her,' whispered Peculiar.

He nodded. Peculiar was right. It was up to him to break the silence with Monity and put things right.

He cleared his throat, 'Monity…' he began, 'Peculiar told me how upset you were when we left you behind. I want to say how sorry I am about not waking you and telling you what was going on. Drabder was right to tell me it was wrong, but I didn't listen,' he paused and she watched him intently, 'I made a mistake… something I seemed to have done a lot of recently, and it was not a decent way to treat a friend… especially someone whom I regard as one of my best friends.'

The words 'best friends' created a warm glow inside Monity.

He leaned towards her and asked anxiously, 'Because you weren't there, shall I tell you what happened, and how we brought back the golden moonbeam in the box right underneath your seat?'

Monity fought the impulse to yell out 'Of course I do!' so she took a deep breath and said calmly, 'Thank you Mailliw for your apology. If you would like to tell me, then I'm more than happy to listen.'

'Go on Mailliw, tell her everything!' said Drabder still beaming, and linked his arm through hers. Peculiar smothered a yawn. She wanted Mailliw to get on with it so she could listen as well.

Mailliw looked at Monity with uncertainty, but when he saw her smile he said, 'Just now, you reminded me of Aunt Foggerty.'

The glow inside Monity increased at the compliment Mailliw had just given her.

***

When the carriage approached Feyngrey, Monity felt Bit awakening. The bat opened her small mouth and yawned.

Monity spoke to her, then opened a window just enough for Bit to slip out and fly away.

'Where's she going?' asked Mailliw, 'It's daylight.'

'I know bats normally sleep during the day, but she went into hibernation with the cold at the Winter Mountains. She's just awoken and rearing to go, so I've told her to fly to your place. When Aunt Foggerty sees her, she'll know we're nearly back.'

'What a good idea! She'll get there before us because we won't be able to go so fast once we're back on the cobbled streets,' he replied.

Sturvald Trotter decreased their flying height and speed, and soon the carriage was only just clearing the tops of the hedges before they bumped down and clattered over the cobbles. People bustling to and from the market square moved aside as the carriage trundled by and made its way home.

The gates were already open and Sturvald Trotter pulled the carriage up in front of the clock tower. Aunt Foggerty was waiting with Bit perched on her shoulder and Mailliw surveyed her wan face and saw the dark circles under her eyes. He leapt out of the carriage with Drabder and towed the black box towards her.

'Have you got it?' she whispered.

'Yes!' exclaimed Mailliw and he became aware of a sloshing coming from inside the black box. The golden moonbeam was no longer a semicircle forming part of a twin. What he had seen with Frija and Snaf was now just a part of his memory. The ice had melted and the golden moonbeam had been released into the water.

'Quickly Sturvald!' said Aunt Foggerty, 'Take it upstairs to Forthright's room.'

Mailliw and Drabder followed close on his heels as he carried the black box into the bedroom and set it down.

On the bed, lay Forthright as pale and as silvery as the moon.

'Forthright!' gasped Mailliw. She did not move. Her eyes were closed. Monity rushed into the room and stopped beside Drabder.

'I'll go an' see to the carriage an' dragons,' said Sturvald and as he left, Monity saw his eyes glistening.

'What do we do now?' asked Drabder.

The sound of Drabder's voice spurred Mailliw into action, 'If I open the container properly, the golden moonbeam will escape. So, I need another plan. Drabder, go and get a metal awl and hammer from the workroom by the clock tower. Monity, get a load of straws from the kitchen.'

They bolted from the room and collided with Dingle and Peculiar. The vampire cat howled when Drabder trod on her paws, but Monity bounced off Dingle and he carried on into Forthright's room. When Dingle looked at Forthright, he gave a small moan and climbed onto the bed. He touched her feet to wake her, but his claws went straight through them.

They heard Aunt Foggerty's walking stick on the floor as she entered the room.

'Are we too late?' asked Mailliw, panic making him rush over to Forthright.

'I don't know Mailliw... I really don't know.'

Mailliw flew to the black box and pulled it closer to the bed. Then he bent over Forthright. She was so ghostly, how were they going to get her to swallow the golden moonbeam? The task reminded him of Drabder drinking the water from the crystal lake, but at least Drabder still had a body they could lift and encourage to drink. There was nothing of Forthright to lift!

Monity brought the straws and gave them to Mailliw. He squeezed the tops of a few and inserted the narrowed tops into the other end of the straws. He was making one long straw to reach from the black box to Forthright's lips. When Drabder handed over the awl and hammer, Mailliw stopped to think. Making a hole in the black box risked losing the golden moonbeam so it was imperative not to make a mistake now. His hands shook.

'Listen carefully. I'm going to make a hole just big enough to insert the straw. Drabder, when I say "now" I want you to push the straw into the hole. Monity I need you to put your thumb over the other end of the straw and keep it there until I'm ready to help you guide it into Forthright's mouth. Does everything make sense?'

Drabder and Monity nodded. Aunt Foggerty watched anxiously as Mailliw took the awl and placed its sharp point against the black box. He took a deep breath... and then brought the hammer down. Nothing happened. He tried again. This time a small dent formed beneath the awl. He gave the awl another wallop, and another, and then the awl broke through.

'NOW!' shouted Mailliw and Drabder speedily plugged the hole with the end of the straw. Monity already had her thumb over the other end.

'Look!' she shouted and pointed to the straw. It shimmered with golden light.

'Don't let go, either of you,' said Mailliw and sprung to his feet. He gently guided the end Monity was holding towards Forthright's lips.

'Forthright... it's Mailliw. We have your golden moonbeam. Can you hear me? I need you to open your mouth.'

He waited for a response, but nothing happened.

'Forthright! Please... please...' he begged and tried to touch her lips to open them. His fingers couldn't feel anything. Desperation clawed his insides, his fingers tried again.

'Please...' he cried, 'please hear me... open your lips Forthright!'

Then it happened.

'Mmm... Mmm...' came so quietly from Forthright's lips, Mailliw almost missed it. He grabbed Monity's hand.

'RELEASE IT!' he shouted.

Chapter 19
Mailliw's Penance

Monity jerked her thumb away from the straw; Mailliw grabbed the end and thrust it between Forthright's parted lips. The golden moonbeam flowed into Forthright's mouth and her body absorbed every part of it.

As she lay on the bed, her body sparkled like a diamond in the sun as the golden moonbeam sought out and mapped the silver moonbeams invading her body. Millions of small sparks and flashes of gold and silver rose up over Forthright and lit up the room. Several sparks zapped Dingle and he shot off the bed, but for the others the scene was quite mesmerising. They watched the sparks of gold and silver merging with each other, embracing and becoming twinned. For every silver, there was a gold and soon they were all paired. They hovered, danced, and flickered like miniature stars over Forthright's body. But as they drifted down onto her skin, they became dust, shimmering, scintillating magical dust! The dust settled and dwindled like a sunset before their eyes, turning gold, pink and ruby in seconds. When the magical dust light faded, substantial colours started returning to Forthright.

'It's working,' said Aunt Foggerty with excitement in her voice, 'it's really working! At last, I'll be able to face Philleas and Agnetha with the knowledge that their two children are safe! Oh, what a blessed, blessed relief!'

Mailliw glanced at his aunt. Her black, gold-flecked eyes welled up with tears, and her face crinkled up with the strange effect of crying and smiling at the same time. He returned the smile and an immense sense of emotion washed over him. When he stepped towards Aunt Foggerty, Mailliw's legs were trembling, his heart pounded against his ribs and his mouth was dry.

'It's wonderful,' she cried, and let go of her walking stick to hug him close to her. Monity stood wiping tears from her eyes, Drabder stood open-mouthed, Dingle crept closer to the bed with caution, still half suspecting another spark to zap him, and Peculiar remembered her bald patches and thought, yes, it had all been worth it.

'Ma... Ma... Mailliw,' came a whisper from the bed. Mailliw shot back to the bed and bent close to Forthright.

'I'm here,' he answered and stroked her hair. He could feel her hair, it was soft and silky and his hand didn't go through it as if it wasn't there... only... Mailliw stared in disbelief. Forthright's brown hair, which had been just like their mother's, was not brown any longer. Mailliw's fingers now trailed gently through jet-black hair that gleamed with the inky blue of a raven's wing in the sun. The shock jolted through Mailliw and he examined his sister for any other signs of change, but he couldn't see anything obvious. Forthright's skin was still pale ivory and her cheeks had their usual soft blush of rose.

'Ma... Mailliw,' Forthright whispered again, 'I nearly... I nearly saw,' she stopped and swallowed, then she tried again, 'I nearly... nearly... saw... where the moonbeams... go...' her voice trailed off and Mailliw could see tears, real salty tears, brimming over her cheeks and onto the pillow.

At last, Forthright was safe and she would be here with him, when their parents came home!

***

It was a couple of days before Forthright was strong enough to come downstairs and she found Mailliw, Drabder and Monity in the library; a library at peace and looking like it had never witnessed the frantic activity of their search for a cure on silver moonbeam sickness.

'Hi,' she murmured as she opened the door. She instinctively put her hands up to her hair as if self-conscious and unsure about her appearance.

Monity squeaked, jumped up, ran to Forthright and put her arms around her.

'Black hair takes a bit of getting used to,' Forthright confessed, 'every time I look in the mirror, I see me looking back at a startled me!'

Mailliw rose from the desk where he had been writing and took Forthright's arm, taking her to the sofa. Drabder just beamed at her.

'Aunt Foggerty says you've had some amazing adventures on my behalf. I'd like to hear them,' she said.

'Sure,' said Mailliw grinning, 'you'd better get comfortable.'

Forthright sat down on the leather sofa, kicked off her slippers and curled her feet underneath a cushion just like their mother. Mailliw was just about to recount the adventures yet again when Aunt Foggerty came in.

'I'm sorry to interrupt Mailliw, but I need to see you right away,' she said. There was a tightness in her voice as if unable to breathe.

He followed her, bewildered. Aunt Foggerty's request had sounded formal and yet she was heading for the informality of the snug.

204

'Please sit down,' she said and took a seat herself.

'You don't look very happy,' he said and wondered if he'd done something wrong, like not tidied his room well enough. Mailliw studied Aunt Foggerty. It was more than that, there was a strange tenseness in her.

'I'm not happy,' she replied, still sounding like she couldn't breathe, 'you see I have a problem. When Sturvald Trotter came back and told me what you had done, I have to admit I was very angry. This time the journey wasn't just you, it was Drabder and Monity as well and I had promised their parents I would make sure you were accompanied by an adult. I also needed to be able to show your own parents we had behaved responsibly. You see Mailliw, I had chosen someone whom I regarded as being the best person for the job. As such, when you left Mr Trotter at Madam Bonbons, I vowed your irresponsible actions would not go without punishment. When you all returned safely, I was so relieved and happy, I didn't even want to think about punishment. However, it seems that Fate has a different opinion. Something has occurred and I cannot ignore it,' as she paused, Mailliw observed the concern in her eyes. 'A pigeon delivered a message this morning. I'd like you to read it.'

Aunt Foggerty handed Mailliw a rolled up piece of paper. He had seen something very similar at Merry Willows the Widow's place. Mailliw read it aloud.

Dear Foggerty,

You recently sent a boy called Mailliw Berry to visit me, for information on finding a cure for silver moonbeam sickness. If he was successful in obtaining a golden moonbeam and was able to save his sister, then you owe me a life debt. I'm calling in the debt and demand you send the boy to me. I'm only asking for one visit. Afterwards, the boy will be free to choose whether he comes to see me again or not. If the boy did not succeed in his quest, I have no claim to make upon you. I am placing my trust in you to be honourable in this matter.

Merry Willows.

Mailliw handed the message back to Aunt Foggerty. He was silent. The pigeon must have come from Merry Willows via Mother McGinty.

'There was another short message as well,' said Aunt Foggerty and handed him another note. It read,

Mailliw, please tell Drabder, Gypsy has given birth to one male puppy. When the time is right, in a few months time, I'll call by with Gypsy and deliver the puppy to him. Please ask Drabder for a name and send it back with the pigeon.

Yours,
Mother McGinty.

'Well, that's good news for Drabder,' said Mailliw and looked thoughtful, 'he said in the ice cavern about Gypsy only having one puppy. I'll tell him so he can reply and let her know the puppy will be called Max. I still don't know how he will convince his father though.'

Mailliw moved to the window and looked out. He dreaded the thought of having to visit Merry Willows again.

'If she wants to know whether I saved my sister or not, why can't we send a message back with the pigeon?' Mailliw asked, 'She doesn't need me to tell her in person.' His voice sounded flat with the strain of trying to sound normal.

'Because it isn't what she's requested. She's asked for you,' Aunt Foggerty replied quietly.

Mailliw had said he never wanted to return but with Aunt Foggerty's reply, he knew he had to go. It seemed like Fate had not finished with him yet. He also realised Aunt Foggerty did not want to ask him, so he had to make it easier for her by offering.

'When do you want me to go?' he mumbled.

'Mailliw, I'm so sorry about this. I should never have vowed a punishment on you. If I hadn't then maybe this would never have happened.'

He watched as Aunt Foggerty wrung her hands.

'I suppose I can assume she doesn't want to kill me, as she's said I'll be free to choose whether I want to visit again or not,' said Mailliw trying to make light of the situation.

'Trust me Mailliw, she won't hurt you, not now.'

'How do you know?'

'I just do,' said Aunt Foggerty gently, 'and as for when you go, I think probably first thing tomorrow morning will be best. You told us after your visit to the Carnivorous Swamp, that Merry Willows gave you a flask of concentrated perfume. Am I correct?' she asked and Mailliw nodded. 'Good, you'll be able to go directly to her then. Dingle won't be going because he won't let Forthright out of his sight and after what happened to Peculiar the last time, I don't think it's wise for her to go with you and another thing, you can't use the flying carpet at the moment. The hole that Merry Willows the Widow caused the last time, has continued to unravel the weave and I haven't been able to find a spell to stop it. The hole is now so big, the carpet is unsafe to use. If I don't find the anti-spell soon, there will be no carpet left! So instead, Norgruk will take you. He's the strongest and fastest flier.'

'Norgruk won't pass out over the swamp will he?' asked Mailliw, remembering her words about dragons and sensitive smells. The thought of falling with an unconscious Norgruk down into the swamp, made him shiver.

'I could travel by broomstick,' he offered, even though he'd never flown such a distance before.

'Just use the perfume for both of you. If Norgruk flies high, he should be fine. It'll be much more convenient than your last visit and I'll feel happier knowing you're not flying alone.'

Mailliw thought that Aunt Foggerty was trying to sound reassuring, but he wasn't convinced.

Mailliw opened the door to leave the snug.

'And Mailliw…'

'Yes!'

'Thank you.'

***

Mailliw took several deep breaths before entering the library.

'There you are!' said Forthright smiling, 'Now come and tell me everything. I can't wait any longer.'

He put on a brave face and sat next to her on the sofa. First, he told Drabder the good news about Gypsy, and then he recounted everything about the golden moonbeam adventure in detail. Forthright never took her eyes off him as he vividly described what the golden moonbeam looked like with its twin. She imagined it in her own mind, almost as if she had been there.

'I am truly, truly amazed,' she said, her eyes open wide as she looked at Mailliw, 'I can't believe you all made it through so many difficulties and… the Scribb! How utterly terrifying!' she said, and shuddered at the thought of such terrible creatures living below the ice, 'I honestly think you must have had Providence on your side! And Mailliw, I'm really sad you won't be seeing Princess Frija again. She must be very lonely with no mother and nobody of her own age for company,' Forthright gave a long sigh, 'Mum and Dad may have to be away a lot, but at least I've got you,' she said smiling at Mailliw, 'and Aunt Foggerty, Dingle, Peculiar, Norgruk, Cleopatra, Drabder,

Monity... and Bit! I'M SO LUCKY AND SO HAPPY TO BE ALIVE!' she yelled at the top of her voice, and they all erupted into peals of laughter.

Mailliw thought it was good for them to be happy at this moment. He wanted them all to enjoy it to the full, especially Forthright, so he kept quiet about having to go to Merry Willows the Widow. He decided to tell them in the morning before he left.

***

In bed, sleep eluded Mailliw. His mind was full of images of the Carnivorous Swamp, the stench, the decayed bodies, the congealed blood, the flies and the knowledge he had to do it again. He tossed and turned until exhaustion took over and he finally slept.

Early the next morning, he put the small flask he had used when he left Merry Willows the last time, into his pocket. He thought about his return journey over the swamp and remembered it had not been too bad. His apprehension from the evening before eased. If the smell of rotting flesh was disguised, then he'd find it easier not to look down. Besides, Aunt Foggerty assured him Merry Willows wouldn't hurt him. This still perplexed him and he was unable to make any sense of it.

Norgruk was waiting in the courtyard, picking out strands of rhubarb from between his teeth. Everyone else was also there waiting to say goodbye to Mailliw. He told them at breakfast and they had been stunned into silence. Peculiar hadn't spoken a word since.

'I'll be fine,' he said, now reaching down and tickling Peculiar behind her ears.

She looked up at him and growled, 'If she harms you, it'll take more than a witch's spell-bolt through a flying carpet to stop me getting at her!'

Forthright stepped forward, 'Mailliw, please take care. I feel so awful about this. It's all my fault! I shouldn't have asked you to look after my moondial, not when the moonbeams were going to be extra powerful… it was too much responsibility when you'd never done it before.'

'Monity is younger than me and she was perfectly capable of looking after her mother's moondial, so I should have been capable of looking after yours. But, I wasn't. I broke it instead,' Mailliw interrupted, 'so, if it's anyone's fault, it's mine and it's my penance.'

Drabder gave Mailliw a hug and let him go quickly. If he held him too long, he might not let him go. Monity reached up, shyly kissed his cheek and then took Forthright's hand.

Mailliw climbed onto Norgruk's back and Aunt Foggerty spoke, 'Mailliw. It's about trust. I broke her trust once, yet despite this she is still prepared to take the risk and trust me in this matter. Trust works both ways.'

Mailliw's heart skipped a beat and he said, 'That's exactly what she said!'

Aunt Foggerty smiled and said quietly, 'Did she now.'

Mailliw took one last look at everyone before Norgruk took off. He did not look back when Norgruk was airborne, in case he changed his mind about going.

Chapter 20
*U*nwelcome *T*ruth

Mailliw was relieved the weather over Lake Gillyfrec looked settled, but he still asked Norgruk if there were any signs of change in the wind colour. Norgruk sniffed and assured him of continuing good weather.

Norgruk had a good flying speed and, without any storms and other delays, they soon approached the Carnivorous Swamp. Mailliw retrieved the perfume flask, poured some of the concentrate into his hands and rubbed it all around Norgruk's ears. Norgruk snorted in disgust.

'You'll be thanking me for this soon,' said Mailliw and rubbed the essence onto his own clothes.

Norgruk flew high over the swamp. The less he saw of flesh eating plants, the better he felt. Mailliw scanned the area and pointed to Merry Willows' island. They drew nearer and Mailliw saw a small black figure working in the vegetable patch. Norgruk swooped low and back around before landing. Merry Willows was already doing her best to hurry towards them and, when Mailliw climbed off Norgruk, the dragon nudged him.

'Is this the hag?' he asked, 'Because if it is, I'll blow her away with one fire breath if you want me to.'

'Shh!' replied Mailliw as Merry Willows hobbled closer.

'You have come!' she said breathlessly.

Mailliw could see her face. She was not wearing her veil like last time.

'Yes. I received your message from my aunt,' he said, maintaining his distance.

'Come, come and I'll make some mint tea.'

Norgruk's eyes lit up at the mention of mint, 'Have you got any peppermint and parsley patties?' he asked hopefully, conveniently forgetting he had just offered to blow her away.

'No, just mint tea.'

They followed Merry Willows and as she led them to her mud hut, Norgruk eyed up the vegetables in the garden.

'Don't you dare,' hissed Mailliw.

'What?' replied Norgruk, 'I was only looking!'

At the hut, Mailliw told Norgruk to wait outside for him. He followed Merry Willows inside and took the chair she offered. When he sat on it the last time, he never thought he'd find himself sitting on it again. Merry Willows bent over the cauldron for hot water to make the tea and Mailliw noticed the locket dangling from her neck.

'You're wearing it!' he said.

'But of course.'

She shuffled round Mailliw and scrutinized him.

'Why did you try to attack me when I left the last time?' Mailliw blurted out. He surprised himself with the question. Merry Willows looked confused.

'You thought... I was attacking you?'

Mailliw saw her shoulders shrink and her face regained the sadness he had witnessed the last time. Merry Willows poured out the mint tea into a goblet for Mailliw and put it on the table. She sat down opposite him and her jaw worked as if agonising about saying something, but nothing came out. Mailliw sipped the tea and waited.

At last she said, 'If that is what you thought, then I'm surprised you even considered coming back.'

'Your letter gave me good reason. My aunt owed you a life debt,' Mailliw stated bluntly.

'Your sister? You saved her then?'

'Yes.'

Merry Willows wheezed out a long sigh of relief, 'Good, very good… it's another thing we have in common.'

Mailliw's thoughts were getting muddled and he was just about to ask what she was talking about when she continued, 'Silver moonbeam sickness. She and I have both had it.'

'Yes, I know,' said Mailliw, 'and you both survived it,' thinking perhaps he was getting the gist of what she was saying.

'Yessss!' said Merry Willows, 'But you don't understand how important it was for her to live.'

'Of course I do! She's my sister!'

'And…' Merry Willows paused and brought her face closer to Mailliw, 'she's my granddaughter!'

Mailliw drew back as if she had slapped his face, 'You're mad! You don't know what you're saying…'

'And you… my dear boy… are my grandson!'

'You are insane and I don't have to listen to this!' Mailliw shouted. He was trying to stop himself from grabbing the old hag and shaking her bones out of her skin.

'You will listen boy… my blood runs through your veins whether you like it or not. Whose lock of hair is in this?' she said thrusting the locket into Mailliw's face.

'Your husband's!'

'Pah! Did Foggerty tell you that?'

'No! She never said exactly. She told us about your husband and so I assumed…'

'Well, you assumed wrong. This is a lock of hair from my child, my son Philleas.'

At the mention of his father's name, Mailliw slipped back off the chair and fell against the wall. He put his hands over his ears to block out her words. Nothing made sense.

'Come boy,' Merry Willows said and offered her hand to help Mailliw get to his feet but he pushed it away. She sank down beside him and opened the locket.

'It's all wrong,' she said, 'I've been here too long.'

'You mean it isn't true?' asked Mailliw hopefully.

'Oh, it's all true. What I mean is… I've been here so long I've lost the knack of speaking tactfully. I didn't plan for it to come out this way. I don't expect forgiveness but I want you to know the truth. Only then can you make an informed decision,' she paused and waited for Mailliw's breathing to become calmer.

'Did Foggerty tell you what I did to my husband?'

Mailliw nodded, 'Yes, she said you cast a spell and fried his brain because he was in love with her.'

'She told you correctly. I was so afraid he would leave and I'd be left alone to bring up our young son, that I acted without thinking and in doing so, I committed a terrible, terrible crime,' she replied wretchedly, 'there's never a day that goes by without me thinking about what I did. Then, when I was sentenced to live here, I intended to bring my husband. His mind was gone and he wouldn't have known any different, but he was killed by a vampire cat, a vampire cat of all things… can you believe it? He couldn't protect himself.'

Mailliw now understood her reaction when Peculiar had flown over the island on the carpet. She must have thought a vampire cat was coming to kill her, so she blasted a hole into the carpet to protect herself.

'Even so,' wheezed Merry Willows, 'I refused to bring our child here. I regarded Foggerty as my enemy, but she was the only person I was prepared to trust with our child. She loved my husband and I hoped she would do it for his sake. We agreed that as far as Philleas was concerned, both of his parents died when he was very young. I gave Foggerty permission to change his name from Willows to Berry, giving the impression she was his father's sister. Until you came with the locket, I had no knowledge of her or Philleas' whereabouts. When I discovered your name, I tried to say you were my grandson. I wasn't attacking you, but I can see how I was so desperate for you to stay, it must have seemed like that to you. After I heard of your sister's sickness, every moment was spent thinking about you and wishing for you to succeed. The only way to find out if you were both safe was to send a message to Foggerty.'

Merry Willows stopped talking. She held the open locket for Mailliw to see the contents. Inside lay a lock of hair so similar to Mailliw's own hair, he could have believed it was his.

Mailliw's mind was whirling. In a matter of seconds, his whole life was turned upside down and he didn't want to believe Aunt Foggerty had lied to his family all this time.

'Why didn't Aunt Foggerty tell us?'

'I made her promise and now I know she kept her word, so you must not judge her for it.'

'She told me you wouldn't hurt me, now I understand why. But what about my father, surely he has a right to know his mother is still alive?'

'I'm not ready for this to go any further than between Foggerty, you and me, not even to your sister. After all the lonely years of living here, just the knowledge that my child has grown up safe and I have two grandchildren, is like a miracle to me.'

Mailliw rubbed his hands over his face and pushed his fingers back through his hair.

'I didn't ask for you to burden me with this and yet you expect me to keep it to myself. How can I look into my father's face with this knowledge and not tell him?' Mailliw asked abruptly.

'Because, for the time being, I'm asking you to understand this is for the best. Foggerty will ask if I've told you and together you will be the keepers of the family secret. I have done what I set out to do when I sent the message to Foggerty. It's now your choice whether you will come and visit again… don't tell me right this moment, I'm not sure I'd be able to bear it if your answer was no. Let me live in hope that one day I'll turn around and you'll be there.'

'I couldn't give you an answer even if you wanted me to. I have to go back and think about all this,' Mailliw said and got to his feet. He pinched the flesh on his arm to see if he was having a bad dream. He didn't want to believe this old witch, condemned to live the rest of her life here, was his grandmother. The pain in his arm throbbed.

'It's time for you to go but I'll give you this just in case,' she said and handed him another small flask of concentrated perfume. Mailliw took it, put it in his pocket and strode to the door.

'I'm returning to my family knowing I'm also leaving family behind,' he said, and as he walked through the door, he heard a faint, 'Goodbye Mailliw.'

For the first time, Merry Willows had used his name. She had not called him 'boy' and Mailliw experienced a fleeting sense of belonging to her and it was a feeling he did not want to acknowledge.

Norgruk opened bleary eyes and smacked his lips, 'I was having a lovely snooze.'

'Well, wake up, it's time to go,' snapped Mailliw.

'What's up with you?'

'Nothing I'm fine!' Mailliw retorted, but Norgruk was certain he was far from fine, especially when Mailliw rubbed the perfume on roughly around his ears, then for the whole journey home, he did not speak one word.

***

216

It was dark and late when they arrived home. Norgruk was starving and went off to the dragons' kitchen in search of food. On their return, Mailliw saw Aunt Foggerty's lit up window and knew she was waiting for him in her room. He went upstairs and knocked on the door.

'Come in Mailliw,' she said.

He opened the door and Aunt Foggerty searched his face, 'So, she has told you who she is?'

Mailliw nodded gloomily.

'Does she want the family to know?'

He shook his head.

'I thought not. It's very hard having knowledge like this, but don't be too harsh on her. She loved your father very much and made the sacrifice to give him up so he had a chance of a good life. I believe he has had, and still has a good life, and I also believe you and Forthright have a good life.'

'I feel so confused and nothing is what it seems,' he said.

'Perhaps not, but sometimes things happen. Fate intervenes and we can't see the reason for it at the time. I think this is one of those times. For myself, I'm glad Merry Willows is alive and knows she still has a family. Forthright is only here because Merry Willows helped you. Your grandmother has a lonely existence, but at least now she has the comfort of knowing she helped to save her granddaughter's life,' Aunt Foggerty paused before asking, 'do you think you'll go to see her again?'

'At this moment I don't know. It's a horrible journey and the swamp is a living nightmare but... the concentrated perfume helps... and... a part of me feels sorry for her.'

'What about sending letters? It's a good place to start,' suggested Aunt Foggerty, 'I think it would mean a great deal to her.'

'Hmm, perhaps get them delivered by Mother McGinty's pigeon. When she brings Max for Drabder I'll ask her,' he said quietly.

'A good plan! Anyway, I have some excellent news for you. Your parents are getting back sooner than they thought. They are arriving in a couple of days, so I'm organising a celebratory banquet for all of us, including Drabder and Monity and their parents. The rooms need decorating with fresh flowers and food needs to be ordered and prepared, so tomorrow is going to be a very hectic day.'

'What shall we tell the others?' Mailliw asked, 'They'll want to know why Merry Willows wanted to see me.'

'We'll tell them part of the truth.'

'Which is?'

'She's a lonely old witch who wanted some company over a cup of tea.'

Mailliw gave Aunt Foggerty a long hug and then went to his room. Peculiar was sitting on his four-poster bed.

'Oh good! You're back, so I don't have to go and sort the old hag out then?' she said.

Mailliw absentmindedly scratched her ears, 'No, not this time, but the reason she didn't like you is because a vampire cat killed her husband,' he said and went to fetch a calendar from a drawer. Peculiar looked thoughtful as she digested this piece of information. Her brain was working as if trying to remember something, but it was too vague. So she dismissed it.

'What are you doing?' Peculiar asked, looking over Mailliw's shoulder as he sat on the bed.

'I'm checking the date of the next full moon because I have a promise to the moon goddess and the sun god to keep. Then I'm going to get a well-earned sleep. With Mum and Dad coming home in a couple of days, it's going to be pretty busy and exciting.'

Mailliw climbed into his four-poster bed and as he turned down the lamp, the room dimmed. He thought about Forthright and how she had been so, so close to knowing where moonbeams go. He got up again, pulled open the metal latch on the window and looked out. Mailliw inhaled the night air. It smelt of warm, dusty cobbled streets mingled with the fragrance of roses from the courtyard garden. It was home! His thoughts went to Frija at her home in the palace… was she lonely? And as he remembered her mischievous grin, Mailliw looked up at the sky. It glittered with stars like a black sequinned evening gown. It was beautiful.

He was about to close the window, when a soft breeze ruffled his hair. Mailliw recognised the touch and put out his hand to catch it. But Fate was too sly, too quick. He heard her whisper, *Well done, well done, you are worthy of success…* and then Fate danced over the chateau roof and was gone. Mailliw closed the window and wondered whose hand Fate decided to touch next and whether Providence would be around to help.

He tiptoed back to the bed, snuggled under the bedcovers and pondered about Merry Willows. Now he knew who she was, he found it impossible to ignore her. He had not asked for the responsibility she had thrust upon him, but Aunt Foggerty was right. Without Merry Willows, Forthright would have died. Being a keeper of the dark family secret, was the price he had to pay for his sister's life.